*"You make it sound like we really are lovers."*

Neil's hand slipped upwards until he was cupping the side of her neck. Raine felt goose bumps dance along her arms.

"I wouldn't be averse to making that part of our story true," he whispered huskily. "What about you?"

Her jaw fell. "Is this what you call behaving like a gentleman?"

"I am being a gentleman, Raine. Otherwise you'd already be in my arms. Like this." He tugged her forwards and Raine was shocked to find herself clamped tightly to the front of his body. She squirmed in an attempt to escape the circle of his arms, but the movement only made things worse. His body was hard as a rock and she could feel the softness of her own curves gladly yielding to every inch of him.

If he kissed her again, she desperately feared she would go up in flames.

# Available in November 2007
# from Mills & Boon®
# Special Edition

# A South Texas Christmas

# STELLA BAGWELL

MILLS & BOON®

*Pure reading pleasure*

*First published in Great Britain 2007
by Harlequin Mills & Boon Limited,
Eton House, 18-24 Paradise Road, Richmond, Surrey TW9 1SR*

© Stella Bagwell 2006

*ISBN: 978 0 263 85661 3*

*23-1107*

*Harlequin Mills & Boon policy is to use papers that are
natural, renewable and recyclable products and made from
wood grown in sustainable forests. The logging and
manufacturing processes conform to the legal environmental
regulations of the country of origin.*

*Printed and bound in Spain
by Litografia Rosés S.A., Barcelona*

To my late mother, Lucille.
Like the Christmas star, you will always
glow in my heart.

## Chapter One

Could this photo be the answer to her prayers?

Only moments before, Raine Crockett had picked up the latest issue of the *San Antonio Express* with plans to scan the news before she got down to the business of her daily schedule at the Sandbur Ranch. But the paper had slipped from her hand and scattered across the floor, exposing a grainy black-and-white picture wedged among the classifieds. Now, she was still staring at the miracle in her hands, wondering if it might finally lead her to the truth about her mother's past—and the identity of her father.

"Knock, knock."

Her friend's breezy voice had Raine jerking her head up and snapping the paper shut at the same time.

Nicolette Saddler, a member of the family that owned the

Sandbur, was like a sister to Raine. This morning she desperately wanted Nicci's advice.

"Thank God you stopped by! I want you to look at something."

Nicolette glanced at the small watch on her wrist. "Sorry, Raine. I don't have time. I have thirty minutes to get to the clinic. I just stopped by to ask you to let Cook know not to set a place for me this evening. I'm going to be working late."

Not willing to let Nicci get away that easily, Raine jumped to her feet and grabbed Nicolette by the arm.

"Raine! I said I don't have time! What—" Her exasperated expression turned curious as she watched Raine shut the door behind her. "What in the world is this about—" She paused as her medical training took over. "You look almost green. Are you feeling ill?"

Raine's hair swished against the tops of her shoulders as she shook her head. Normally she was a quiet, serious-minded young woman, a bookkeeper who kept her nose stuck in the incoming and outgoing invoices of the Sandbur. It wasn't like her to get emotional. But the photo had filled her with hope and excitement.

"I'm not sick!" Raine's office was inside the Saddler family's ranch house where anyone, especially her mother, might be passing by, so she spoke in a hushed voice, "I want you to look at this." She jerked open the paper and thrust it at Nicolette.

A deep frown marred the woman's forehead as she scanned the paragraphs beneath the photo.

"What do you think? Could it be my mother?"

"Maybe. I don't know. This was taken years ago. Lord, look at that big hairdo! And the dangling earrings! Your mother wouldn't be caught dead looking like that now. Still—" She paused. "I have to admit, it does resemble her."

Another burst of optimism surged through Raine, in spite of her attempt to stem it. This photo was probably just another of one missing person among thousands. And Raine's mother wasn't actually lost. She was living here on the ranch, safe and sound, just as she had been for the past twenty-some years. It was Esther Crockett's past—and all her memories of Raine's father—that had been lost.

Nicolette groaned. "Raine, I really don't want to get into this."

Raine understood why her friend didn't want to get involved. Nicci didn't want to encourage a search that would only cause deeper rifts between Raine and her mother. Well, Raine didn't want another fight with her mother, either. But she wanted—needed—answers, and as far as she was concerned, this photo was too important to simply toss in the trash.

"Am I crazy for thinking this might be Mother—before she lost her memory?"

Nicolette pointed to the brief information beneath the photo. "The woman went missing back in 1982. Why would anyone start searching now?"

"Maybe they've searched before—in other areas of the country. But just think, Nicci, the timing would be right. I was born that year, the year my mother lost her memory. And this woman does resemble Mother. I'm not crazy about that, am I?"

Nicolette's expression changed to one of concern. "No, honey, you're not crazy. But you've tried this before. By now you ought to realize what a long shot it would be for this—" she tapped the paper with her forefinger "—to be your mother in her younger days. This woman was obviously a glamour girl! Esther always looks like she just stepped out of a Victorian novel!"

Raine grimaced. It was true that Esther Crockett's appearance was somewhat dowdy. And up until Raine had become an adult, Esther had also insisted that her daughter appear and behave in the same conservative fashion.

Little by little, Raine was doing her best to cut the thick ties her mother had used to restrict her all these years. But the separation wasn't nearly fast enough to suit Raine. She was going to turn twenty-four next month. She was a grown woman now and she wanted to be her own person and live life her own way without fearing her mother's disapproval. Most of all, she desperately wanted to find her father, even if her mother was dead set against the search.

"You're right, Nicci. But Mother could have been different, before," Raine argued on a hopeful note. "After all, she got pregnant with me. There must have been a man in her life."

"True." Nicci's eyes were full of sympathy. "You really want to find your father, don't you?"

Raine nodded as a hard lump of emotion collected in her throat. Ever since she'd been old enough to ask about her father, she'd been told there was no way of finding him. Esther didn't remember that part of her life and, moreover, she refused to allow Raine to search for anything that might lead her to the man.

Blinking at the film of tears in her eyes, Raine said, "More than anything. What if I have brothers or sisters somewhere? I think about that all the time. It drives me crazy that Mother won't talk about it or help me search."

Shaking her head, Nicci handed the paper back to Raine. "Well, I guess there's always a slim chance you could accidentally stumble onto some sort of genuine information here. But you'd be running a big risk in trying! The last time you did something like this—well, everyone on the ranch remembers how furious your mother was when she found out."

Biting down on her lip, Raine paced around the room.

"You don't have to warn me about Mother. We've had so many fights about this that, frankly, I'm sick of trying to reason with her."

"What does that mean?" Nicolette questioned warily. "That you *are* going to call the number in the paper?"

Raine's casual shrug belied her spinning thoughts. "Maybe—I don't know yet."

To hear her mother tell it, Raine should be more than content with her life. She had a nicely furnished office with an antique oak desk, leather chairs and a couch made of beautiful Corriente steer hide raised here on the Sandbur. Potted plants shaded the wide windows and an elaborate stereo system supplied her with music while she worked. She received a very adequate paycheck every week, plus plenty of benefits to go with it.

The accounting degree Raine had obtained two years ago was now paying off. Her job on the Sandbur was one that most any young woman would be envious of. She had a nice apartment in town and a social life, if she wanted it. But no matter how hard she tried, Raine couldn't dampen the longing she had to find out about her mother's past and her father, who had to be out there somewhere.

Nicolette nodded at the paper. "Why is an attorney instead of a private investigator taking the calls? Could be the woman in the photo is a criminal."

Raine refused to consider that idea. "Then it couldn't be Mother. She's too straitlaced for that kind of past."

Nicolette rolled her eyes. "Raine, you can't know what

kind of person Esther was twenty-five years ago! You could open up a nasty can of worms with this thing!"

Raine tightened her lips line. "You're trying to discourage me."

Nicolette threw up her hands in a helpless gesture. "I'm only trying to point out the downfalls. Especially if Esther discovers what you're up to."

Raine reached out and plucked the paper from her desk. "Maybe I can do this without her knowing about it. At least for a while." Raine locked it away in the bottom drawer of her file cabinet.

"What are you doing that for?" Nicolette asked. "There are newspapers everywhere on this ranch, including your mother's house. She's probably already spotted the picture."

"I don't want anyone other than you knowing that I saw it."

"I'm getting worried now! This isn't like you! You don't normally keep things from your mother. At least not something this important."

Raine swiped the air with her hand. "Those are the key words here, Nicci. *Something this important.* This is my family we're talking about—my father!"

Nicolette's worried expression changed to one of resignation. "I know now how empty I would feel if I didn't know who my father was. And I've always thought it strange that Esther doesn't want to know who she used to be or where she came from. What woman in their right mind wouldn't want to find the man that fathered her child?"

Nicolette's question was one Raine had been asking herself for years now, but a reasonable answer had never come to her.

"I don't understand it, either," Raine said with a sigh. "I think she's afraid. You just talked about opening a nasty can of worms. Well, I think that's how your mother feels. But in my opinion, no one can truly step into the future if one doesn't know her past." Raine was no longer just talking about her mother.

As Nicolette left, Raine returned to her desk chair and dropped her head in her hands.

*Oh, Mother,* she silently wailed, *why can't you understand that I need to know who my father is before I can ever have a family of my own? It would all be so much easier if you would help me search for him rather than threatening to disown me if I even tried to look.*

The shrill noise of the telephone jerked her back to the present and she cleared her throat to put on her best business voice. "Sandbur Ranch, business office."

"Raine, it's Matt here. I just wondered if you'd managed to find those vaccination papers on the bull we brought in yesterday? The vet will be here this morning. I need them."

Raine shoved all thoughts of her mother and the newspaper article from her mind. "Sure thing, Matt. I have them right here. Would you like for one of the maids to bring them to your office?"

"Hell no!" the man barked in her ear. "Every damn time one of them shows up at the barn it takes me an hour to get the boys back to work and their minds on their business. I'll come after the papers myself."

"No need for that," Raine quickly offered. "I can run them over to you."

"Don't even think it. You're worse on the guys than the maids," he said, then he hung up before Raine could make any sort of reply. Which wasn't surprising. Matt Sanchez was all business and spent nearly every waking hour of his life making sure the cattle on the Sandbur were the best in Texas.

He was a good man to work for, as were the other family members who ran the Sandbur. For more than forty years, two sisters had made this ranch one of the best and biggest in south Texas. Elizabeth Sanchez and Geraldine Saddler had forged their families and succeeded in keeping the property prosperous by insisting that everyone work together.

Raine couldn't help but be envious of the close-knit siblings and cousins. In good or bad times they were always there for each other. What must it feel like to be surrounded by loving relatives?

If you had the gumption to stand up to your mother and call that attorney, maybe you would find your own family.

The prodding little voice inside Raine's head caused her gaze to swing to her file cabinet. Should she? Might the call lead her to her father?

Until she found the courage to pick up the phone, Raine could only wonder.

Later that same day in Aztec, New Mexico, Neil Rankin was about to step out of his law office to head to the Wagon Wheel Café for lunch when his secretary answered the phone.

Pausing at the door, he said, "I'm already gone."

Scowling at him, Connie grabbed the receiver with one hand and held up the other in a gesture for him to wait.

"What did you say your name was? Miss—" She quickly scribbled on a pad, then pushed it around for Neil to read.

Darla's photo!

Neil rolled his eyes. This past week he'd had more than a dozen calls pertaining to Darla's photo and all the callers had been certified nut cases. He wasn't in the mood to deal with another one. Not when his stomach was growling and the sheriff of San Juan County, who also happened to be a good buddy, was waiting to have lunch with him.

"Quito is already at the Wagon Wheel," he mouthed to Connie. "Take the caller's name and I'll call back."

Connie shook her head at him. "Of course he'll speak with you, Ms. Crockett. Just a minute and I'll transfer you to his personal line."

With her palm tightly clamped over the receiver, she jabbed the phone in his direction. Neil cursed beneath his breath. He wasn't a detective. He was a lawyer who normally dealt with simple cases like writing wills or reading abstracts. Dealing with inquiries about an ice cold missing persons' case was not his style.

But Neil had taken on the task to help his childhood friend, Linc Ketchum. The rancher had gone without a word from his estranged mother for nearly twenty-five years. It had been only recently that Linc's new bride had encouraged her husband to search for the lost woman.

As for Neil, he didn't hold a lot of hope for finding Darla Carlton, but he was a man who stood by his promises and he'd assured Linc and Nevada that he wouldn't stop looking until he'd turned over every stone on the path.

"This one sounds legitimate, Neil," Connie said with a rush of excitement. "This is what you've been waiting for. I can feel it in my bones."

"You're going to be feeling something else in your bones if I plant my boot in your backside," he warned jokingly, while silently hoping that Connie was right. He was getting mighty tired of all the false leads he'd gotten since this search for Linc's mother had started.

Connie chuckled at her boss's harmless threat. "You're too

much of a sweetheart to do something so mean, Neil. It's why I've worked for you for the past ten years."

Groaning, he grabbed the phone from his secretary's plump hand. "Neil Rankin here."

"Uh, this is Raine. Raine Crockett. I'm calling about the article you put in the paper—about the woman you're searching for."

The voice sounded light and sweet and young, and the thought quickly ran through his mind that a mischievous teenager might be on the other end of the line.

"Okay. Where are you calling from, Ms. Crockett?"

After a short pause she said, "The Sandbur Ranch. It's located north of Goliad, Texas. Do you know where that is?"

There was an eager note in her question, as though she was hoping she'd found a transplanted Texan on the other end of the phone. The idea put a faint smile on Neil's face. "Sorry, Ms. Crockett. I've only visited Texas twice in my lifetime and both times were to Dallas."

"Oh. Well, I'm far from Dallas, Mr. Rankin. The ranch is about fifty miles south of San Antonio."

The mention of the Alamo city caught his attention and he planted his hip on the corner of the desk while he picked up a notepad and motioned for Connie to hand him a pen.

"I see," he said to the young woman. "So what prompted you to call me, Ms. Crockett? Do you know Darla Carlton or Jaycee?"

"No. At least, I don't think so. I'm calling—well, to be honest, I'm not sure I should have called you at all. I could be wasting your time."

"Don't worry about it. No one else does," he said with false cheeriness.

Connie frowned at him while he doodled on the notepad resting next to his hip.

"Okay," the sweet voice replied. "I called you because the woman in the picture resembles my mother."

Neil's sandy-brown brows pulled together to form a line across his forehead. "Is your mother's name Darla Carlton?"

"No."

"Was she ever married to Jaycee Carlton?"

"No. Not that I'm aware of."

"Is your mother missing?"

There was a long pause in his ear followed by a tiny sigh. The sound told Neil this woman was troubled and he realized he hated the idea. Particularly when she sounded so nice. But, hell, he could hardly help every troubled soul in the world. Even if she had the voice of an angel.

"If your mother isn't missing, then you obviously know who she is and where she is, right?"

"Well, not exactly…"

Her words trailed away and Neil was surprised at the disappointment flooding through him. Something about this young woman had made him hope for her sake that she had a connection to Darla Carlton. But it didn't sound as though that were the case.

"Look, Ms. Crockett, I'm sorry to cut you short, but I have a luncheon appointment. And I really don't see any point in us continuing this conversation."

He could hear a fierce intake of breath on the other end of the line and the next thing he expected was the sound of the receiver clicking the phone line dead. But that didn't happen. Instead the young woman's voice changed from sweet to clipped and cool.

"I've been waiting twenty-four years to find my mother's lost identity, Mr. Rankin. Surely your lunch appointment can wait for five more minutes."

Her words knocked the air from him and for a moment all he could do was grip the phone and stare at Connie's curious face.

"You—what do you mean?" he finally asked in a rush.

She hesitated, then said, "It's too complicated to go into now. Go to your lunch, Mr. Rankin. You can call me back later."

"No! Wait!" he practically shouted. "Please don't hang up. I'm—sorry if I seemed short. I really am interested, Ms. Crockett."

Silence met his apology, but at least the phone line was still connected. Finally she said, "I'm sorry, too, for being so curt, Mr. Rankin. You've got to understand that this is difficult for me. My mother would be very upset if she found out I was doing this. And I hate going behind her back."

"You say her identity was lost?"

"That's right. Twenty-four years ago. But I don't really want to go into the whole story over the telephone. Is there any way I could meet with you?"

Neil's mind was suddenly spinning. He wanted to hear this woman's story. "Sure we could meet. If you're willing to travel up here to New Mexico."

"Oh. That's—out of the question."

She sounded disappointed and Neil had to admit he was feeling a bit deflated himself. As a lawyer he had the impression her story needed to be explored. And as a man he would like to see for himself what sort of woman Ms. Raine Crockett was.

"Why? Is there some reason you can't travel?" he asked.

His questions were met with another long hesitation, then she said, "I can't leave my job right now, Mr. Rankin. And I don't have a feasible reason to give my mother for traveling to New Mexico."

"You're underage?" He was worried now that his first impression was correct.

"I'm almost twenty-four, Mr. Rankin—not underage. I just happen to love my mother and I don't want to do anything that might…hurt her."

How could finding the woman's past possibly hurt her? Neil wondered with confusion. But he didn't voice the question to Ms. Crockett. She was obviously a cautious little thing and he didn't want to put her off.

"Well, surely you could come up with some excuse that wouldn't raise eyebrows," he suggested.

"I can't think of one. You see, I've never traveled on my own and—" She paused, then went on in a disgusted way, "Oh, this was a bad idea anyway. Let's just forget it."

Neil jumped off the corner of the desk. "Ms. Crockett, why can't we discuss this over the telephone? It would be much simpler for both of us. Why don't I go have my lunch and I'll call you when I get back? You won't even have to be out the expense of another phone call," Neil suggested.

"Wait just a moment," she said in a suddenly hushed tone. "Someone is coming into the room."

Frowning, Neil started to ask her what that had to do with anything, but she must have partially covered the receiver with her hand. He could hear the muted sound of voices in the background. The conversation went on for less than a minute and then she came back onto the line.

"Mr. Rankin, are you still there?"

"Still here."

"Great," she said with a measure of relief, then, "I'm sorry about that. You see, my mother works in the same house as I do. That was her. She's going out this afternoon. I think— maybe it would be better if you did call me back. At least I could give you a brief rundown."

Neil had the feeling he was agreeing to some sort of clandestine meeting or something worse. But he was already this far into this strange exchange. He couldn't drop it all now. He'd be curious for the rest of his life.

"All right, Ms. Crockett. I'll call you back in about an hour. How's that?"

"Fine. I'll give you my extension number. But if someone other than me does happen to answer, just say that you're calling to—to talk to me about a computer I'm thinking about purchasing."

Now she was prompting him to make up stories, he thought incredibly. Something smelled very fishy about this whole setup.

"I'm a lawyer, Ms. Crockett. Not a computer salesman."

"Please! Just do as I ask. If you can't be covert about this, then there's no use in us going on."

He looked at Connie and rolled his eyes. The secretary shook her finger at him.

What the hell, Neil thought. At the very worst, Ms. Raine Crockett was trying to set him up, but for what or why he couldn't guess. He would have to find out for himself.

"All right. I can be discreet," he promised.

"Good. Let me give you the number."

Neil took down the telephone number, then added a last warning, "Ms. Crockett, before you hang up, let me tell you right now that if I were you, I wouldn't get my hopes up."

"I wouldn't know how to do that," she said, then clicked the phone dead in his ear.

## Chapter Two

The moment Neil dropped the receiver back on its hook, Connie asked, "What was that? Or should I ask *who* was that?"

"Some woman down in south Texas," Neil said wonderingly.

Connie was enthralled. "So? What do you think?"

With a wry shake of his head, Neil looked at his secretary. "You know, when Nevada first came to me about finding Linc's mother, I never thought the search would turn into me dealing with people who have more problems than this ole boy knows how to deal with."

Frowning, Connie said, "You're making her sound like a mental case—or something worse."

Neil peeled the phone number from Connie's notepad, folded the paper, then stowed it away in his shirt pocket.

"How do you know she isn't? You don't know what was said on the other end of the line."

"I don't have to know the whole conversation," Connie argued. "The woman is obviously searching for someone she loves. You could show a little more sensitivity, you know. What's the matter with you, anyway? If people didn't have problems we'd never have any clients."

Neil had practiced law for thirteen years. Once he'd passed the bar exam and gotten his license, he'd gone to work in Farmington. Not a huge city by any means, but compared to Aztec it had been like moving from the secluded countryside to downtown Manhattan. The firm had specialized in wrongful lawsuits and he'd hated the experience so much that for a brief time he'd considered giving up law completely. Until he'd come back home to Aztec and decided to open an office of his own where he could help people with an array of needs rather than constantly suing someone.

His clients trickled in sporadically and sometimes not at all. But that was all right with Neil. He didn't want to be one of those harried men who died before they ever had a hand on a retirement check. Like his father had.

"Yeah, yeah. I need to be a *nicer* person. This afternoon when I call the woman back, I'll try to be more sympathetic." As he hurried to the door, he shot her a wicked grin. "And don't look at me in that shameful way, honey. You know how I hate to disappoint you."

Rolling her eyes, Connie motioned for him to leave and chuckling under his breath, Neil shut the door behind him and headed down the sidewalk toward the Wagon Wheel.

For early December, the day was mild. Most often, this time of year brought brutally cold weather to this northern corner of the state. It wasn't unusual to see snow and even blizzard conditions, so the warmth of the weak, wintry sun shining down on his broad shoulders was an unexpected pleasure.

The Wagon Wheel Café was situated off Main Street and had been in existence for more years than Neil had been alive. It was far from the nicest eating place in Aztec. The vinyl booths were worn and the Formica bar running the length of the room had lost its red and white pattern from all the elbows and dishes sliding over it. But the down-home, friendly atmosphere and good food made up for any shortcomings. Once Thanksgiving had passed, the waitresses had cheered up the place by hanging Christmas bells and glittery tinsel from the ceiling. Poinsettias sat on every table and behind the bar a CD player constantly spun songs of the season.

During the weekdays, Neil always ate lunch here. But he didn't often get to lunch with the busy county sheriff. And now that Quito and Clementine were married and trying to start a family, he saw his old friend even less.

When Neil entered the café, he immediately spotted Quito sitting in a booth situated by a plate-glass window overlooking the adjacent street. A stranger to Neil was standing at the edge of the table talking amiably to the sheriff, but as soon as he walked up to the booth, the other man politely excused himself.

"Sorry if I interrupted something," Neil apologized to his friend as he slipped into the seat. "And before you start in—yes, I'm aware that I'm late, but it couldn't be helped."

Quito, who had a mixture of Navajo and Mexican blood, was a handsome man of rough features and a body built like a small bull. Neil had often wished he had just half of the sheriff's charisma. It was no wonder that the man had easily held his office for the past fifteen years.

"I'm not griping," Quito replied. "But I was beginning to wonder."

"Have you ordered yet?" Neil asked.

"No. I waited for you."

Before Neil could reply, a waitress appeared at the side of their table and the two men quickly ordered the blue plate special. Today it was pork roast with brown gravy, mashed potatoes, corn and cherry cobbler. Not a dieter's dream, but Neil didn't have to worry about any flab on his six-foot frame. At least, not yet. But he was thirty-nine years old. Who knew what middle-aged maladies might strike him next year?

"So were you flooded with clients this morning?" Quito asked once the waitress filled their coffee cups and left the table.

Neil laughed. "Not hardly. Other than me, I think Connie's the only one who's been in and out of the front door this morning."

Amused by his friend's response, Quito shook his head. "You don't appear to be too worried about it."

Neil reached for his coffee. "No need to worry. Worry can't change anything. Besides, I never wanted to be rich."

Which couldn't be more true, Neil thought. He'd never been a man obsessed with acquiring a fortune. He lived modestly, on a place out of town, where the only neighbors he had were coyotes and sometimes bear. He'd purchased the land with money that his father had left him when he'd died of a sudden heart attack. James Rankin had only been forty-five years old at the time. His father's premature death was an everyday reminder to Neil that money couldn't buy happiness or immortality.

"Well, you'll never be destitute," Quito remarked fondly. "So if a client didn't keep you at the office, what did?"

"Connie!"

"Your secretary? What's the matter with her?"

"Nothing. She answered the phone," Neil quipped.

Quito chuckled. "Isn't that what you pay the woman to do?"

"I pay her to do what I tell her to do. And I told her not to answer the phone," he said with a grimace. "On top of that, she made me talk to the caller."

"What a hell of a thing for her to do," Quito said with wry humor.

Seeing that his friend was practically laughing, Neil grinned. "Okay. Call me crazy, but I've had a hell of a week. I'm not a private investigator, Quito, but ever since I put that damn picture of Darla Carlton in the *San Antonio Express,* I've had to try to play Mike Hammer."

Quito chuckled. "You're showing your age with that reference. And that shouldn't be so hard for you, Neil. You already have the playboy part down."

"You're as sharp as a tack today, old buddy," Neil retorted, while thinking the sort of experience he'd had with women wasn't likely to be helpful with Ms. Raine Crockett. She didn't sound like the type who could be easily charmed by a man. "So why don't you advise me as to how to deal with nut cases?"

Quito glanced at him. "Is that what this last caller was, too?"

Neil released a weary breath and started to answer, but the waitress appeared with their food. Neil waited until she'd served them and the two men had started to eat before he continued the conversation.

"Actually this one wasn't a kook. In fact, she sounded pleasant enough, only a little strange. And two things she said did intrigue me."

"The caller was a woman?"

Neil nodded as the conversation with Raine Crockett played over in his mind. He realized he was eager to talk with her again. And not just because she might accidentally be a lead to Darla Carlton. There had been something innocent and vulnerable in her voice. Her words had touched him in a way that had taken him by complete surprise; a fact that he wasn't about to share with the sheriff. Quito would think he was crazy and Neil would probably have to agree with him.

"A very young woman," Neil answered. "Her name is Raine Crockett."

"And what was so intriguing about this Raine Crockett?" Quito asked, then added, "I might be able to help."

"I'm probably going to need it," Neil told him as he picked up his fork and shoveled it into the potatoes and gravy. "First of all, she said she was calling from a ranch north of Goliad, Texas. That's not all that far from San Antonio."

Quito nodded with deduction. "That's where Linc's step-father was from."

"Right," Neil responded. "Now add that to the notion that this young woman said her mother's past identity had been lost."

Quito frowned. "What the hell does that mean? The mother doesn't know who she is?"

Neil turned a palm upward in a helpless gesture. "Don't know yet what it means. And this young woman was reluctant to explain anything over the telephone." Scared was more like it, Neil thought, and he was eager to find out why. "But she had the timing right. Her mother apparently lost her memory twenty-four years ago. That's when Darla disappeared."

"Could just be coincidence," the sheriff told him in a dismissive way.

"Could be," Neil agreed. "But I'm calling her back this

afternoon and I'm going to do my damned best to get some answers from her."

Quito was silent for a few moments as he ate and thought about Neil's words. Then he warned, "You'd better be careful, Neil. There's plenty of con artists out there just waiting to pounce on people searching for missing family members. You might turn around twice and realize she's taken you for a ride."

"No chance," Neil said with a shake of his head. "I'm not that dumb. At least, not where women are concerned."

His friend grunted with amusement. "Since when?"

Neil chuckled. "All right," he conceded. "I've made a few bad choices in my lifetime. But the lessons have made me wiser. Never believe a pair of pretty blue eyes."

Quito glanced across the table to Neil. "What about green ones? Or brown? Or gray?"

Laughing, Neil held up a hand. "Whoa, buddy. I can only deal with one color at a time. And I haven't seen Raine Crockett's yet."

A week later, Neil shoved up the cuff of his white shirt to expose the face of his watch. It was past twelve thirty. Far past. And so far he had not seen any sign of Ms. Raine Crockett.

Maybe the young woman was one of the con artists that Quito had been warning him about, Neil thought, as he studied the people milling about him. Maybe she'd lured him down here to San Antonio just for kicks, just to watch him squirm and know that she'd caused him to lose time and money.

Restless now, he rose from the wrought-iron bench and walked over to the river's edge. At this section of the river walk in downtown San Antonio, the nearby shops were richly decorated with Christmas trees and colorful blinking lights.

Shoppers were thick and people carrying parcels were strolling the sidewalks while enjoying the warm afternoon.

This morning in New Mexico he'd left blowing snow and temperatures in the twenties. When he'd stepped off the plane at Stinson Municipal Airport, he'd been hit with sunshine and balmy south winds. If Raine Crockett turned out to be one more kook, he could at least say the weather and the scenery had been an enjoyable break from winter in Aztec.

And speaking of scenery, he thought, as he noticed a slim young woman walking quickly in his direction, he could look at this sort of Texas rose all day long. Honey-brown hair swished and bounced against the tops of her shoulders as her long, shapely legs carried her forward. Black high heels were strapped around her ankles and a sweater type dress of powder blue covered her shapely body.

Black sunglasses shielded her eyes from the bright Texas sun, but even so, he could see that she was beautiful, like a graceful rosebud among a patch of prickly pear.

He was still admiring the woman when he realized she was walking straight up to him. *Powder blue.* She was wearing powder blue, he thought with sudden dawning. This was Raine Crockett. The woman he'd been waiting to meet!

While he tried to gather his shocked senses, she stopped a few feet from where he stood next to the ragged trunk of a Mexican palm tree. Her smooth forehead was creased with uncertainty as she studied him.

"Pardon me, sir," she said. "Is your name Neil Rankin?"

The south Texas accent slowed her words and made his name sound more like a melody. He felt his heart jerk with odd reaction.

"That's me," he said. "Are you Ms. Crockett?"

Nodding, she slipped the glasses from her face and offered her free hand out to him. "Yes, I am. Hello, Mr. Rankin."

Her hand was small and warm inside his. He shook it, then held it firmly between the two of his.

Smiling faintly, he met her gaze with a directness he'd acquired in law school. She had green eyes, he noticed instantly, a cool, willow-green that reminded him of early spring when the air still had a nip to it.

"Thank you for meeting with me." She let out a long breath that told Neil she must be nervous about this rendezvous. Well, he could tell her that he wasn't exactly calm himself. He hadn't been expecting to meet with a woman like the one standing before him. He'd expected someone with average looks, not an ingenue in a siren's clothing.

"No. I should be the one thanking you, Ms. Crockett. I know this whole thing has caused you a lot of inconvenience."

Hell, Neil, what has come over you? he silently cursed himself. *He* was the one who'd been sitting around in airport terminals, shuffling luggage and booking a hotel room. *He* was the one who'd had to leave his law office and put off more important and profitable clients.

His being here was his own fault, though. He was the one who'd allowed Ms. Crockett to persuade him to fly down here to San Antonio when he should have stuck to his guns and told her a big, flat-out no. He should have told her he couldn't go traipsing off to another state just to check out a woman's hunch.

"It will all be worth it, Mr. Rankin, if Darla Carlton turns out to be my mother. And I want to thank you. Very much. I realize I was asking too much of you to make this trip. But I didn't know of any other way."

She sounded sincere enough and Neil pushed away the annoyance he'd been feeling since early this morning when he'd first boarded the plane to make this trip.

After a quick glance around him, Neil gestured to the empty bench he'd been sitting on earlier. "Why don't we sit down so we can talk? Or better yet, while I was walking here to meet you, I noticed a restaurant not too far back along the river. Would you like coffee or something to eat?"

"I would love a cup of coffee," she replied. "I was in such a hurry to get away from the ranch this morning I didn't have time to drink any."

"All right," he said with a smile and reached for her arm.

She stiffened the moment he touched her and Neil wondered if she wasn't accustomed to having a man escort her or if the reaction was something directed at him personally. In either case, he kept his fingers firmly around her elbow as he guided her down the sidewalk in the direction from which he'd come.

By the time they reached the café, she had relaxed somewhat. He could feel the muscles in her arm losing their rigidness. She even smiled when he asked her if she would like to sit at one of the outside tables near the water's edge.

"That would be lovely," she told him.

He guided her to a vacant table, a round, tiny piece of furniture that was made for two people who wanted to sit close. The chairs were made of bent wire with pink padded seats. All around them were more tables that were positioned on terraces of ground that eventually climbed to the café building itself. Willows, palm trees and bougainvillea bursting with peach-gold blossoms shaded the patrons and provided a landing place for graceful mourning doves and chattering mockingbirds.

"It's like summer down here. You're very lucky to have this sort of climate," he told her as he pulled out one of the chairs and helped her into it.

She murmured her thanks, then asked, "Is it cold where you came from?"

She smelled like an angel, Neil thought. Or at least what he imagined the scent of an angel would be: flowery, sweet and warm. As he moved away from her, he forced himself not to breathe in too deeply. He didn't want the scent of this woman to dally with his head. But something told him it probably would anyway.

He answered, "Snowing. In fact, I was a little worried that the flight would be delayed."

While he took the seat across from her, she pushed her handbag beneath her chair, then straightened and shook her silky brown hair back from her face.

"I'm glad it wasn't delayed," she told him. "I would have had to come up with some sort of excuse to spend the night in San Antonio. And I don't like fibbing to my mother."

"Why fib in the first place?" he asked. "You're both grown women. And if you'll excuse me for being blunt, it seems a bit ridiculous. This hiding you're trying to do."

Her soft pink lips pursed with disapproval. "I tried to explain over the telephone, Mr. Rankin—"

"Please," he interrupted, "call me, Neil. There's no need for us to be formal with each other, is there?"

No need, except that this man was shaking her up like a south Texas windstorm, Raine thought. Dear Lord, she hadn't expected Mr. Neil Rankin to look like a film star. She had imagined him to be around fifty years of age, but he had to be at least ten or fifteen years younger than that. Thick blond hair streaked with threads of light brown and platinum was brushed smoothly to one side of his head. Eyes as blue as the sky were set beneath darker brows and lashes. His white smile was a bit lazy and bracketed by two of the most adorable dimples she'd ever seen on a man. Just looking at him left her a bit tongue-tied.

"Of course not. Call me Raine."

"And you can call me Neil. Or anything else you'd like," he added teasingly.

"Neil will be fine," she said a bit stiffly and then wished she could slap herself for being so awestruck. Neil Rankin was just a lawyer, after all. And as for male hunks, she'd seen a few of those before, too. There wasn't any need for her to get all slack jawed over this one.

Footsteps sounded behind her and she glanced around to see a waitress approaching their table. Raine couldn't help but notice how the young woman was eyeing Neil with an appreciative eye. But that shouldn't surprise her. He cut a dashing figure in his white shirt and green patterned tie.

The two of them ordered coffee and pecan pie. While they waited for the waitress to return with the food, Raine wondered how she could explain anything about her need to find her father when all she could think about was the way this man was making her heart do a complete runaway.

"You told me on the telephone that you'd never traveled on your own," he said. "How did you manage to drive up here without lifting your mother's eyebrows?"

Raine's cheeks burned. It was embarrassing that this man had the ability to make her feel so naive and inexperienced. Even though Esther had kept her on a tight rein, it wasn't as if she'd been shut away in a convent for the past twenty-four

years. She'd spread her wings once and had a brief relationship during her college days. That horrible experience had left
her very wary of men in general.

"Uh, when I said that, I meant traveling for a long distance
alone. The ranch is only about a fifty-mile drive from here. I
do come up to the city on occasion to shop—and other things.
And since Christmas is coming I had a good excuse for a
shopping trip."

His brows had lifted on the "other things," but Raine
didn't bother to elaborate. Suddenly Neil Rankin's view of
her had become all too important and she realized she didn't
relish him getting the idea that she was a stay-at-home-stuck-
in-the-mud kind of person. She didn't want him to know that
a wild night on the town for her meant sharing a movie and
a box of popcorn with a male friend, who was far more safe
than exciting.

From the tiny distance across the table, Raine watched a
faint smile touch the corners of his mouth and she found
herself studying his lips as though she'd never seen a pair of
them on a man before. But then she hadn't. At least, not a pair
of lips that looked like Neil Rankin's. They were as hard and
masculine as his square jaw and she couldn't help but wonder
how many women had touched his face, kissed his lips. Too
many, she figured.

"I see," he said. "Well, I'm glad this trip won't cause a
problem for you."

Maybe not a problem with her mother, Raine thought. But
she was definitely having one with him. He was wrecking her
senses and she couldn't seem to do one thing about it.

She swallowed as the nervousness in her stomach went
from a flutter to an all-out jig. "Look, Mr., uh, Neil," she

began haltingly, "I may have given you the wrong impression about myself."

"Really?" His brows inched upward as he leaned casually back in the little iron chair. "What sort of impression do you think I have?"

She breathed deeply while asking herself why she hadn't thought all this through before she'd made the call to Neil Rankin's law office. Instead she'd made the call and this trip without telling anyone, even Nicolette. And now she was sitting here feeling as though she was about to jump off the edge of a rocky cliff.

"Well, you're probably thinking I don't make a move without my mother's consent."

Her small fingers were playing nervously with the napkin lying in front of her. Neil wanted to reach across the table and take her hand in his. He didn't like the idea that she was uneasy with him and he wanted to reassure her that he was on her side and that the two of them were in this thing together.

"Not really," he said in an easy, teasing manner. "I don't see any strings attached to that pretty blue dress you're wearing."

A tiny smile lifted the corners of her mouth and then as she looked across the table at him, the amused expression on her face deepened. "Believe me, it used to be that bad. Before I finally grew up and moved away to go to college. When that happened, Mother was finally forced to cut some of the strings."

As Neil's gaze roamed her lovely face, he suddenly realized there were lots of things he would like to know about this woman. He got the feeling that up until now her life had not been typical. And that would probably be an understatement, what with having a mother that wasn't aware of who she really was or where she'd come from. Lord, Neil couldn't imagine how that would be. And even though his father had been a remote figure in his life, the idea of never knowing him was incomprehensible.

"You haven't told me about your job. What do you do?" he asked in hopes she would freely offer information about herself.

The waitress arrived with their pie and coffee. Once the woman moved away and the two of them were eating, she answered, "I have a degree in accounting. I'm the bookkeeper for the Sandbur Ranch."

So she'd gone through the long, arduous task of college, only to take a job back home. Maybe she hadn't cut as many of those parental strings as she believed, Neil mused. Or maybe the Sandbur was where she felt most comfortable. If that were the case, he couldn't blame her. After working those first few months in Farmington, he'd thought he was going to end up on a psychiatrist's couch

"The Sandbur…it's a big place?" he asked.

Raine nodded. "The property consists of several thousands of acres. It runs around two thousand mama cows. A hundred head of bulls and two hundred and fifty head of horses."

Not quite the size of the T Bar K back home, Neil thought, but damn close. "You never wanted to move away?" he asked curiously. "Like up here to San Antonio? A young, beautiful woman like you could have most any job you set your sights on."

It was an effort for Raine to keep her mouth from falling open. She wasn't used to men calling her beautiful. Especially not a sinfully handsome lawyer who looked like he probably jetted around the world with any exotic creature he wanted on his arm.

Stop it, Raine scolded herself. This man was here in San Antonio with her because of business and nothing else. Quit thinking about his personal life. Quit thinking about him period.

Struggling to focus her attention on the slice of pie in front of her, she said, "I love the ranch. It's where I've always wanted to work. I'm not a—city-type girl."

"Oh. Then you must be happy on the Sandbur," Neil replied, but actually that wasn't all he wanted to say about the matter. In fact, he wanted to go a step further and ask her why she wasn't married and if she had a special guy in her life at the moment. But that was none of his business. And what this woman did in her spare time shouldn't interest him at all. But it did, he realized. Even though she was far, far too young and innocent for the likes of him.

*Beware those green eyes, Neil.*

Even as Neil looked across the table at Raine Crockett and felt a little part of him melt like a warm candy bar, he could hear Quito's warning in his head.

## Chapter Three

Clearing his throat, Neil sipped his coffee and decided it was past time that he brought their conversation down to the real nitty-gritty of this meeting. He hadn't flown all the way down here to Texas just to enjoy the charms of a beautiful ingenue. Not that he wouldn't fly a thousand miles to lunch with an attractive woman. Neil had been known to do plenty of extravagant things to capture the hand of a fair lady. But Raine Crockett was off-limits. He expected she would be the sort that would leave a lasting impression on a man's heart. And Neil definitely wasn't in the market for heart problems.

"So tell me," he ventured, "have you tried to hunt for your mother's past before?"

A grimace tightened Raine's lips. Just the memory of that time still had the power to hurt her. She'd been so confused and angry with her mother for not understanding her need to find the identity of her father. And since then, not much had changed with their stilted relationship. That was one of the main reasons Raine had decided to follow up on the photo in the newspaper. If she could discover the truth of Esther's past and where her father might be, then maybe it would tear down the terrible wall between her and her mother.

With a single nod, she said, "Shortly after I graduated college I hired a private investigator, but Mother eventually found out about the whole thing and put a quick stop to it. She was furious with me. In fact, none of us on the ranch had ever seen her so angry. If I'd been living with her at the time, she would no doubt have thrown me out of the house. But by then I'd moved into an apartment of my own in town."

"Oh. You don't live on the ranch, but your mother does?"

She glanced at him and saw that he was surprised. No doubt he'd been thinking her mother tucked her into bed every night, she thought ruefully.

"That's right. Esther has worked for the Sanchez and Saddler families ever since I was a baby. She lives in one of the smaller houses on the property. If she had her way, I would still be living there with her. But the two of us get crosswise with each other from time to time," she admitted regretfully. "It's best we're not together too much."

Neil held the same attitude about sharing a house with a woman. Too much togetherness was a bad thing. Tempers flared and cross words were flung until all the pleasure was taken out of having a companion in the first place. All too often he'd watched his mother and father go at it as if they were bitter enemies rather than husband and wife. He didn't want that for himself. Ever. Just give him a few sweet, intimate hours with a woman and then he wanted to be left on his own, before all the fighting had a chance to start.

Shifting on the small, uncomfortable chair, he tried to push the sad memories of his parents from his mind. "So you still haven't mentioned any of this to Esther?"

"No. Why borrow trouble?" she asked glumly.

He studied her thoughtfully as one question after another popped into his head. He wasn't a detective, but, more often than not, a lawyer had to think and act like one. Asking the right questions meant success or failure in the courtroom. With Raine, Neil figured he was going to have to go gently. In more ways than one.

"It doesn't bother you to go behind your mother's back like this?"

Her gaze slid from his face but not before he saw a pained expression fill her green eyes.

"Actually it breaks my heart. Mother worked hard and raised me single-handedly. She loves me," she told him in a quiet, strained voice. "I don't want to do anything to hurt her. But I…more than anything, I want to find my father. I want him to be a part of my life. She can't tell me anything about him. And she refuses to help me. So I have no other choice but to search on my own."

Neil could feel her pain and he realized he wanted to help this young woman as much as he wanted to help his old friend Linc.

"I have to be frank, Raine," he began in a thoughtful tone. "It strikes me as very odd that your mother doesn't want to search for her past life. Most any woman would want to know if she still had a husband, a family somewhere. Isn't she curious? I sure as heck would be."

Raine turned back to face him and Neil could see the hopelessness etched upon her soft features.

"I realize it's strange, Neil. That's why we've argued so many times over this thing. The only reason she'll give me is that she's afraid there could have been something wrong in her past life and she doesn't want to uncover it. In other words, fear of the unknown."

"Hmm. Well, we know one thing. There was a man in her life. Otherwise, she wouldn't have been pregnant with you."

Raine thoughtfully traced her forefinger around the rim of her coffee cup. In Neil's newspaper article it had stated that Darla Carlton's husband, Jaycee, had been found dead in a wrecked car between Progreso, Texas, and the Mexican border. Ever since Raine had read that bit of information she couldn't help but wonder if the man might have been her father.

"Maybe this Jaycee could have been my father," she mused aloud. She looked at him, her green eyes full of skepticism. "But how would I ever know? With him buried—" The doubts in her eyes vanished as she stared at him with sudden excitement. "DNA," she blurted quickly. "If Jaycee Carlton had other children, I could have my DNA tested against theirs!"

Neil looked at her with regret. "I'm sorry, Raine. Jaycee didn't have any children. As far as I know, Darla was the only woman he was ever married to."

"Oh." She tried not to be disappointed, but she knew the emotion was most likely showing on her face. "Then maybe I have wasted your time by having you to come down here."

Neil grimaced. He wasn't about to tell her that there was an offspring of Darla's that could supply genetic testing. But before he suggested such a thing to Raine or Linc, he wanted to gather concrete evidence that this was a case worth following. Besides, a blood test would clear up the matter much too quickly for his liking, Neil suddenly decided. Raine Crockett was one sexy female. Now that he was down here, he wanted to enjoy himself and get to know her much better. And the easiest way for him to do that was to stick around for a few days and pose a few personal questions, he thought with wicked pleasure. As long as he kept things light and playful, there shouldn't be any harm come to either one of them.

"Don't be so negative," he told her. "I've only just gotten here. There's lots of research we need to do before we think about throwing in the towel. Are you up to telling me some of the story right now?"

His question prompted her to straighten her shoulders, as though to tell him that she wasn't one of those weak-willed women who swoon over the least little stress. Neil wondered if he'd managed to stumble onto one of those rare women who happened to be strong as well as beautiful.

"Of course, I am," she said with renewed conviction.

"Okay," he said as he shoveled another bite of pie into his mouth. "Then lay it out to me."

Raine took a bite of her own pie in hopes it would calm her jumping stomach, but even before she swallowed the sweet concoction, she knew the only thing that was going to ease her nerves was to put miles and miles between herself and Neil Rankin.

"Since we talked on the phone, I've tried to think of anything and everything that might be important. But I really don't know where to start. At the beginning, I suppose. When Mother woke in the hospital."

Neil nodded. "When was this?"

"The latter part of October, I think, 1982. It was Halloween, she's said, but with all her injuries she was feeling more tricked than treated."

"Tell me about her injuries."

As Raine sliced off another bite of pie, she answered, "I'm not exactly sure what the extent of her injuries were. I do know she suffered some sort of trauma to the head, maybe due to a car accident, but maybe not. One leg was broken and several of her ribs. Obviously the head injury was the reason for her amnesia. At first, the doctors believed whatever caused her injuries would surface in her memory. But it didn't," she added regretfully.

"How do you know her memory hasn't returned?" Neil asked pointedly.

Raine's brows rose to two high peaks as she stared at him. "What is that supposed to mean?"

"Exactly what it sounds like," he told her, then reiterated his question. "How do you know that your mother hasn't remembered and is keeping the fact from you?"

Raine sputtered with disbelief. That idea had never crossed her mind. To even think such a thing about her mother swamped her with guilt.

"Don't be ridiculous," she said stiffly. "Mother would never lie to me!"

His direct gaze didn't waver from hers and Raine shivered inwardly. This man was not only doing strange things to her body, but he was also turning her thoughts in a frightening direction she didn't want to go.

"You're certain about that?" he asked softly.

Anger sparked her green eyes. "I'm very sure," she answered. "Mother would never lie to me. Unless she—" Raine broke off as an idea struck her. Then she finally said in a choked murmur, "Unless she was trying to protect me from something. Then she might hide the truth."

Neil stifled a sigh. The last thing he wanted to do was upset this woman. No matter how painful the possibilities, she needed to look at this matter with open eyes.

"I haven't met Esther yet, but in most instances, it's the general nature of a mother to protect her young."

Horror, confusion and finally disbelief traipsed across her face and Neil realized he was giving her a lot to chew on in just a brief short of time. Besides, no child wanted to believe a parent would deliberately lie to them.

Feeling unusually soft, he decided to let that subject rest. "Well, let's set that notion aside for the moment and go back to her time in the hospital. Have you ever seen the police records on this case? Where did they find her? How?"

"No to the police records. But I did search the newspaper archives in Fredericksburg for a story." Raine reached for her purse. "I brought a copy just in case it might be helpful to you." She handed the photocopy to Neil and waited while he read the short article posted in the *Fredericksburg Standard:*

Two weeks ago, a local rancher, Louis Cantrell, discovered an injured woman lying at the edge of Highway 87 approximately three miles south of Cherry Spring. At first it was believed the woman had been involved in a vehicle crash, but the police verified to the press today that the woman had been beaten with a blunt object and tossed onto a grassy shoulder of the highway.

Presently the woman, whose age and name have yet to be determined, remains in a coma in a Fredericksburg hospital. The Gillespie County sheriff's department is asking the community for help in solving this case. If anyone thinks they can identify this woman, please contact Sheriff Madison at—

A telephone number ended the piece, and after Neil scanned the whole story one more time, he placed the paper onto the tabletop and tapped it with his forefinger.

"You implied there wasn't any reason Esther might be afraid to find her past." He shot her a challenging look. "What do you think this is? If she was beaten and left to die, someone obviously had it out for her."

Refusing to believe that anyone would want to harm her mother, Raine quickly shook her head. "Wait a minute! You're jumping to conclusions. The police couldn't positively determine what caused the injuries to my mother. She could have fallen from a car."

Neil couldn't relent, even though it was obvious that the idea of Esther being beaten was torturous to her. "Then why didn't the driver of the vehicle stop, pick her up and rush her to the hospital?"

The logical questions caused Raine's shoulders to slump with despair. "I don't know," she mumbled. "Why are you trying to make something sinister out of this?"

Hating the pain on her face, he reached across the table and touched her hand in an effort to reassure her. "I'm not trying to be mean, Raine," he said gently. "We have to look at all sides of this case. And a beating is definitely sinister."

Neil's suggestions about her mother's accident were shocking to Raine. But not nearly as surprising as the warm touch of his hand upon hers. True, he'd held her arm as the two of them had walked here to the restaurant, but that had been the action of a gentleman. This was far more intimate and inviting and the fact that he was touching her in such a way was enough to make her whole body quiver with awareness.

"But we don't know if it truly was a beating," she argued while carefully avoiding his gaze. Neil Rankin didn't miss anything and she didn't want to give him the chance to look into her eyes for very long. If he did, he just might see how much upheaval he was causing inside her. "Mother *could* have been in a car accident."

"Then where was the car? Did they find any sort of broken-down vehicle near the area where she was found?"

She shot him a brief glance, then fixed her gaze on a bougainvillea bush growing a few feet beyond his left shoulder. "No. The police found nothing. Not any sort of clue."

Desperate to ease the fire licking up her bare arm, Raine eased her hand from beneath his and cradled it around her coffee cup.

Watching her, Neil wished she hadn't pulled away from him so quickly. Her hand had been incredibly soft and he'd found that touching her, even in that simple way, had given him a rush of male excitement far above anything he'd felt in years. What could that possibly mean? he wondered wryly. His taste was turning toward young innocents? Lord, help him.

"Okay. Let's try another angle. Where did she go once she recovered enough to leave the hospital in Fredericksburg?" he asked with more patience than he was actually feeling.

"Down here to San Antonio. She stayed in a Catholic convent until I was born. After that, she found a job clerking in a bank. Eventually she put enough savings together to rent her own apartment and make a home for herself and me. She says the past was gone. She had to focus on the future."

"Hmm. I can understand that. To a certain point." Neil swallowed the last of his pie as his gaze slid over Raine Crockett's lovely face. Her skin was on the pale side, but sun-kissed enough to tell him she didn't hibernate indoors. He could only wonder what shade she would be beneath her blue dress. "So when do you think I can meet with your mother?"

Raine stared at him as her mind worked furiously. She'd not been expecting him to suggest something like this. She'd thought he would take the information she'd given him and go on about the investigation on his own.

"I—I don't know…it couldn't be wise," she finally managed to get out.

Rolling his eyes with impatience, he said, "Look, Raine, I understand that you don't want to step on your mother's toes, but you can't just tie my hands. If that's the way you plan on doing things, then I might as well head back home."

Anger tightened her lips. Who did he think he was? she asked herself, someone who could just barge into her private life whether she wanted him to or not? "Maybe you should do just that," she said with slow deliberation. "Now that you're here, I'm not so sure I've done the right thing."

Neil leaned across the tiny table so that their faces were only inches apart. Raine clasped her hands together in her lap to prevent them from trembling.

"I thought you were serious about this. I didn't travel a thousand miles just to hear you say you've changed your mind!"

It was easy to see that she'd angered him, Raine thought. His blue eyes sparked and his voice was as taut as a guitar string. But the idea certainly didn't distress her. From the moment he'd walked up and introduced himself, he'd been upsetting her.

"I haven't changed my mind…exactly," she corrected him. "When you asked to see my mother…well, I didn't realize that would be necessary. Can't I show you a photo instead?"

His brows lifted. "You have a recent one with you?"

Nodding, Raine reached for her handbag. "It's not an extreme close up of her face, but I think you'll see the resemblance."

She rummaged around in her small black handbag until she found what she was looking for. Neil watched as she pulled a snapshot from a long white envelope and handed it to him.

Taking the photo from her, he turned it right side up. The woman staring back at him appeared to be in her sixties. Her hair a light color somewhere between blond and gray. She was a tall woman with a figure that he suspected was once a real head turner, but now there were extra pounds around her waist and on her hips. She was dressed casually in slacks and a short-sleeved blouse that could have been purchased off any discount store rack. If this was truly Darla Carlton, then she'd lost her taste for the finer things.

Neil had only been a young teenager when Linc's mother, Darla, had left the T Bar K, but he still carried memories of the woman. For one thing, she'd been very pretty with a sort of delicate air about her. One day he and Linc had entered the house to grab colas from the fridge when they'd come upon her weeping. She'd been wearing a lavender satin robe edged with Spanish lace. The scent of roses had clouded around her as she dabbed a handkerchief to her eyes and tried to smile at her son and his friend. He'd thought she was one of the most beautiful women he'd ever seen.

Linc had been embarrassed that they'd caught his mother

still dressed in her robe at one o'clock in the afternoon. But Neil had been intrigued and had thought about the woman for days afterward.

"Neil?"

The sound of her voice calling his name caused Neil to push away his old memories and glance up at her. She gave him a wan smile that was full of nerves and in that moment, Neil knew he had to come up with a perfectly viable excuse to follow Raine to the Sandbur.

"I was wondering what you think?" she persisted. "Do you think it might be her?"

Neil placed the photo on the tabletop while promising himself he would never purposely lead this woman on just so he could spend time with her. Hell, he had all sorts of girlfriends back in San Juan County. He wasn't that desperate for a woman. Only this one, a little voice whispered in his head.

"I can't be sure," he answered truthfully. "There are some similarities about the two women. The height and the shape of the face. Your mother is a heavier person than Darla Carlton was when she went missing."

"Twenty-five years usually adds some pounds to a woman," Raine replied with a grimace, then added, "You don't think it's her, do you?"

Neil gave her his brightest smile. "There's always a chance it could be her. We need to do more investigating. If I could see your mother and talk to her it would be a big help."

It was all Raine could do to keep from jumping up from her chair and running as fast and as far as she could from this smooth-talking lawyer. He was going to be trouble. Not only with her mother, but with her. Just looking at him made her feel like a simpleton. How could she possibly keep her senses in check around him?

"She'd chase you out of the house if she had any sort of suspicion that you were an attorney or private investigator." Raine chewed on her bottom lip as she contemplated the situation. "We'll have to be more subtle than that."

Neil let loose a wry chuckle. "Subtle. You mean we'll have to lie to her, don't you?"

The frown creasing her forehead grew deeper. "Don't try to make me feel any guiltier than I already do," she answered. "There's no other way to handle it. You'll have to come to the house as—" She broke off as her mind searched for some feasible excuse to invite him into her mother's home.

"Your love interest," Neil finished for her.

Raine's mouth fell open as her heart thumped loudly in her ears. "My...what?" she asked with a gasp.

Neil laughed softly. "You heard me. I'll be your new sweetheart. Anything wrong with that?"

## Chapter Four

"Just about everything is wrong with that!" she blurted out loudly.

Neil glanced around him to see if Raine Crockett's outburst had garnered any attention. Thankfully there was no one sitting near them, except for an elderly couple, who was grinning at Neil as if to say they understood all about lovers quarrels. Well, at least the two of them had already fooled someone, Neil thought wryly.

Bending his head toward her, he said with hushed sarcasm, "Since you've protested so loudly, I suppose you have a better plan. You still want me to be a computer salesman?"

Neil a salesman? Now that Raine had met him in the flesh, the idea was laughable. And how in heck could she ever explain her association with a man who came across as an American version of 007?

She regarded him thoughtfully. "That would never work. Mother doesn't own a computer. She hates the things. Besides, you don't look like a computer geek."

"Thanks," he said with dry humor. "Then maybe I should rent a spray truck and pretend that I'm a termite exterminator."

Raine waved a dismissive hand at him. "That wouldn't work, either. She had the house checked recently for termites."

Neil had only made the suggestion as a joke, but she'd taken it seriously. She was taking *everything* about this matter way too seriously and that worried Neil. In spite of his eagerness to spend more time with this beautiful Texas rose, he didn't want to get himself mixed up in some sort of family squabble. There was nothing more dangerous than standing among fighting relatives.

Sighing, he said, "I don't like the idea of lying and sneaking." He added, "That's not the way I work."

He was looking at her with a bit of disgust and Raine could feel his disapproval all the way to her bones. She told herself it shouldn't matter how he viewed her, just as long as they discovered the truth. But as she studied Neil's perfectly chiseled face, she realized his opinion of her mattered very much.

"Believe me, Neil, I normally don't go around…fibbing to people. It's just that I understand how my mother's mind works. If she has any suspicion that you were a lawyer, P.I., or anything like that, she'll clam up tight."

He rubbed a thumb against his chin as he regarded her for long, silent moments. Raine could feel the sweep of his blue gaze and like an idiot she began to wonder what it might feel like if he were looking at her with adoration, as if she were the only woman in the world for him.

*Stop it!* She silently scolded herself. *You're acting like a ninny.* The man was here on the behalf of another client. He didn't really care if her mother was Darla Carlton. He was simply doing a job. And the very last thing he would be doing was looking at Raine as any sort of love interest. Not when he could probably pick and choose any woman he wanted.

As for Raine, she'd never been overrun with male pursuers. She'd been a shy, skinny teenager, all arms and knees and braces on her teeth. Esther had been a strict mother with very modest ideas. She'd insisted that her daughter dress down to avoid attention from boys her own age. Getting involved in that sort of relationship would only cause her trouble and misery, Esther had often preached to Raine. To say the least, her high-school years had been dull and lonely. She'd felt like a freak on the outside looking in.

Raine had not been the sort to disobey or talk back. Esther was her only parent. Her only family. She'd never wanted to hurt her mother in any way, even when it meant that Raine was miserable herself. Her one defiant streak had been the short fling she'd had in college and its disastrous failure had only proved to Raine that she'd been so overprotected she didn't know how to have a love affair.

But that had been during her adolescent and ensuing teenage years. Now that she was a grown woman, things were different. She couldn't dismiss her need to find her roots, in spite of her mother's encouragement to let the past rest. After the fiasco she'd gone through with the private investigator and her mother's fury, she'd tried to do a little discreet searching on her own, but she'd gotten nowhere. It wasn't until last week, when she'd found Darla Carlton's picture in the paper that she'd felt any sort of real hope again. Working with Neil Rankin might prove to be difficult under her mother's eagle eye. But, if she ever wanted to find her father, it was a chance she was going to have to take.

"Raine? Did you hear me? Do you want to go on with this or not?"

Neil's questions broke into her rambling thoughts, and as she looked at him, she nodded haltingly, then with enthusiasm. "I do. I really do. And it if means we have to cozy up to each other in front of Mother, then so be it. I'm a pretty good actress. I won a leading role in a college play. I think I can make her believe that we're—in love."

The corners of his mouth turned downward. She made it sound like being close to him was going to be hard work. Neil wasn't accustomed to that sort of reaction from a woman. Normally they were all more than eager to snuggle up against him. Obviously Raine was going to be a challenge, but Neil had to admit he was looking forward to the task.

"You make it sound like this will be a role for the Oscar."

Picking up her coffee, she tried to appear casual, but her stomach was fluttering and if her fingers hadn't been clutched around the cup, her hands would have been shaking.

"Trust me, Neil, the roles will be difficult for both of us," she told him. "Mother isn't accustomed to me bringing home boyfriends."

Neil smiled inwardly at the idea of him being Raine's boyfriend. He hadn't been one of those since he'd taken Destiny Granger to the high-school prom.

Reaching for his coffee, he asked in a teasing tone, "Why? Don't you have any?"

Her green eyes were solemn as she lifted them to his face and just for a moment, for a flash of time, the look on her face reminded Neil of his friend Linc Ketchum. Dear Linc, his longtime buddy, who'd watched his mother walk away and never come back. Could it be that Esther Crockett truly was his long lost mother and Raine his sister?

No! Don't even go there, Neil. It was much too early to be having such thoughts. And not for anything would he get Linc's hopes up needlessly. No, if he believed something about Esther Crockett resembled Darla, he was going to keep the notion to himself until something more concrete came along.

"I have dated," she admitted. "But not very much. And only one guy on a regular basis. But that only lasted a few weeks."

Surprise crossed his face and she said, "I've been busy getting a college degree in accounting. I haven't had time for men." Plus she wasn't ready to get her heart broken all over again, she thought dismally.

"Hmm. You sound like you don't want to make time, either. Does your mother know about your lack of social life?"

A cynical laugh popped from Raine's mouth. "Let's put it this way. If I never married, Mother would be a happy woman."

Neil rolled his eyes upward toward the banana leaves shading their table. And if Claudia, his own mother, had never married she would have probably been happier. Certainly she wouldn't have ruined his father's life with her constant nagging for more, more, more. His mother's quest for the material "good things" had turned Neil against money and women. The only way he wanted either of them was in small doses.

"Then Esther obviously isn't going to welcome me into her home," he stated, then glanced at her with regret. "Raine, she's obviously going to be suspicious of me. Or at the very least resent my presence in your life. Under those circumstances, I can't see me getting the woman to open up about her past."

Raine suddenly forgot that she needed to keep her distance from the man. She reached across the scant space between them and grabbed onto his hand. "Neil, please," she pleaded. "Don't give up on this. On me. You're here. And I have an intuition that something is going to happen. Something will turn up—some sort of information that will help us both."

She couldn't have said it better, Neil thought. Something *was* going to happen. He was going to end up plunging into deep water with this woman and if he wasn't very careful he just might not be able to swim to a safe shore.

But her soft little hands wrapped tightly around his felt so vulnerable and the pleading light in her green eyes pierced him with a need to protect her and please her. Dear Lord, it wasn't possible to fall for a woman in the length of time it took to drink a cup of coffee, was it?

Hell, don't worry about that, Neil argued with himself. He'd wanted the excuse to spend time with this beauty and now she'd handed it to him and more.

Groaning inwardly, he said, "All right, Raine. We'll give this a try. But the minute a war breaks out between you and your mother, I'm outta here. Got it?"

Nodding, she smiled a slow, shy smile that melted his insides to a bunch of worthless goop.

"Yes. I understand," she said a little breathlessly.

Neil could see renewed excitement building on her face and the sight made him almost forget he was fifteen years older than her.

"So when do we start?" she asked.

"What about tonight?" he suggested. "I've rented a car. I can follow you to the ranch. How far is it?"

"About fifty miles. An hour and a half of driving will get

you there. But it's safer not to make the trip after dark. That's when all the deer and wild hogs decide to cross the highway."

His brows met in the middle of his forehead. "Wild hogs?"

Raine suddenly realized she was still holding on to his hand. The fact embarrassed her and she ducked her head as she moved her hands away and pretended to snap her handbag closed.

"Yes, wild hogs," she replied. "You know. Like a big pig with tusks and tough bristles sticking up on their back."

"These hogs don't belong to anybody?"

Raine laughed. "Not hardly. The farmers and ranchers hate them because they eat the crops and forage that would normally go to cows and horses. People hunt wild hogs all the time. And they are good to eat."

"Then they're not protected like our bear is in New Mexico," he said the obvious.

Raine shook her head, then dared to smile at him again. "No. But don't feel too badly. They manage to keep their population high."

Chuckling at her implication, Neil motioned for the waitress to bring their check.

Raine attempted to pay for her half of the small snack, but Neil refused her money. After he'd settled the account and tipped the waitress, he rose to his feet.

"Are you leaving?" she asked with a bit of dismay.

"Not without you."

He reached for her elbow to help her out of the chair and once again Raine felt the skin on her arm burning, her cheeks stinging with wild, unchecked heat. Even if she was accustomed to men touching her, Neil Rankin would still make her blood sizzle like raindrops on hot pavement.

"I—where are we going?" she asked.

Hearing the slight panic in her voice, he asked, "Raine, are you—frightened of me?"

Her eyes darted up to his handsome face. "Why no. Of course I'm not afraid. Why would I be?"

His expression turned grim as he guided her away from the café. "Probably because I'm a strange man that you've never met before. I could be an imposter. I could be a killer who lures women from their safe places."

"Stop it!" she spurted the words back at him while at the same time she jerked her elbow away from his cupped hand. "You're not being a bit funny."

Neil's brows arched. "I wasn't trying to be."

She heaved out an unsettled breath that caused the material of her powder-blue dress to move against her small breasts. Neil felt the man in him perk up with far more interest than he should be feeling.

"I know who you are. *I'm* the one who called your office. You're a lawyer," she said, then added, "Albeit, I'm not sure how good of one. And now that we're on the subject, I've been wondering why you're the one doing this search for Darla. Why didn't your client hire a detective instead of a lawyer?"

His glance down at her face was totally patronizing. "Because my client happens to be a very close friend. And I'm the only one he's willing to trust with such a personal matter."

"Oh. Your client is a he?"

Neil's smile was a bit wicked. "Yes. Why? Were you going to be jealous if it had been a woman?"

He was teasing of course, Raine thought. There was no way he could suspect the upheaval he was causing inside of her.

"I don't think we've known each other long enough for me to be—feeling that sort of emotion," she said coolly.

Neil chuckled as it dawned on him just how refreshing her prim attitude was after the willing, experienced women he'd known in the past.

"Well, give it a few days," he teased. "Maybe I can turn you a little green by then."

Her eyes flew to his face as he looped his arm with casual ease through hers. "Days?" she sputtered. "Aren't you going back to New Mexico tomorrow?"

Frowning, he urged her onto the paved walkway that edged the river. Boats of all shapes and sizes decorated with Christmas wreaths and blinking lights were floating by. Many of them were filled with tourists enjoying the warm sunshine and the sights of San Antonio.

"Not hardly. I just arrived."

She balked in her tracks and he turned to look squarely down at her upturned face. She looked worried. No, Neil decided, she actually appeared frightened.

"You mean this investigation—or whatever you want to call it—is going to take more than one meeting with my mother?" she asked with disbelief.

Careful to keep his expression smooth, he urged her to continue walking forward. "The day is beautiful, Raine. Let's walk and talk and get acquainted with each other. I don't want to go into this evening blind. I need to know a little bit about my new lover."

The last two words were said with a purr that caused a shiver to race down Raine's spine. Oh, this man was way too smooth for a country girl like her, Raine decided. She was going to have to watch every step she took, every word she said, and even then she wasn't sure she would be safe from his charms.

"We—we're not going to pretend to be lovers!" she said in a voice pitched with fear. "That's carrying things a bit too far, don't you think?"

With a soft chuckle, he patted the little hand resting on his forearm. "Not really. You're an attractive young woman and I'm a man. Put the two together and something usually boils up."

Pursing her lips to a disapproving line, she stared straight ahead. "Maybe in some cases. But I have no intention of doing any boiling. In the kitchen or anywhere else," she added for good measure.

Her comment only produced a laugh from him and the sound was so light and contagious that Raine couldn't help but tilt her head around to him and smile.

"Okay," she conceded. "What do we need to know about each other?"

He shrugged with nonchalance, but deep inside Neil was shocked at how very interested he was in this woman's life. She was different, very different from the women he'd known in the past. There was something sweetly naive about her. Yet on the other hand there was a sultriness to her green eyes that made him think she wasn't all soft innocence. She was taking a big risk of ruining her relationship with her mother in order to go after what she wanted—a father. Obviously she was a woman who would hold on tight to her dreams. But was a father the only man she had in her dreams of the future? Neil wondered.

"Oh, just the simple things," he told her. "Like where you grew up. Your likes and dislikes, education, anything and everything. Remember, we're supposed to be *close*."

Raine released a long, pent-up breath. "Close! Neil, I've never introduced a man to my mother before. She's going to start getting ideas that we truly are serious. She's going to question me all about you, then start warning me how dangerous you are."

Neil chuckled. "I'm a lawyer. I'm always dangerous," he teased.

She rolled her eyes. "And are you always this lighthearted? Aren't you ever serious?"

"Do you mean with women or my work?"

"Women—uh, work. Both," she finally added in a fluster.

"I don't get serious with women," he said. "But I do with my work."

Slowly she digested his comment as they strolled along the river's edge. It didn't surprise her to hear this man admit to being a confirmed bachelor. Everything about him screamed that he was as free as an eagle. But Raine did wonder why he'd chosen the single life. She couldn't believe it was simply for sinful pleasures. He was more complex than that. "So you're not married?" she asked.

"Never considered the idea. What about you?"

Raine suddenly felt loneliness press heavily upon her shoulders. "No. I haven't yet met a man who's made me want to take that much of a step. And I'm not sure that I would know how to be a good wife."

His face was perplexed as he glanced down at her. "That's an odd thing for a young woman like you to say," he said.

Raine focused her attention on one of the boats drifting lazily by them. The vessel was filled with a young couple and two children that were obviously their offspring. The little group was the perfect, happy family, she thought. They probably even lived in a two-story house in the suburbs or maybe a hacienda in the country. They had cats and dogs that had the run of the house and the yard, and were treated like family members, too. This coming Christmas would be very special at their home. Lots of relatives would gather. There would be eating, dancing, joking and plenty of laughter.

"Raine? Are you still with me?"

She suddenly noticed a hand waving up and down in front of her face and with a burst of embarrassment she realized she'd been daydreaming about the very thing she'd always wanted.

"Uh—I'm sorry. What were you saying?"

"I was asking why you had doubts about being a wife."

She kept her gaze carefully away from him and on their surroundings. She didn't want him to see just how lost and afraid she felt when it came to dealing with men and the idea of having a family.

"I guess what I'm trying to say is that I…it's always just been my mother and me. I don't know what it's like to have a man living in the house. I've never seen my mother be a wife. We're creatures that live by example, and so far I haven't been given any. I really don't know much about the opposite sex."

He smiled gently down at her. "Well, don't feel too badly. I'm much older than you and I don't know much about what makes a woman tick. The only thing I'm sure about is that I wouldn't want one hanging around the house all the time telling me what and what not to do."

Surprised by his callous remark, Raine brought her head back around to his. "That's a terrible, chauvinistic remark."

He shrugged one shoulder again and for the first time since she'd met him, Raine watched a steely expression creep over his face.

"It probably is terrible," he agreed. "Connie, my secretary, is always telling me I'm jaded. But I saw what my father went through with my mother. No matter how much he gave to her, whether it was material things or himself, it was never enough. He worked himself to death to try to please her."

She looked at him with new regard. For some reason, she'd come to the conclusion that he probably had one of those perfect families she'd always dreamed about. A family with a mother that was loving and encouraging and a father who'd always been there for him with a steadying hand. "Your father died?"

Neil nodded soberly. "A heart attack. He was only forty-five—a very young man."

"That's so—tragic. What about your mother? Is she still living?"

Neil nodded. "Oh, yeah," he said, unable to keep the sarcasm from his voice. It was a rare occasion that he and Claudia visited on the telephone and even more rare that they visited each other in person. But he didn't feel guilty about the fact. She was happy living the high social life. Neil was only an afterthought to her. "About the time I graduated high school she got married again. To a politician. Thank God I was headed off to college by then and didn't have to be a part of their family. Now they live in Santa Fe where he works at the state capital."

"What about siblings?"

He sighed. "No. I'm all by myself."

She nodded glumly. "Me, too. And I hate it. There have been so many times I've wished and prayed that my mother would remarry and give me a sister or brother. It never happened. She wants no part of a man."

"Hmm. Well, I can understand that. She doesn't know what happened to your father. In the back of her mind she might believe he tried to hurt her. Or maybe she believes he's still alive and she wants to wait for him to return."

"Do you actually think my mother's husband or companion—whatever he was—tried to hurt her?" Raine asked quickly. That was another idea that had never come to her before now. It made her see that Neil's judicial mind was constantly branching out in different directions. Forget about hiring a private investigator, she thought. Neil Rankin was much better than a gumshoe would ever be.

A few feet ahead of them was a low, wooden bench shaded by a clump of banana trees. Neil guided her toward it. "Let's sit," he suggested. "Unless you'd rather go somewhere inside?"

Raine shook her head and allowed him to help her onto the bench. "This is fine. Just lovely," she assured him. "It's not too often that I get up here to San Antonio. I always enjoy it whenever I do."

"Do you normally make the trip by yourself? Or do you bring friends along?" Neil asked as he settled himself next to her.

"Usually there's someone with me. My mother. Or sometimes Mercedes or Nicolette comes along with me. They're daughters of one of the families who own the Sandbur, the ranch where I work."

Now that the two of them had stopped walking, Neil had released his hold on her arm. Raine realized she felt an immediate disconnect and almost wished he would reach for her hand. Even though he heated her blood in a way that was totally sinful, there was something about his strong touch that made her feel as though everything was going to turn out okay, that he would move hell and high water to make it that way.

"So you and your mother both work for the Sandbur ranch," he commented. "How long has Esther been associated with the ranch?"

Raine watched with appreciation as he crossed his long

legs out in front of him. He was wearing a pair of starched khakis and a pair of chocolate colored cowboy boots made of ostrich leather that most any Texan would be proud to wear.

"Esther first went to work for the ranch many years ago when I was only a toddler. So the place has always been home to me. That is, until I moved into my own apartment."

His brow puckered with confusion as he held up a hand. "Wait a minute. I thought you told me she got a job as a clerk in a bank right after you were born."

Raine nodded. "She did. That's where she met the two sisters who own the ranch. Elizabeth and Geraldine. Most of their fortune was deposited in the bank where my mother worked and they were periodically coming in to do banking business. Mother got acquainted and somehow the sisters lured her to the ranch to cook and keep house."

Perplexed, Neil shook his head. "But she was a bank clerk. Why would she want to go from filing bank documents to cleaning house? Wasn't that a step down?"

A soft laugh passed Raine's lips. "Not really, when you stop to think that the sisters paid her twice the amount of what she was making at the bank. Plus they allowed her to live in one of the ranch's rent houses for free. In fact, she's still living in that same house. It's getting old now. But then so is the big house and its twin on the hill."

Neil was certain he'd never seen such shiny hair in his life. The sun sparked the strands and turned it to the color of molten honey. He felt like a kid wanting to reach out and grab a piece of hard candy.

"Tell me about the sisters. Are they still running the ranch?"

"No. A few years back, Elizabeth Sanchez passed away. Her husband is still living, but physically disabled. Geraldine

Saddler is still going strong, but she's a widow now and has handed her reins over the ranch to her son, Lex. He and Elizabeth's two sons, Matteo and Cordero, also help. They have sisters, but only one presently lives on the property and she had a job outside the ranch."

"These three men are cousins?" Neil asked as he tried to keep the information Raine had given him straight in his head.

Raine nodded. "That's right. The sisters married. Elizabeth became the wife of Mingo Sanchez and Geraldine married Paul Saddler."

"So," Neil said after a moment, "your mother has worked for these two families for many years?"

Raine looked up at him and felt her heart give a little jolt. He had to be one of the sexiest men she'd ever laid eyes on. His sandy-blond hair contrasted with his darkly tanned skin, but not nearly as much as his blue eyes. They were that light color of blue of a sparkling, mountain lake on a summer day, the sort that invited a hot body to jump right in.

"That's right. And now I also work for them. The whole bunch is like family to us. Especially since—" She broke off, her lips twisting with pained regret. "Since my mother and I are the only real family we have," she finished.

For the first time since the two of them had met, it struck Neil as to just what this young woman had gone through because of her mother's lost memory. She didn't know where her roots had started or if the man who'd sired her was still alive. She could only wonder and dream about having a sibling out there somewhere, a person who probably didn't even know they had a sister in Texas.

And then he thought of his buddy, Linc Ketchum. The man had been deeply hurt when his mother had remarried and walked away from him and the T Bar K ranch in New Mexico. For years his friend had bottled up the pain and lived mostly like a hermit. If Nevada Ortiz hadn't come along and shown him true love, he would still be living that way, Neil thought.

His gaze traveled over the gentle slope of Raine's cheekbone, the smooth, straight line of her nose and finally the soft curve of her full lips. She was young and full of life. She would have so much love to give to a man and their children. He didn't like to think of her wasting these precious years searching for the past and being too scared to step into the future.

Impulsively Neil reached for her hand and lifted it to his lips. As he kissed the soft skin of her fingers, her eyes flew wide, her lips parted.

"What are you doing? Practicing for tonight?"

Smiling, Neil leaned closer and pressed another kiss on her warm temple. "Yeah, I'm practicing," he murmured. "Or something like that."

## Chapter Five

His lips were injecting some sort of twilight drug into her temple. What else could be the reason for this sensation of floating? she wondered dreamily.

A set of strong, warm fingers suddenly curved around her shoulder, the faint rasp of a five-o'clock shadow brushed against her cheek. She sensed more than saw his lips descending upon hers. But she was too tranquilized to do anything but let him have his way.

For long moments she could only respond to the thrill of his hard lips moving over hers, the sinfully delicious taste of his stolen kiss.

Then nearby laughter drifted across from the river, reminding Raine that the two of them were in a very public spot and practically necking like a pair of teenagers.

Raine jumped out of his arms as though he was an

exploding firecracker and backed several steps away from the bench.

Neil stared at her, a sleepy, sexy grin adorning his face. "Oh, now, what's the matter, honey? Why are you looking at me like you'd like to throw a dagger at my chest?"

Was she? Raine felt more like cuddling back up to his side and the shock of that realization must have put a glower on her face. She drew in several long breaths and tried to calm her roiling senses.

"What do you think is wrong with me?" she asked in a strained voice. "You behaving like Romeo isn't part of the deal! In fact, you'd better decide right now whether you want to flirt or do your job!"

Neil laughed. He couldn't help it. Not when she was so beautiful and the words coming out of her mouth were so sweetly outraged.

"I thought it had everything to do with my job. We are going to be lovers, remember?" He just had to remind her.

Groaning with frustration, Raine moved back to the bench and plopped down on the far end away from him.

"Maybe you should be the one remembering," she retorted. "We're going to be lovers *only* in pretense. And if you can't agree to those terms, then we'd better call it quits right now!"

Neil scooted toward her, but only for a short distance. He realized if he slid too close, she'd be back on her feet in a flash. "Raine! There's no need for you to get so bent out of shape. It was just a tiny get-to-know-you kiss. It couldn't have been all that offensive, could it?"

There hadn't been one damn thing offensive about it, Raine thought. That's why she was so upset. Even if he was stronger than a jolt of tequila, she couldn't start swooning over this man.

"No. There was nothing wrong with your kiss. It's your brashness and this attitude that you think you can touch me—in a familiar way."

She was getting way too worked up about this. But then, so was he, Neil realized. Only he was worked up in a far different way. Kissing Raine had been too darn good for his own peace of mind. He wanted to repeat the act. Over and over. And already he was imagining what it would be like to have her naked and trembling in his arms.

"All right, Raine," he said gently. "I promise to behave myself. But I'm going to warn you right now, whenever we're in the presence of your mother, we're going to have to give her some sort of physical display. The first time you start behaving as though I have smallpox then she's going to smell a fish."

He was right, of course. But how was she going to handle having him touch her, Raine wondered, when that little kiss of his was enough to make her shake?

Jutting her chin with more confidence than she felt, she glanced at him. "Look, you just worry about your end of the bargain and I'll hold up mine. Like I said, I can act when there's a need for it."

Act? Yeah, right. As long as Neil Rankin believed she was acting, Raine tried to assure herself, then everything would be all right.

"And I can be a gentlemen when needed," he replied, his blue eyes narrowed on her face. "So there shouldn't be a problem, should there?"

Shaking her hair back, she tilted her head to a regal angle. "None that I can imagine," she lied.

He rose to his feet and offered his hand to her. "Now that

we have that settled, I think we'd better head to the ranch. Don't you?"

Raine wasn't all that anxious to show up on her mother's doorstep with Neil on her arm. But dallying around here in San Antonio with the man might prove to be even more dangerous. Especially if he decided to try some of his "practicing" again.

Placing her hand in his, she allowed him to pull her to her feet. "You're probably right," she answered. "The drive will take at least an hour and like I said before, it would be better to get there before dark."

"Good. Where are you parked?"

She pulled her hand from his and motioned in the direction from which they walked.

He nodded. "So am I. Let's go," he urged.

As they retraced their steps along the riverbank, Raine expected him to reach for her hand or loop his arm through hers. Instead he kept an appropriate distance between them and his hands to his sides. The fact that he was sticking to his promise should have pleased her, but instead she felt flat and just a little disappointed. A realization that troubled her greatly.

As it turned out, Neil's dark green SUV was parked only a few cars away from Raine's white pickup truck. Before they climbed into their respective vehicles, Raine gave him brief directions of how to follow her out of the city and onto the main highway that would lead them to the Sandbur.

Neil had no problem keeping up with Raine in the busy city traffic. She was a cautious, by-the-book driver and before long they were beyond the suburbs of San Antonio, traveling south on Highway 181. At first, the hill country was lush and green and dotted with plenty of spreading live oak and huge pecan trees. But later, as the miles passed behind them, the area grew flat and much more rugged and arid. Cacti, yucca and mesquite trees began to appear and where the grass had been thick and green, now it was thin and spotty.

By the time they turned off the main highway and headed west on a farm to market road, few house places could be found and traffic was practically nonexistent. Eventually the landscape turned even more isolated. Miles passed before a living creature of any sort appeared and that came in the form of white Brahman cattle. With the sighting of the cattle, Neil also noticed the fence separating the land from the highway changed from sagging hog wire to sturdy strands of barbed wire strung tautly along fat, cedar post. No doubt they were on Sandbur land, he decided. Even behind the windshield of his SUV, he could feel the mystique of the a huge old ranch, especially one that had been handed down through generations of family.

Once they reached the entrance of the ranch yard, Neil expected Raine to pull over and share the next step of the trip with him, but she surprised him by simply driving on through the iron gates and onto a narrow graveled road that led through a series of barns, outbuildings, and livestock pens.

A half a mile passed before a huge house on the far right appeared. The two-story structure was made of rough, pale green stucco trimmed in dark wood and roofed with matching wooden shingles. The porch running along the front was elaborate with several wooden pillars supporting the overhang. A quick glance at the place was all Neil had time for before they moved past the ranch house, but it was enough to see an assortment of brightly colored lawn furniture interspersed with potted flowering plants adorning the porch.

As they traveled on, more cattle pens fabricated from iron pipe appeared on both sides of the narrow road and then another huge house appeared to their left. The structure sat several yards back from the road and was shaded with live oaks, Mexican palms and weeping willows. Compared to the home they had just passed, the red brick house wasn't quite as elaborate, but almost. It, too, had two stories, but the style was more antebellum than Mexican.

Apparently the "sisters" had done quite well for themselves, Neil couldn't help thinking, as he kept one eye on Raine's taillights and the other on the rich surroundings of the Sandbur.

Just past the red brick, Raine turned to the left and traveled another quarter of a mile. When she finally brought the truck to a halt, Neil could see they had stopped in front of a small house with pale yellow siding. As he cut the vehicle's engine, he noticed a black dog leaping off the small square of concrete porch and racing toward the chain-link fence surrounding the yard.

While the dog barked a vicious warning, Neil waited in the vehicle until Raine walked over to his window before he climbed out to join her.

"Is this where your mother lives?" he asked.

Even in the dusky twilight, he could see a weary, nervous expression on her features, and he realized she was dreading the moment Esther Crockett laid eyes on him.

Casting a wary glance at the house, she nodded. "Are you ready for this?"

She made it sound as though he was about to face a judge who'd already decided he was guilty as hell and needed maximum punishment. Surely the woman couldn't be that bad, Neil considered. And if she truly was that difficult to deal with, then it was about time Raine stood up to her.

"I couldn't be more ready," he said, then grinned at her. "But maybe you'd better forewarn me before we go inside. What am I?"

Before she could answer, the front door decorated with a wreath of pine cones, opened on the house and a woman stepped onto the porch. The black dog raced back to her, but kept up its barking.

Stepping closer, Raine lifted her mouth close to his ear. "On the way down here, I called my mother and told her we were coming. I said that you're a financial advisor and we first met over the phone when I needed some advice about tax shelters for the ranch."

Bending his head, he replied in a hushed tone, "Sounds good enough to me. Just don't ask me to do any rapid calculations in my head."

The woman on the porch called out, "Raine? Is that you?"

Raine slipped her arm through Neil's and tugged him toward the house.

"Yes, it's me, Mother," she answered. "And I've brought someone with me."

Esther Crockett was a tall woman somewhere in her early sixties. Dressed in dark slacks and a plain white blouse, her graying blond hair was pulled severely back from her face and wrapped in a coronet at the back of her head. The corners of her mouth were turned downward and Neil could only wonder if the expression was a reaction to him or if she wore a permanent frown on her face.

At the foot of the porch, Neil stood on the bottom step and reached a hand up to Esther.

"Hello, Mrs. Crockett. I'm Neil Rankin," he introduced himself.

The woman cast a skeptical glance at her daughter, then settled it back on Neil's face before she extended her hand to greet him.

"Nice to meet you," she murmured stiffly.

The woman's handshake was as lukewarm as her greeting, but Neil didn't allow her attitude to put him off. He'd already expected as much.

Smiling with as much authenticity as he could muster, he said, "And it's very nice to meet you, Mrs. Crockett. Raine has talked so much about you that I feel I already know you."

The woman's brows slowly inched upward, then shot up to greater proportions as she watched Raine join him on the step and wrap both arms around him as though she couldn't bear to be an inch away from him. Neil decided right then and there that pretending to be Raine's lover was going to be far more pleasant than he'd ever expected. After all, there was nothing better for a man's ego than to be adored by a beautiful woman, even when the adoration was only make-believe.

Esther didn't make any sort of reply and Raine was the first to break the short, awkward silence.

"Mother, do you think you might ask us in? Neil and I have just driven down from the city and we'd very much like something to drink."

The older woman stared in dismay at her daughter, but only for a moment. Turning, she opened the door behind her and gestured for the two of them to enter the house.

Once inside, Neil took a quick glance around the small living room. The space was neat and furnished modestly. Along the north wall, centered in the middle of double windows, a small Christmas tree sat on a table. The sight of the holiday tradition gave him hope. After all, with a Christmas tree in her house, Esther couldn't be a complete scrooge. Neil's attention turned to the beautiful woman dangling on his side, then on to the stern older one motioning for them to take a seat on the couch. It was incredible to him that Raine had been born from such a woman. They looked nothing alike and where Raine radiated sweetness and beauty, Esther Crockett seemed to emit bitterness.

"I have to admit, Raine, that I'm very surprised you brought a—friend home with you." She stood in the middle of the room, staring at the pair of them as though they were a pair of teenagers who'd stayed out past their curfew. "When you left this morning, you didn't say anything about meeting someone."

While Esther stood and stared, the two of them took seats close together on the couch. Neil blatantly continued to hold Raine's hand and at Esther's remark, he squeezed it slightly. In response, Raine looked at him with a tiny smile that spoke of silent conspiracy.

"I know," Raine said, turning her attention to her mother. "But I wanted to surprise you."

Raine's gaze drifted back to Neil's face and he gave her a slow wink. The sexy gesture burned her cheeks and suddenly she was remembering the wild, delicious taste of his lips and how hard and fast her heart had beaten as he kissed her.

Jerking her gaze back to her mother, she gave her a starry-eyed smile. "I'm sure this is a surprise—"

"Surprise?" Esther interrupted curtly. "I certainly wouldn't describe it that way. More like a lightning strike. You haven't mentioned having any sort of boyfriend." She stopped long enough to narrow her eyes on Neil's face. "Is that what this young man is to you?"

Neil pressed himself closer to Raine and enveloped her hand between both of his. If she took the gesture as a sign of support from him, he couldn't exactly tell, he only knew that the soft, pleading look in her green eyes struck him right in the heart. Dear Lord, it was incredible how much he already wanted to help her.

Raine tried to laugh, but wound up clearing her throat more than anything. "Well—first of all, Neil is a financial advisor for a brokerage firm in San Antonio. That's how we met. Over the telephone. I was needing advice on tax shelters for the ranch and—well, Neil had some wonderful suggestions." She turned a melting smile on him. "Once we got to talking we hit it right off, didn't we, darling?"

As far as Neil was concerned she could have taken her acting talents further than a college play. She was so convincing he was actually beginning to *feel* like her lover.

"That's right, Mrs. Crockett. Something about your daughter's voice attracted me and then when we finally met in person, well, I was instantly smitten." At least that much was the truth, Neil thought.

Esther's expression was more than skeptical. Her features were etched in stone. "You've done a good job of flooring me, Raine. Why haven't you mentioned this man before?"

*This man.* She couldn't even use his name, Raine thought crossly. That would make it all seem too permanent and real for her mother. But then why the heck should it bother her if Esther acknowledged Neil in an unkindly fashion? He wasn't really her love interest. He was just a man digging for the truth. But Esther wasn't aware of that. To her mother, he was simply her daughter's love interest. And if she was anywhere close to the mother that Raine wanted her to be, she would be welcoming Neil with open arms instead of skepticism.

Raine answered, "Because I wanted to wait until I was certain my feelings for Neil were serious before I brought him here to the ranch to meet you."

Esther moved forward until she was practically standing over them. Her gaze was sharp and probing as she settled it on Raine.

"And now you're telling me that you *are* serious? Just suddenly out of the blue?"

Raine thanked God that Neil was holding her hand tightly. His touch strengthened her and reminded her that she wasn't in this thing alone.

She cast him a nervous smile and he leveled a crooked grin back at her that said he understood her mother's third degree and everything would be okay. The tension inside her was suddenly replaced with unexpected warmth.

"That's right. Except that this whole thing with Neil and I isn't sudden. We've been seeing each other for some time now. And I thought with Christmas coming it would be a nice time to tell you about him."

Esther appeared incensed. As though her adult daughter seeing a man was something akin to criminal behavior.

"You mean all those times you've traveled up to San Antonio you were seeing him?" She waved a hand at Neil. "I thought you were going shopping!"

Yeah, shopping for a man, Raine wanted very much to say. But the sarcasm would be lost on Esther and, anyway, Raine wasn't that sort of daughter. Smiling gently, Raine settled her eyes back on Neil's face. "I was going shopping. Neil just happened to be going with me. And now—well—I can't keep it from you any longer." She glanced at her mother. "I'm so much in love with Neil that he has me considering marriage. I even have my eye on a wedding dress that I saw in a little boutique on the river walk."

After that shocking confession, Neil fully expected Esther to explode. He was pretty stunned himself. Yet the older woman merely shook her head in amazement and said, "We'll talk about all of this later, Raine. Right now I'll go get a light supper together for you and Neil. Why don't you take him out on the back patio? With the sun already down, it should be cool out there."

"Thank you, Mother," Raine told her. "But I should help you in the kitchen. Neil won't mind."

With a dismissive wave of her hand, the woman turned and started out of the room. "No. You two go on. I'll bring it all out to the patio whenever I have it ready."

Once Esther had disappeared from the room, Neil bent his head close to Raine's and exclaimed in a loud whisper, "What in hell are you doing? I've gone from a lawyer to a financial advisor and now a fiancé!"

"Sshh! She'll hear you," she scolded, then pulling him along with her, she jumped to her feet. "Come on. Let's go outside where we can talk."

The two of them left the house by way of the front entrance and once they were outside, Raine led him around the side of the small yard until they reached the back and a rectangular patio made from red brick. The area was partially covered with a roof that extended from the house, while the other was shaded with several fat palm trees and an oleander bush dotted with hot pink blossoms.

Raine gestured for him to take a seat in one of the lawn

chairs situated around a glass-topped table, but Neil shook his head. Instead he took her by the arm and led her behind a cove of flowering bushes where the two of them couldn't be spotted from any of the windows in the house.

"All right," he said, "why don't you explain what all of that was about. I sure as hell didn't come down here with the intentions of playing the role of your fiancé!"

He was angry. A condition that was very uncharacteristic for Neil. But he couldn't help himself. For Raine to give her mother the impression that she was considering marriage with him was a little too scary for Neil's liking. Even if she had said everything with her fingers crossed behind her back. Just hearing a woman link him with the word marriage made him more than nervous.

Shaking her head, Raine looked up at him with disbelief. "Neil, you're the one who said we had to be a convincing couple!"

Even though he was trying to concentrate on her words she was standing so close that the front of her body was brushing against his and shooting streaks of fire straight to his loins. "I did say that," he agreed, his voice dropping to a husky tone. "But don't you think you're taking things a bit far? Making Esther think we're lovers didn't have to include the idea of marriage."

She sighed and the soft sound rippled across his skin like the touch of a finger. The desire to reach out and brush his knuckles against her cheek, to pull her into his arms and bury his face in the side of her neck was playing with his senses, making it difficult to remember why he was here and what the two of them were really supposed to be doing.

"What's the matter with you?" she whispered fiercely. "I thought you were game for all of this. Are you trying to tell me that you're getting cold feet?"

The mere mention of the word cold, while everything inside him was heating to the boiling point, was enough to push Neil over the edge. Behaving as a gentleman was the last thing on his mind as he took her shoulders in both hands and jerked her forward.

"If you think I've gone cold then maybe I should enlighten you," he murmured as he settled his arms around her back.

Surprised, her head fell back while her hands lifted against his chest in a defensive gesture.

"What are you doing?"

Her low, huskily spoken question put a wicked grin on his face.

"Showing you what it's like to play with fire."

Raine could see the kiss coming and realized she should swing her head aside, push out of his arms, do anything to avoid it. But she couldn't seem to make her body do any of those common sense things. Instead she closed her eyes and waited for his lips to settle upon hers.

When they did, she felt her breath stop in her throat, her heart leap across a giant chasm then take off in an all out sprint. A tiny moan sounded in the back of her throat and then the last of her resistance fluttered away like wilted rose petals on the breeze. Her hands flattened and softened against his chest, then slid provocatively up his shoulders, while her mouth opened to the search of his lips.

Back and forth his mouth rocked over hers until his tongue slipped between her teeth. Like an automatic switch, her body melted against his and his hands slipped from the small of her back to the rounded curve of her hips.

With one little tug their loins were pressed tightly together, her breasts were squashed against his hard chest. Heat was rapidly suffusing every particle in her body and she knew if he didn't stop soon her senses would be totally lost to him. Then just as her knees were growing mushy, he finally lifted his head and looked down at her.

His nostrils were flared and beneath the splay of her hands, she could feel his lungs expanding as he dragged in several calming breaths. As for herself, she wasn't sure she'd ever breathe properly again. Her head was reeling and parts of her body were tingling with urges that turned her cheeks red with embarrassment.

"Still wondering if I'm getting cold?" he murmured the question.

Raine was forced to swallow before she could make her throat work and even after that her voice was hardly above a whisper when she finally spoke. "You…didn't have to take things that far to make your point, did you?"

His gaze was purely sensual as it slipped over her shadowed face. "Probably not. But I enjoyed every minute of it."

*Chapter Six*

Neil's admission was enough to shake her out of the fog of desire that had settled over her, though she pushed out of his arms with far more determination than she was feeling. "We'd better get over to the patio before Mother finds us," she muttered as she stepped around the edge of the bushes and back into the open area of the yard.

Chuckling lowly, Neil followed on her heels. "And what would be wrong with that?" he asked. "To hear you tell it, we're getting married. Engaged couples do kiss—among other things."

Raine refused to look at him as she walked quickly over to the nearest lawn chair and slipped onto the seat. "I thought you were a lawyer, not a wolf," she replied coolly.

Neil laughed easily as he sank into the chair next to hers. "Honey, most people consider the two animals close cousins."

He was teasing her and Raine figured she should probably be laughing and making an effort to lighten what had just happened between them. But she'd been staggered by the feelings Neil had invoked in her. Even now her whole body felt as if it was glowing and sending out a bright neon message to him that continued to flash the words "make love to me."

Thankfully, only a few silent moments had passed between them when Esther appeared carrying a tray. As they helped themselves to finger sandwiches, chips and lemonade, the other woman took a seat directly across from them and scanned Raine's pale face before moving on to Neil.

"So, Mr. Rankin, do you have family?"

The question was blunt and more interrogating than conversational, but Neil managed to keep an easy smile on his face as he answered the woman's question.

"My father passed away several years ago, but my mother is still living in Santa Fe, New Mexico. I don't have any siblings, but I do have a few aunts and uncles strung across the States. What about yourself?" Neil asked casually.

Beside him, he could hear Raine's slight intake of breath and realized she was walking a tight rope between staying in her mother's good graces and searching for her father. The idea that Esther could be so insensitive and self-centered angered him greatly. But it didn't surprise him. Not when for years he'd watched his own mother demand to be the center of the universe.

Esther's whole body visibly stiffened and for a moment he thought she was going to get up and leave their little party, but then she released a long breath and smoothed a hand over her hair with just enough flair to remind Neil of an actress on the silent screen. Maybe he and Raine weren't the only ones doing some pretending, he mused.

"Hasn't Raine told you about my…memory loss?" she asked. "I mean, if you two are close enough to be considering marriage, you surely know about her family."

He could feel Raine's gaze boring a hole in the side of his face, but he continued to study Esther as he replied, "Yes. Raine has told me about your unfortunate accident. And I'm so very sorry that something so awful had to happen to you, Mrs. Crockett. I just thought that perhaps some of your lost family might have managed to find you since your memory failure."

Clearly affronted, Esther leaned back in her chair and crossed her legs. As she did, Neil did his best to try to equate her to the fragile, beautiful woman he remembered meeting on the T Bar K that day he'd been visiting Linc. But try as he might, he couldn't envision them being the same woman. In his opinion, it wasn't possible for a person to change *that* much.

"Isn't it obvious that Raine would be the first person I would tell if something like that had happened?"

Not if you wanted to hide something from her, Neil thought. To Esther, he said, "Sorry. That was a stupid question."

The woman heaved out a breath as though she were attempting to relax, yet Neil couldn't help but observe her toe nervously tapping the air. Was she worried about exposing something about herself, or simply worried that her daughter had found a man? Neil wished he had the answers.

"Well, Raine and I have found a family here on the ranch with the Saddlers and the Sanchezes, haven't we, sweetheart?"

Neil glanced to Raine and noticed she was incredibly pale. Especially after the warm pink that had flushed her face after their kiss.

Hell, Neil, that was far more than any kiss, he corrected himself. The exchange between them had been more like a minor earthquake and his body was still reeling from the aftershocks.

"Yes. That's right," Raine answered dutifully. "We're all like one big family around here."

Sure it was good to have close, loving friends, Neil thought. In fact, without his buddies back in Aztec, his life would be pretty solitary. But that wasn't the sort of family Raine was really searching for. She was a conventional woman. She wanted a father and siblings to complete the circle of her family. Maybe they were out there and maybe they weren't. Either way, if Esther wanted to do the right thing, she'd step to the plate and help her daughter find the answers.

"Well, if you ask me, there is such a thing as miracles. And who knows, maybe you just might start to remember things," Neil said to Esther in an optimistic tone. "And that would surely make Raine happy."

The older woman looked at him stonily. "I wouldn't hold my breath. I haven't remembered anything in twenty-four years. And I don't figure there will be any miracles happening around here in the future."

From the corner of his eye, he could see Raine bending her head. Whether her reaction to her mother's response was from embarrassment or pain, Neil wasn't quite sure. But there was one thing he was certain about: her sadness bothered him far more than he wanted to admit.

Turning his gaze back on Esther, it was on the tip of his tongue to suggest that she might try praying more, but he kept the remark to himself. After all, Esther was the only real family Raine had and he didn't want to cause any more unease between the two of them than there already was.

Abruptly, while Neil's thoughts were vacillating between

Raine's needs and Esther's stiffness, the woman rose to her feet. "You two enjoy the rest of your meal," she said to the two of them. "There's something in the house I need to attend to."

After Esther disappeared into the house, Raine leaned back in her chair and rubbed a thumb and forefinger across her forehead.

"God, why does she have to be this way?"

Hearing the utter despair in her voice, Neil scooted his chair closer and reached for her hand. As he squeezed her fingers, he wanted to tell her that she needed to stand up to Esther Crockett, she needed to remind her mother that she was now a grown woman and she didn't appreciate her bitter, demanding attitude. But he was the last person to be giving family relations advice, he reminded himself. Especially when he was barely on speaking terms with his own mother.

"Don't let it bother you, Raine. Everything will be okay. I'll be gone from here in a few days and then I'm sure she'll go back to normal." Whatever normal was for Esther, he thought grimly.

Dejected, Raine looked at him. "Your leaving won't necessarily appease her. Remember, she'll be thinking we're engaged and she'll be hounding me to give you the boot."

One corner of his mouth turned upward. "Then by all means, when that time comes you can give me the boot."

Sure. That was easy enough for him to say, Raine thought. Just end this farce of a relationship as though it didn't mean anything to her.

*It doesn't mean anything, Raine. Remember, you just met the man.*

The little voice racing through her mind stopped her short. This was all just a playact and soon Neil would be out of her life. She had to quit thinking about him in a personal way. She had to stop dwelling on their reckless embrace. But the memory of those moments seemed to have already been branded in her mind and the more she thought about the way she'd kissed him, the more she recognized that her response had been more than physical desire.

True, the touch of his lips had set off a fire inside her, but beneath the flames she'd felt something strong and sweet, a connection to another human being that she'd never felt before. The realization frightened Raine to the very core of her being because she knew if she let her guard down, even for a minute, this man was going to walk away with her heart.

The emotions roiling inside Raine made it impossible for her to look at him directly. Instead she kept her eyes focused on their entwined hands.

"So. What do you think now that you've met my mother? Do you think there's any chance that she might be Darla Carlton?"

"It's a bit early to be asking me that, don't you think?"

She darted a glance at him from the corner of her eye. "Probably. I guess I'd just like to hear your initial opinion."

Neil kept his sigh to himself. The last thing he wanted to do at this moment was to squash Raine's hope. He was quickly beginning to see how very important this whole search was to her. Yet common sense told him that the chances of Esther and Darla being the same person were more than great. How would a woman who'd once been married to a New Mexican cattle baron end up here in Texas working as a housekeeper? It didn't add up to him, but then strange things did happen in the world. And anyway, he had to have an excuse to stay a few more days, Neil decided. After the kiss

Raine had given him a few minutes ago, he wasn't about to walk away. The afterburners from that brief connection were still scorching him.

"Okay," he answered. "In my opinion the chances are slim. But I came here to investigate and we won't really know for sure until I can come up with answers to some pertinent questions."

Raine nodded, her expression clearly worried. "That's what I was thinking, too. But I really don't know how you're going to go about asking questions, Neil. You see how my mother is."

"Don't start fretting now. Your mother isn't the only person around here that might shed a bit of light on things. I'll get some answers. It might just take a little longer, that's all."

Raine looked at him squarely and her eyes were shaded with sad resignation. "I'm sorry she's been so curt with you. Just try not to take it personally. No matter what sort of man I brought home to meet her, she'd resent him."

Wanting to soothe her somehow, Neil's thumb caressed the top of her hand. "Don't worry about me, Raine. I have a thick hide. I'm just wondering why your mother doesn't want you to have a man in your life. Most mothers are jubilant about their daughters marrying and having children. I hate to say this, Raine, but in many aspects, your mother is—rather strange."

She sighed and there was such a lonely sound to it that Neil's heart winced.

"You don't have to tell me that. It's something I've lived with for as long as I can remember. From the time I was a very small girl, Mother has done all she could to control me. During my adolescent years she was so overly protective that what few little friends I had were forced to spend time with me here on the ranch or not at all. I wasn't permitted to go to their homes or, God forbid, spend the night at a pajama party.

My clothes always had to be sedate. And above everything, I was never to do anything that might draw attention to myself."

He studied her face in the waning light as he tried to imagine her as a young child, wanting and needing to feel as if she belonged with her peer group, but having her spirit tamped down by a controlling mother. The image was disturbing to Neil. Almost as much as his own memories as a child and the sound of Claudia shouting unreasonable demands at his father, of things being thrown and broken, of James's low voice attempting to placate her and the haggard sadness he constantly wore on his face.

"I can't imagine what your teenage years must have been like," he murmured as he tried to push away his own dark memories.

Stirring, she pulled her hand from his and rose to her feet. Neil watched her amble aimlessly around the patio. She was still wearing the same powder-blue dress she'd had on when they'd met at the river walk. The soft fabric clung to her curves like a gentle hand. Her whole appearance was both sexy and sophisticated, making it quite obvious that she'd emerged from her mother's thumb. But Neil wondered at what cost.

"They weren't pleasant years, I can tell you that much. While my friends were dating and choosing prom gowns I stayed at home and dreamed."

Since Neil was a guy, he couldn't fully appreciate the importance of those things to a teenage girl, but he had a fairly good idea. It would be like him being kept off the debate team, when he'd fancied himself as being the best arguer in the whole high school.

"You mean she wouldn't allow you to go to your prom?" he asked with disbelief.

Raine shook her head as she absently fingered the leaf of a rosebush climbing a post supporting the patio roof. "Oh, I had permission to go. But I didn't. Being a dowdily dressed wallflower was not my idea of a good time." Her face was a picture of puzzlement as she walked back over to where Neil remained seated in the lawn chair. "Sometimes I wonder if my mother had some sort of bad experience with a man. Something she hasn't told me about. That's the only thing I can imagine to explain why she's so averse to me getting into a relationship. Maybe she thinks I'll be hurt like she was. What else could it be?"

He turned one hand up in a helpless gesture. "I'm just a lawyer, Raine, not a therapist. And I'm not good with family issues. I'm more of a one-on-one guy."

He didn't have to tell Raine that bit of information: she'd encountered it firsthand and she was already inclined to believe he'd changed her life forever. Just looking at him sitting here in the twilight was enough to make her heart thud with longing, a longing too deep to be rational.

Annoyed with her reckless thoughts, she busied herself with picking up their paper plates and dirty glasses. "If you're finished eating, maybe we'd better go inside. She's probably in there stewing."

Neil rose to his feet and reached for the tray before Raine had a chance to. "Yeah. It's probably time I head over to Goliad and find a motel room."

Raine paused long enough to look up at him and suddenly all the attraction she'd been feeling for the man tumbled into one hot image. Him in a motel room, undressed and in bed. Her in his arms.

"I—I wished you didn't have to drive anymore tonight. I'm

sure Geraldine would be glad for you to stay in the ranch house with her."

With a brief smile of appreciation, Neil shook his head. "The woman hasn't even met me yet. And I don't want to start intruding on anyone here on the Sandbur. It won't hurt for me to drive fifteen miles or so."

He started toward the back entrance of the house and Raine followed alongside him. "I'm going to be indebted to you for life," she said. "You're going to a lot of trouble just for me."

They reached the door and he turned his head to glance at her. "Remember, Raine, there's someone else I'm doing this for, too."

In other words, he wasn't going to all these extra lengths just for her, she thought. The reminder hit her like a whack in the face, yet she told herself that she'd needed it. She had to stop all these personal thoughts she was having about the man.

"Yes, you're right," she said with a forced smile. "So I won't feel too guilty about making you work overtime."

She opened the door and the two of them entered the house. They found Esther in the kitchen making a fresh pot of coffee. The moment she heard their footsteps, she glanced over her shoulder and Neil was mildly shocked to see something close to a smile on the woman's face.

"I thought you might want some dessert and coffee," she explained. "Cook made red velvet cake for supper and I brought plenty home with me."

Neil placed the tray on the cabinet counter, then glanced to where Raine stood next to a wooden dining table. She looked as perplexed by this development as he felt. "That's very nice of you, Mrs. Crockett. I'd enjoy a piece of cake before I leave."

Clearly surprised by his announcement, the older woman turned to stare at him. "Leave? You're planning on leaving the ranch tonight? I got the impression you were here for a little visit."

"Neil needs to rent a motel room," Raine informed her.

Esther's gaze switched quickly from her daughter over to Neil. "That's not necessary," she said quickly, her expression guarded. "I have plenty of room here for you and Raine. There's no need for either of you to drive over to Goliad tonight."

While Neil was trying to digest Esther's unexpected offer, Raine said, "Neil will be staying for more than one night, Mother."

Shrugging, Esther turned her attention back to the double sink where a handful of dishes were soaking in soapy water. As she picked up a saucer and swiped a sponge over its surface, she said, "No matter. He's welcome to stay a few days."

Neil's gaze slipped over to Raine and he could see by the stunned look on her face that she was just as astonished as he was. He could also see she was troubled about something. Probably worrying that Esther would discover the real reason for his being here on the Sandbur, he figured.

Moving to Raine's side, he slipped an arm around the back of her waist and gave her a little reassuring smile. She acknowledged his touch with a glance, but didn't return his smile.

"That's awfully generous of you, Mrs. Crockett," he said to Esther. "Thank you."

"Yes, thank you, Mother," Raine added stiffly. "It will make it much easier for Neil and I to spend time together."

Neil gently pinched her side to get her attention, then made a motion with his head for the two of them to exit the kitchen.

"Uh, Raine, could you show me the bathroom? I need to freshen up before we have cake and coffee with your mother," he said.

With a wary glance at him, she said, "Sure." And then to her mother, added, "We'll be back in a few moments."

Raine nudged him toward an open doorway on the opposite side of the room and once the two of them were out of the kitchen and back into the living room, she pointed toward a short hallway. "The bathroom is right there on the right," she informed him.

"Yeah, I see." Neil took her by the arm and pulled her along with him until they were both standing in the darkness of the hallway where he was sure they couldn't be seen or heard by Raine's mother. With one hand retaining a hold on her shoulder, he admitted, "I did need to find the bathroom. But I thought we should talk. You looked almost sick in there when your mother invited me to stay. What's the matter? Are *you* getting cold feet now?"

Even though they were standing in the darkness, she didn't chance looking at him. Her face was hot and no telling what he might see in her eyes. "Let's not go into that again," she murmured.

"Then what's worrying you? And don't tell me you're not worried. I could see it all over your face."

Dear God, was she becoming that transparent? Raine wondered. But no, if she was wearing all of her feelings on her face, then he would know her worries had little to do with her mother and a whole lot to do with staying under the same roof with him when he was constantly touching her, looking at her as though he adored her. It was more distraction than an inexperienced woman like her could handle.

"Well, actually I guess I am a little concerned," she said slowly. "I can't figure what Mother is up to. Inviting you to stay here is almost too nice. I'm afraid she's doing it so she can pick you apart."

Neil gave her a wry smile. "Honey, she's doing it so she can keep an eye on us. If you go back to your apartment in Goliad and I go to rent a motel room, then she can't be sure that the two of us won't wind up in bed together. Here under her roof, she can make sure we don't."

As Neil's words began to sink in on her, Raine's face grew even hotter than it already was. She didn't know what was more embarrassing—her mother's manipulation, or the fact that Raine had already envisaged the two of them in bed together.

"Oh Lord, I should have expected her to be thinking along those lines. But I guess I keep hoping she'll start to treat me as a grown woman." Groaning, she shook her head. "Looks like that hasn't happened yet."

Neil squeezed her shoulder. "Don't worry about her motives," he urged. "She's actually helping our cause. I'll be right here on the ranch—with you," he added.

The low, suggestive tone of his voice sent warning signals clanging in the back of Raine's head and she choked back another groan before he could guess how much he was affecting her. "You make it sound like we really *are* lovers."

His hand slipped upward from her shoulder until he was cupping the side of her neck. Raine felt goose bumps dance along her arms and bosom.

"I wouldn't be averse to making that part of our story true," he whispered huskily. "What about you?"

Her jaw fell and she whispered loudly, "Is this what you call behaving like a gentleman?"

He chuckled. "I am being a gentleman, Raine. Otherwise, you'd already be in my arms. Like this."

He tugged her forward and Raine was shocked to find herself clamped tightly to the front of his body.

She squirmed in an attempt to escape the circle of his arms, but the movement only made things worse. His body was as hard as a rock and she could feel the softness of her own curves gladly yielding to every inch of him.

If he kissed her again, she desperately feared she would go up in flames. "Neil—you…"

"Raine. The coffee is ready."

The sound of her mother's voice calling out to her was enough to break Neil's hold on her and she backed away from him with a sigh of relief. Or was the sudden surge of feelings inside her more like regret? Dear Lord, the man was making her crazy!

Glancing up at his grinning face, she muttered, "I'll see you in the kitchen."

She turned to go, but before she could slip away from him, his hand reached out and caressed the length of her arm.

"Relax, Raine. You look like a storm is about to blow in."

No, she thought, the storm had already hit. Now she could only hope the damage left behind wouldn't be the remnants of her heart.

## Chapter Seven

The next morning Raine was in the kitchen pouring a cup of coffee when she heard footsteps on the tile behind her.

Knowing it was Neil, she braced herself as she added cream to her cup, then turned to face him. This morning he was dressed casually in Levi's and a blue plaid shirt. The color made his eyes just that more vivid and the worn jeans outlined his long, muscular legs much more than the dress pants he'd been wearing yesterday. He looked rugged and sexy and far too potent for any normal girl to handle and especially a girl who'd spent most of the night tossing and turning and trying to get the man out of her mind.

"Good morning," she greeted.

Smiling, he walked over to the cabinet where she was standing. "Good morning. Got any more of that?" he asked, inclining his head toward her coffee cup.

"A whole pot." She opened the cabinet and took down a green cup that matched hers. As she filled it with coffee, she said, "I was just wondering whether I should wake you up before I left for work."

Neil glanced at his watch. "Am I late? It's only seven-thirty."

Smiling faintly, she handed him the cup. "We don't keep lawyer's hours here on the ranch, Neil. Matt would say we're already burning daylight."

"Matt?"

"Matteo Sanchez. He's the general manager of the ranch and oversees the cattle operation."

"Oh, yeah, I remember now. You said something about two more family members running the ranch, didn't you?" Neil asked. "Sorry I don't remember their names. Yesterday was a long day."

Smiling faintly, Raine turned back to the cabinet. "Matt's younger brother, Cordero, manages the ranch's working remuda, plus the horses that are trained and sold. And their cousin, Lex Saddler, does a little of everything in between, including sales and shipping."

"Hmm. So the ranch truly is a family operation," Neil mused aloud as he tilted his coffee cup to his lips.

"Very much so. It's been that way for nearly a century, I think." Raine opened a loaf of bread and dropped four pieces into a toaster. As she watched the coils inside the appliance heat to a bright red, she decided she was worse than the toaster. She didn't even have to be plugged into electricity to feel a sizzle. One look from Neil was enough to heat her. Even now, with her back turned to him, she could feel his eyes on her and just the thought left her cheeks warm, her heart beating fast.

She glanced over her shoulder. "I thought you might like to walk over to the barns with me this morning and meet the guys. That is, if I'm lucky enough to find them all on the ranch at one time."

He smiled. "Sure. Since I'm practically your fiancé, I need to see what sort of competition I have here on the ranch," he teased. "I hope all three men are married."

Even though she understood Neil was just being playful with her, she couldn't stop the warm, gentle feeling settling over her. It was nice to hear him speak as though she was attractive, as though she was a woman that any man would cherish.

"No. None of them are married. Matteo is widowed and has a daughter. The other two guys are still single. But believe me, I'm like a little sister to all of them. They've watched me grow up here on the ranch."

The bread popped up and while she began to butter each piece, Neil glanced around the homey kitchen. The room was small enough to make it feel cozy, yet large enough for two people to cook at the same time. He thought of his own kitchen back home and tried to remember the last time a woman had been in it. Too long for him to clearly recall. He'd learned early on in his young life that if you shared a bit of hearth and home with a woman they tended to get clingy, and fast. Now that he'd gotten older and wiser, he avoided any sort of domestic scene with a woman. It was easier that way.

Maybe he was breaking his own rule with Raine, he admitted to himself. But this time with her was only going to last a few days at the most. Besides, she wasn't interested in hanging on to him. Her thoughts were zeroed in on finding her father. He was as safe as a baby cradled in its mother's arms.

"Where's Esther?" he asked.

Raine carried a plate of toast over to the table then fetched saucers for the both of them. "She goes to work very early. Usually around five-thirty or six so that she can help Cook over in the Saddler house."

"Which house would that be?" he asked as she handed him a knife and fork.

"The first house on your right after you drive onto the property. It's the hacienda-styled one with the red-tiled roof. The Sanchezes live in the red brick."

She took a seat kitty-cornered from his and pushed a jar of homemade dewberry jam toward him. Neil slapped a layer on a piece of the toast as he flashed covert glances at her.

Somewhere between last night and this morning he must have forgotten exactly how beautiful she was. But a few minutes ago when he'd walked into the kitchen and she turned to look at him, he'd been reminded with an impact that had struck him like the punch of a fist.

Raine wasn't a glamour girl, the type that Neil was normally attracted to. No, with her subtle makeup and fresh innocent face, she was far from being the sultry temptress. So when Neil looked at her and thought she had to be the most beautiful woman he'd ever seen, it confounded him, even scared him.

She wasn't supposed to look this good, he thought. Her golden-brown hair was pulled into a simple ponytail and she was wearing a basic white shirt over a pair of blue jeans and tan cowboy boots. There wasn't anything ultrafeminine about her attire, but it was damn sexy the way the jeans outlined her curvy little butt and long, strong legs. The shirt was unbuttoned down to the V of her breasts and every time she moved the slightest bit, Neil found his gaze locked on the honey smooth skin and the slight, tempting shadow of cleavage.

Clearing his throat the way he wanted to clear his mind, he asked, "Did you talk with your mother this morning before she left the house?"

Her expression went flat. "Only for a few minutes."

He glanced at her as he bit into the toast. "How was she?"

Raine shrugged. "She didn't mention you. It was like last night never happened. But I could tell beneath her small talk that she was reeling from it all." She picked up a piece of the toast, then with a sigh lowered it back to her saucer. "I'm really beginning to feel awful about this whole thing, Neil. Maybe I should just fess up and tell her why you're really here."

"No!" His response came out so quickly Neil almost shocked himself and he looked across to Raine to see she was staring at him. She was probably wondering about his fierce reply, and frankly, Neil was wondering about it himself. A million little voices had been telling him there were going to be problems ahead with Esther Crockett and this game of deception that he and Raine were playing. Yet spending time with Raine and hoping against hope that he might actually help find her lost father was beginning to mean much more to him than escaping an ugly confrontation with the woman.

Quickly he said, "We've already come this far, Raine. Let's not mess things up now. If she's as adamantly against searching for her past as you say she is, then she'd demand that I leave the ranch without giving me the chance to ask anyone questions. Don't you see we've got to keep on with what we've started? That is, if you still want to try to find your father."

Her expression changed to sudden desperation and she nodded. "You can't imagine how badly I do want to find him. He's not just a part of my past, he's a part of me. I want to know where I came from before I start thinking about having a family of my own. Otherwise, it's like I have no legacy to pass on to my children. And you're right, Neil, we can't quit this charade now. But I feel so…horrible about deceiving her."

"Don't think about that part of it. Just think how relieved and happy she'll be once I'm gone from here and out of your life."

Wearily Raine pinched the bridge of her nose, then gave him a wobbly smile. "I'm sorry I'm putting you through all this. I didn't even offer you a proper breakfast."

*If she'd handed him a cardboard doughnut, he would have been happy to eat it just as long as she was sitting here beside him.*

Hell, Neil, he silently cursed himself, now wasn't the time to revert back to adolescence. He wasn't here to get all dreamy-eyed over a woman fifteen years his junior. As far as that went, he wasn't going to let himself get dreamy-eyed over any woman, including Raine Crockett.

"Don't worry about it. I know my way around the kitchen," he said.

And more than likely the bedroom, too, Raine thought, as she watched him quickly down a piece of toast. The whole image of Neil making love to her or any woman was enough to rev up her feminine engine. But try as she might, she couldn't seem to make her thoughts about him go in a different direction.

Last night after everyone had retired and the house had gone quiet, she'd lain awake in bed while her mind replayed over and over the moments she'd spent in his arms. Wisdom told her he'd only been playing with her. And from what she could gather about him, she doubted he would ever be serious about any woman. So why had his kisses *felt* serious? she asked herself. Why couldn't she look at him and forget about the way he'd made her feel?

Pushing those troubling questions out of her head as best she could, Raine swallowed the last of her coffee. "It's getting late," she explained. "If you're finished, we'd better be going. There's an office down at the main barn that the men use. I'll take you by there before I go on up to the Saddler house. That's where I work," she went on to explain.

"All right," he agreed, then rose and carried his cup and saucer to the sink.

Raine scooped up what was left on the table and joined him at the sink. Quickly she rinsed everything clean, put the dishes away and turned off the coffee machine. She didn't want to give her mother anything to complain about. Even something as petty as two dirty cups and saucers.

Outside, the two of them climbed into Raine's pickup truck and drove the short distance to the main barn, a huge metal structure situated at least a quarter of a mile from the Saddler house. On one side of the barn, a maze of cattle pens made of iron pipe covered, at the very least, two acres of land. On the opposite side of the building was a large corral filled with a dozen or so horses.

Apparently this autumn season had been dry for the area. The ground in the horse pen was like loose powder and as the animals trotted around in the warm morning air, dust boiled from their hooves and hung above them like a brown cloud.

In spite of it being December, the weather was quite warm, the sun already bathing the low hills of the ranch in a golden glow. Raine parked beneath the skimpy shade of a mesquite tree growing at the edge of the horse corral and the two of them climbed to the ground. As Neil glanced around him with interest, he spotted two men coming from the nearby barn.

Raine noticed them, too, and immediately motioned for them to join her and Neil. Then glancing around to where he was standing just behind her shoulder, she informed him. "That's Lex and Cordero. Maybe Matt is around here somewhere and we'll catch him, too."

Two tall men dressed in jeans, boots and hats, and appearing to be somewhere in their thirties, began to amble in their direction. As the pair made their way across the dusty lot, Neil stepped up beside Raine and slipped his arm around the back of her waist.

She shot him a brief glance. "Is that necessary?" she asked under her breath.

Smiling, Neil whispered down at her, "To keep things looking authentic. We want these guys to believe we're a couple, don't we?"

She sighed. If only his embrace was real, she thought, and the warmth of his arm would always be there when she needed love and support. But this was an act, a fairy tale that would eventually have to end. Why did the idea leave her feeling so bereft?

"I suppose it's necessary," she replied.

"Then you'd better get rid of that frown running down the middle of your forehead," he whispered.

He'd barely gotten the words out when the two men joined them in the shade of the mesquite. By now Raine had plastered a happy smile on her face and she quickly made introductions.

"Neil, this is Lex Saddler and Cordero Sanchez," she said with a gesture to each man. "Guys, this is Neil Rankin. He's— uh—"

A lost expression suddenly stole over her face and Neil quickly stepped in.

"I'm Raine's fiancé," Neil finished for her. "Glad to meet you both."

While assessing both men, he shook their hands. The two were equal in height, with rugged physiques and dark brown hair. Both had similarly striking features and green eyes, with Cordero's being a darker hazel of the two. As Neil studied their faces, the odd sensation that he'd seen these men before crept over him. But how could that be when he'd never been in this part of the country?

Neil's mind whirled with the possibility as both Lex and Cordero were staring at Raine with great surprise.

"Why, you sneaky little thing," Cordero was the first to speak. "You've been telling us you didn't even have a boyfriend! Now here you bring a fiancé home to the ranch. What gives?"

"Good Lord, don't be questioning her, Cord!" Lex scolded his younger cousin. "She deserves our congratulations!"

Stepping forward, Lex jerked Raine away from Neil's grasp and gathered her up in a tight bear hug.

"Way to go, honey! This is wonderful news!"

Not wanting to be left out, Cordero pushed Lex aside and pulled Raine into the tight circle of his arms. "That's not the way to do it, cuz," he said to Lex, then sweeping off his Stetson, he bent his head and kissed her soundly on the lips.

"Congratulations, little one," he murmured through a wide grin. "I hope you're very happy."

Neil, who'd never been the jealous sort in his life, suddenly wanted to reach out and snatch Raine away from both men.

"I'm going to make sure Raine is very happy," Neil spoke up.

The one called Cordero chuckled with pleasure. "You sound pretty sure of that."

Neil had made the statement with plenty of conviction, he

admitted to himself. And where his attitude had come from he didn't know. He didn't have any long-term ideas about Raine. And there wasn't any need to go overboard with this fiancé thing. So why was he standing here sounding like a lovesick, possessive male?

Before he could even think about answering those questions, Neil reached out and tugged Raine back to his side. She stumbled in the process and he steadied her with a tight hold on her waist.

His actions caused her to glance sharply up at him and he smiled lovingly down at her. "I'm pretty confident I can make Raine happy," he said.

The man called Lex was grinning from ear to ear. "Well, this is great news," he said. "And about time, too. Matt and I had bets on whether Raine was going to enter a convent or simply stay single the rest of her life. Especially since she never showed any interest in dating. Guess she had both of us fooled."

The two cousins laughed over this idea, whereas Raine appeared completely embarrassed. As for Neil, the men's comments were beginning to make him wonder if Raine had actually lived such a solitary life. Dear Lord, she could possibly still be a virgin! But Neil didn't want to think about that possibility. He wasn't in the habit of seducing young, innocent women. No matter how beautiful or sweet or sexy.

"What's going on? Is someone planning a barbecue?"

The sound of another male voice behind them caused Neil to look over his shoulder. A third man, dressed in a black cowboy hat and pair of worn batwing chaps was rapidly approaching the group. As Neil studied him, he didn't have to guess that the man was Matteo. He resembled his brother

Cordero, and from his authoritative stride, he appeared as a man in charge.

"Matt, wait till you hear our little darlin's news," Cordero called to him. "She's getting married!"

The man, who appeared slightly older than the other two, stopped in his tracks and stared at both Raine and Neil.

"You're kidding!"

Raine looked up at him and Neil could see troubled shadows in her eyes. He squeezed her side with reassurance and smiled down at her.

"Tell him, honey. There's no need for you to be bashful about it," he urged, while wondering what his beloved secretary, Connie, would think of his performance as Raine's fiancé so far. She'd probably recommend he try out for the local little theater. Either that, or scold him for enjoying the role a bit too much.

"No. He isn't kidding, Matt. Uh, I've brought Neil home to meet Mother and I wanted y'all to meet him, too."

Matteo stepped up and offered his hand to Neil. "Hello. I'm Matt Sanchez."

Neil shook the other man's hand. "Neil Rankin. Nice to meet you."

Even as Matteo turned his gaze on Raine, he could see the man was still sizing him up, trying to decide if Raine had picked someone worthy of her love. And it suddenly became obvious to Neil that these people considered her family.

The idea made Neil wonder if part of what Esther had said might be right. Maybe the Saddlers and the Sanchezes were family enough for her and Raine. But no. Linc Ketchum was surrounded by loving cousins, yet that didn't make up for the fact that he'd been without a mother for more than twenty years. Linc needed to find Darla Ketchum.

Just as much as Raine needed to find her father, whomever he might be.

*Linc! Ross! Seth!* The names shot through his brain like zaps of lightning. Now he understood why these cousins had seemed familiar to him. They possessed the same strong, rugged builds, dark hair and green eyes as the Ketchum men back home in New Mexico. And the impish grin on Cordero's face could have been a replica of Ross's.

*Whoa, Neil!* Just pull back on the reins and take a deep breath, he ordered himself. These people didn't have any connection to the Ketchum family of the T Bar K ranch. Or did they? Could it be possible?

Raine didn't know what was putting such an odd look on Neil's face, but she figured her own appearance was even more strained than his. None of this pretense was sitting well with her. She loved these guys. They were just like her brothers and now they believed she'd found the love of her life and was planning to get married. Oh why, why had she ever said such a thing to her mother last night? she asked herself. It had been a sudden impulse. A result of too many kisses and not enough time to think past them, she realized.

"Neil is a financial advisor from San Antonio," she heard herself saying. "We met over the telephone and then later I started driving up there to see him."

Matteo chuckled. "And Lex thought you made those trips to San Antonio to visit a convent. He had this idea that you wanted to become a Sister."

She did, Raine thought, but not the sort that Lex was thinking of. She wanted to truly be someone's sister. Or maybe discover that she had a sister of her own out there somewhere. If all this fibbing could help her do that, then it had to be worth it, she told herself.

Raine smiled at the ranch manager. "I was thinking more along the lines of being a wife," she told him.

The cousins laughed and so did Neil. Matteo leaned forward and kissed her cheek.

"Congratulations, little darlin'," he said, then asked, "Have you two set a date?"

"Not yet," Neil spoke up. "But I'm pressing her for one."

Dear Lord, he was good at this game, Raine thought. Far too good. The day had only just started and already she felt as if she should head to town and start shopping for a wedding gown.

"You going to be around the ranch for long?" Lex asked Neil. "Maybe we can throw you two a party? I know Mom is going to want to celebrate this news. It will give her another excuse for another Christmas party."

"Oh, no!"

Raine's outburst had all four men turning to look at her and she felt her cheeks immediately turn red-hot.

"I mean—Geraldine shouldn't go to that much trouble just for us," she quickly tried to explain.

"I'm not certain how long I'll be here," Neil told the other man. "At least for the next few days."

"Good. That will give Aunt Gerry time to put something together," Cordero spoke up. "We like any excuse to have a shindig around here."

"That's right," Matteo said, then added, "and while your fiancé is here, Raine, I don't want you working. You need to spend time with him—show him around the place."

Raine's mouth fell open. Not in a million years had she

expected the boss men to make this big a deal of her so-called engagement. But then she hadn't been thinking straight last night when she'd popped off to her mother about marriage. The words had passed her lips impulsively, without giving her time to think of all the ways it would affect tomorrow and the days afterward.

"Oh but—but there's all sorts of work that I need to be doing," she protested. "Someone needs to be in the office to answer the phone and there's—"

"Sara is fairly competent with the phone and she does a good job taking care of Mother's personal accounts," Lex interjected. "She can sit in for you for the next few days."

Raine felt awful. She rarely asked for time off, and when she did, she always made sure her absence would be short and that someone would be readily available to take her place. She didn't want to cause anyone on the ranch undue problems.

"Sara has her own duties and—"

Lex interrupted her with a loud chuckle. "Believe me, Mom knows how to write a check and post it in a ledger. She and Aunt Elizabeth could both give lessons in accounting and neither one of them had a day of college."

The cousins all chuckled at this idea and as Raine's gaze slipped from one man to the next, she realized that she couldn't protest or make any more excuses than she already had. To do so would appear more than odd. They expected her to be walking on air and dying to spend time with her husband-to-be. She had to keep playing the game, even if it meant she and Neil were literally going to be thrown together.

"Okay," she said with a forced smile. "If you guys are going to give me some time off, then I certainly will accept your offer. Thank you."

"Yeah, I want to thank you all, too," Neil said as he grinned broadly down at Raine and hugged her close to his side. "This will give me even more time to spend with my little honey."

The cousins assured him he was more than welcome and after plenty of handshaking and back slapping, the men eventually left the couple and went on about their work.

Once the two of them were alone again, Raine looked up at Neil and sighed.

"What are we going to do now?" she asked bewilderedly. "Those guys think we're getting married. I'd bet every last dollar I have that at this very moment Lex is going straight to his mother to give her the news. By tonight, she'll have a party planned. And Mother—"

"Will what?" Neil interrupted. "What can Esther do? Cause a horrible scene in front of everyone here on the ranch? I doubt it, Raine. Now quit worrying. From what Cordero said, they have parties here on the ranch for any little reason. It won't be a big thing."

She groaned with dismay. "No big thing? You don't know anything about the Sandbur. Everything they do here is big and noticed by all. I think—" She lifted her forefinger and tapped it against his chest in a gesture to reinforce her words. "You'd better ask your questions as fast as you can and make a hasty exit before things really get out of control."

Grabbing her hand, Neil lifted the puncturing finger to his lips and kissed it with outrageous leisure. "And leave my beautiful bride-to-be? Don't count on it, sweetie. As far as I'm concerned, the fun is just starting."

## *Chapter Eight*

Rolling her eyes toward the heavens, Raine plucked her hand from Neil's grip and stepped around him.

"Come on," she muttered while trying to get her fluttering nerves back under control. "Let's get in the truck and I'll drive you around the place."

Nodding dutifully, he opened the driver's door and helped her onto the seat before he walked around the vehicle and climbed into the cab to join her.

While she started the engine and pulled away from the mesquite tree, he gently asked, "Will you tell me one thing? Are you going to stay angry with me throughout this tour? Or can I settle back and enjoy it?"

Raine looked over at him and discovered an absurdly charming smile on his face and even if it meant her sudden death, she couldn't stop herself from smiling back at him.

"I'm not angry. It's obvious that you're a complete and utter flirt. I'm learning not to take you seriously. Besides," she added with a nonchalant shrug of one shoulder, "it's not like we're officially engaged and I'm going around showing them a big diamond on my finger."

Her words prompted him to sit up on the edge of the seat. "A ring! I wasn't thinking. Maybe I should drive into town and get one for you."

The thoughtful tone in his voice told Raine he was actually serious and she stared at him in dismay. "No! That's the last thing I would allow you to do. Engagement rings are expensive and then you'd be stuck with the thing. Unless—" She broke off, her expression wry. "You gave it to a real fiancée later on."

Neil shot her a look of surprise, then dismissed her suggestion with a laugh. "Not a chance. I'll never have a fiancée, bride, wife or anything close to the above. I'm a man who's perfectly happy to go through life all by myself." His eyes narrowed on her profile as she headed the truck on past the big barn. "Uh, now that you've brought it up, I think we'd better go into town and get a ring. It might help ease the tension with your mother. A ring might show her that I have real intentions of taking care of you."

Raine jammed on the brakes and the truck bounced to a stop. "That is—" Neil said as he rubbed the back of his neck, "if I don't have to be hospitalized with a permanent whiplash."

"Damn it, Neil, you're making me crazy," she practically yelled at him. "This isn't real. Get it? All that talk with the cousins, it was just a bunch of hogwash. You're not going to be taking care of me. In a few days, you'll be going home, for Pete's sake!"

Leaning across the seat, he placed his palm against her

brow. "Calm down, honey, you're getting so worked up you feel feverish. And you don't have to remind me that we're playacting. I'm not delusional. And, by the way, didn't I just tell you I'd never have a real fiancée?"

The touch of his hand on her face made Raine go instantly still and for a moment all she could think about was sliding from beneath the steering wheel and falling into his arms. She didn't have to wonder if he would hold her or even kiss her. He was a man who'd be more than glad to oblige her physical wants. But that's where things ended with Neil. And instead of reminding him that they were playing fairy tale, she'd better start reminding herself.

Soberly she nodded. "That's right. You've made that point very clear. That's why it's ludicrous for you to be talking about buying an engagement ring for me."

Pulling his hand away from her, he leaned back to his part of the seat and looked out the passenger window. "I don't want people thinking I'm cheap. Or that I don't care enough about you to buy you a ring. If I'm going to stay around here for a few days, I want them to look at me and think you've found yourself a decent man. We both deserve that much, don't you think? And quit worrying about the cost. I'll write it off my taxes as a work expense."

Put like that, the notion did make sense, Raine thought. And why was she worrying about this man's expenses anyway? He had a client somewhere who was probably footing the bill for this whole trip. Someone, like her, who wanted to find a family member, or a loved one. Could it be that person had known her mother in the past? she wondered. She hoped. Yet she understood the chances of that were slim to none.

"All right. If you want to buy some sort of ring for me, I

won't argue. Just don't get gaudy on me. I am a Texas girl, but you can see by looking at me that I'm conservative."

He looked around at her and smiled, although she noticed the expression wasn't lighting his blue eyes like it normally did. The idea that she might have fallen in his opinion bothered her, but she tried not to dwell on it. He was here to do a job, not feed her damaged ego.

Easing her foot off the brake, she gassed the truck forward onto a dirt road. As they passed a pole barn with several tons of stacked hay, she said, "I'm sorry if I'm being difficult, Neil. I just feel so—like a phony." She glanced at him, her expression vaguely hopeful. "If you want, we'll go into town tomorrow and get the ring."

He glanced at her briefly, then turned his attention back to the windshield and the landscape in front of them. "Sure," he said. "We'll go tomorrow and have lunch while we're there."

For the next few minutes the truck went quiet as they rocked over the rough track of road. Neil stared out at the huge patches of prickly pear and twisted mesquite trees and wondered what in hell was coming over him. He didn't know why he'd made such an issue over the ring. Whether she had one or not shouldn't mean anything to him. Good Lord, he was going home soon. Probably by the end of the week. So why was he throwing himself into this role with so much fervor? he wondered. He couldn't be falling for Raine. No. Even if he wanted to fall in love with a woman, he wouldn't know how. He'd closed the doors on his heart a long time ago.

"Neil, may I—ask you something personal?"

Her question roused him from his thoughts and he glanced over at her, a whimsical expression on his face. "Why not?

We've already been—personal with each other," he pointed out in a husky voice. "No need for you to be shy with me now."

A sweep of pink color painted her cheeks. "No. I guess not. I was just wondering—" She shot a quick glance at him then turned her gaze back to the road ahead. "Why are you so adamant about remaining single? I know you told me a little about your mother and how she affected you, but surely there's more to your thinking than that."

Wasn't seeing your father driven into the ground enough to warp a person? Neil wondered. Uncomfortable now, he shifted on the seat. "Because I like my life just the way it is. Why tamper with something that isn't broken? A person might end up making things a lot worse."

She nodded slowly, thoughtfully. "Yes. That's sort of the way I feel about it. Why borrow trouble when you don't have any? But then I start asking myself if that's a coward's way of dealing with things. And then I begin dreaming about how much I would like to have a family to share the rest of my life with. Don't you? Or would you rather spend your golden years alone?"

"Golden years?" he asked with a humorous grin. "Honey, I'm not *that* old."

She grimaced. "I didn't mean it that way. I just meant— well, for the rest of your life."

"For the rest of my life," he repeated dryly, "I sure as hell don't want someone around making my life miserable."

Slowing the truck, she stared at him with a wounded gaze. "I thought you liked women. You've certainly given me every indication of it."

A faint smile twisted his lips. "I adore women. In small doses."

Deep lines of disapproval marred her forehead. "In other words, you consider them playthings and nothing more."

Frowning, he stared out the window. "You make me sound criminal, or something."

She sighed. "Sorry I asked. It's none of my business anyway."

She was right, Neil thought. His views on women sure as heck weren't any of her business. And yet, it bothered the hell out of him to think she was viewing him as a piece of pond scum or something even lower.

"Look, Raine, I respect women. Some of my best friends are female. I just don't want to sit across the breakfast table from one every morning."

Her nostrils flared. "Afraid you might have to cook breakfast for her?"

Neil let out a humorless laugh. "If only that was enough to keep a woman happy," he said with a bitterness he couldn't hide.

She didn't make any response to that and Neil found himself irritated that she'd dropped the debate. He wanted, needed to defend himself. He wanted her to understand that his heart wasn't made of stone. He just had practical views.

For the next few minutes, the road they were traveling began to curve until the truck finally topped out on a short hilltop dotted with several spreading live oak trees.

Raine parked beneath the drooping branches of one and motioned to the scene in front of them. "Want to get out and stretch your legs?"

Nodding, Neil joined her at the front of the truck and gazed out at the endless range below. It was rough country covered with thorny vegetation, rattlesnakes, fire ants and no water except for the occasional tank filled by a windmill. But the grass was thick and almost knee high in places.

"The land probably looks wild and worthless to you," Raine said, "but it raises some of the best cattle in the state."

She sounded proud and Neil could understand why. Since a small child, the Sandbur had been the only home she'd known. The Saddlers and Sanchezes were her stand-in family. Her roots here were deep.

"In my corner of New Mexico, the land is rough and dry. It's high desert country and is so barren in spots that it takes acres and acres just to feed one cow. The grass appears to be more plentiful around here." He gazed toward the western horizon. "Are there any more houses or buildings farther out on the property?"

"Not in this direction. If you'd like we can drive on," she suggested.

Shaking his head, he turned to face her, his gaze solemn as he studied her face. "Maybe later. Right now I want to say something."

Sensing he was getting serious, she squinted warily up at him. "If it's something about this engagement thing, I don't want to hear it. We've beaten that subject to death, don't you think?"

He reached for her hand and was relieved when she didn't pull back. Rubbing the tips of his fingers over her soft skin, he said, "It's not about that. It's—what we were talking about a few minutes ago. I shouldn't have been so short with you. Forgive me."

Her features softened as her eyes fluttered up to meet his. "Don't apologize. You were only being honest."

The corners of his lips drooped downward. "A little honest. But not totally."

Her brows arched with curiosity, yet she contradicted the expression by saying, "You don't have to explain. Like I said, it's none of my business."

He groaned with misgivings. "This isn't something I go around discussing with anyone, Raine. But there are times when I feel very alone and I imagine what my life will be like ten years from now, then twenty, and so on. I wonder if there will be anyone around who'll care. I think about children and wonder if I'm ruining my life by not having any."

Surprise flickered in her eyes. "Do you like children?"

A wan smile tilted the corners of his lips as he thought of the Ketchums back home and the babies they were quickly adding to their families. Oh, yes, he was envious of his good friends. Even through the hard times they were surrounded with love and shoulders to lean on. "I enjoy being around my friend's children. And I think it would be great to have a son or daughter, or even both. But—"

"The idea of having a wife outweighs the need for children. Is that it?"

A long breath eased from him as he looked at her with a measure of regret. "I guess you could put it that way. Sounds chauvinistic, I know. But I'm living proof of what happens to a child when their parents' marriage is miserable."

Sadness slipped across her features. "And you blame your mother for the problems in your parents' marriage?"

Glancing away from her, he looked out at the Brahman cattle grazing along the nearby fence. The huge, grayish-blue-colored cows and calves were strong and fierce looking, yet Neil knew if they were taken from this warm climate and placed in the frigid temperatures that swept across the T Bar K in winter, they would all perish. Like the Brahmans, he understood that not all people could survive in certain situations. His mother was one of those people.

"She's a needy person, Raine. Some people are just like that.

They can't help themselves. I used to be very bitter about it. I used to blame her outright for my father's death. But I've gotten past that. Now I just think it would be better for me if I live the single life. No kids to mess up. No wife to make demands."

No kids. No wife. No love. No heartache. In many ways, Raine could understand his thinking. Since her college days, she'd actually run from any man who'd wanted to get closer than a kiss on the cheek. Why take the chance of putting herself through the pain and humiliation of being used again, she often asked herself. And yet there were deep holes inside of her. Holes that she realized would never be filled up unless she had a mate by her side, a man to give her love and children.

"I understand, Neil," she said simply. Then gently she squeezed his hand and smiled. "C'mon. I'll show you a bit more of the ranch and then we'll go to the Saddler house and you can see my office. I'll bet it's not nearly as fancy as yours."

He laughed then, and the sound filled her with warm pleasure.

"My office is a little log cabin with two rooms. The front room is where my secretary greets clients. The back room is where I work. You can't count the restroom, it's more like a closet."

She smiled at his description. "It sounds charming to me. I wish I could see it some time."

A provocative light glinted in his eyes. "Why don't you fly back to New Mexico with me and I'll show you all my stomping grounds?"

Why didn't she? Raine asked herself. She was a grown woman. She could go anywhere she wanted. The ranch gave her two weeks paid vacation, which she'd not yet taken this year. So her job wasn't an issue. The real and only reason she couldn't make the trip was that he was a dangerous man, at least to her common senses. Already he was spinning her thoughts and emotions in all directions. If she were to spend that sort of private time with the man, he'd have her heart sitting right in the middle of his palm.

"I'd love to see where you live, but I don't think that would be the best thing for me to do right now. Besides," she added with a grin in hopes of lightening her words, "if I showed up, all your girlfriends might get angry with you."

He laughed loudly and then as his humor faded to a smile, his hand came up to cup the side of her face. "If I actually did have a girlfriend, she'd take one look at you and be as jealous as hell. And she'd have damn good reason to be."

His hand was warm and tender against her cheek and for a moment Raine wanted to believe he wasn't a man who flitted from one woman to the next. She wanted to lean into him, feel his arms come around her, feel his lips take hers with breathless persuasion. But he'd just told her clearly that being with any woman on a long-term basis was not his style. So where would that leave her? With a few magical days and a broken heart, she figured.

Clearing the tightness from her throat, she eased back from him. "I, uh, think it's time we moved on. There's a lot more of the ranch to show you. And I'm sure Geraldine will be expecting us to show up soon."

Not waiting on his reply, Raine turned and hurried to the truck. She didn't want to give him, or especially herself, the chance to repeat the kisses they'd shared last night.

Raine drove the two of them back to the main ranch yard and for the next hour, she showed him the barns and horse stables and a few of the prize colts that were raised on the

Sandbur. Along the way she introduced him to several of the ranch hands, most of whom were Hispanic and spoke only broken English. By the time they reached the Saddler house, the morning had grown warm and the humidity felt like a wet blanket around Neil's shoulders. His shirt was glued to his chest and his back whereas Raine didn't appear to be affected by the tropical climate at all.

"I really shouldn't be meeting Mrs. Saddler looking like this," Neil said as the two of them stepped onto the long portico that framed the entire front of the house. The outdoor furniture grouped along the spacious wooden floor was probably worth more than every stick of furniture in Neil's house. But then he'd never been big on decorating. As long as he had a place to eat and sleep, he was content, a trait in him that his mother had always abhorred.

"Don't be silly. She's used to seeing working men with dirty hands and sweat on their backs."

"Yeah, but I haven't been working and you look as cool as a cucumber."

Smiling with encouragement, she took him by the hand and urged him up to the door. "You're not accustomed to being in warm weather in December."

Rolling his eyes, he lowered his lips to her ear. "That's right. But I'm supposed to be. Remember I live in San Antonio, not in Northern New Mexico."

"Oh. I'd almost forgotten," she said with a bit of surprise. "Well, if she mentions that you seem overly heated we'll tell her you have to take some sort of medication that makes you sweat."

Shaking his head, Neil chuckled under his breath. "Now you're going to paint me as sickly. What a hell of an impression I'm going to leave on these people."

"Don't worry about it," Raine replied. "Like you said, you'll be gone in a few days anyway. And I can always tell them I decided to end our engagement because you turned out to be a little weird."

"Thanks," he said drolly.

Raine knocked on the carved wooden door and soon a young Hispanic woman with two black braids and a wide smile ushered them into the house.

"Miss Geraldine is in the parlor, Miss Raine. She's been waiting for you and your man to arrive."

"Thank you, Alida," Raine told the woman as they followed her out of the foyer and into what appeared to be a long great room.

At one end, the floor stepped down three steps before they entered a short hallway. Two doorways down, the maid turned through an open archway and Neil instinctively reached for Raine's hand.

This time she clutched it tightly and Neil realized she was almost as nervous to introduce him to Geraldine Saddler as she had been her mother.

The parlor, as Alida had called it, was much smaller than the great room and far cozier. A couch and two armchairs covered in a rose-patterned chintz were positioned in front of a large rock fireplace. Off to the left of the room near a row of paned windows was a wide oak desk with a telephone, inkpad and a small pot of Christmas cactus sitting on one corner. To the right of the room near an arched window was a tall Virginia Pine decorated with gold and red ribbons and hundreds of candy canes.

Mrs. Saddler was sitting in a leather chair behind the desk and as Neil took in the sight of the older woman, he realized he was looking at one of the last true matriarchs of the

Sandbur. She was dressed in a white peasant blouse and a tiered skirt of lavenders and blues. A squash blossom necklace made of red coral adorned her neck, while heavy silver earrings with the same stone hung from her ears. Her hair was platinum-gray and pulled sleekly back from her face and pinned in a tight twist at the back of her head. In her early sixties, Neil couldn't help but notice that she was still an attractive woman. Yet that wasn't the thing that had his eyes riveted to her smooth face—it was the tiny mole situated at the corner of her mouth. The facial mark looked exactly like the one on Randolf Ketchum, Linc's late father.

*There you go again, Neil, trying to link these people to the Ketchums. Wake up and quit acting as though you're in the Twilight Zone.*

He and Raine walked to the middle of the room and waited for the older woman to leave the desk and join them. While she approached them, Neil ignored the little voice in his head and assessed the rest of Geraldine Saddler's physical appearance. She was tall and slender with an active spring to her step. But it was her face that struck him most. She had high, slanting cheekbones like Victoria and a variation of green eyes that ran in the Ketchum family. But how could there be a connection? It wasn't possible. Or was it?

"Good morning, Geraldine. I hope we're not disrupting your morning," Raine greeted her.

"It would have been more disrupted if you hadn't shown up," she said with a wide smile. "Lex has already given me the news and frankly, I couldn't be more excited or pleased."

Leaning forward she gave Raine a quick hug and kiss, then reached out a hand to Neil. "I'm Geraldine Saddler. Raine's second mother if you want to know how the cow eats the corn around here. And I suppose you must be Neil."

Neil warmly shook the woman's hand. "That's right. Neil Rankin. It's very nice to meet you, Mrs. Saddler. I hope you'll forgive my appearance. Raine has been showing me around the ranch." Thankfully, now that they were in the air-conditioned house, his shirt had begun to dry.

"A grand place, don't you think?" she asked with a proud smile.

"Very grand and very beautiful. I can see why Raine loves it here."

Geraldine motioned for the two of them to take a seat. Neil, still gripping Raine's hand, led her over to the couch and settled himself close to her side.

"Raine you have certainly floored me with this news," the older woman said as she eased into one of the armchairs. "You must certainly be able to keep secrets. I would have never guessed you'd been seeing a young man."

"Raine is bashful about these things, Mrs. Saddler. I had to urge her to break the news," Neil said.

From the corner of his eye, he could see Raine's lips twitch.

Geraldine settled a concerned look on Raine. "Well, I can understand Raine's feelings. She has her mother to contend with. Who, by the way is helping Cook right now. After Lex told me the news I immediately notified the kitchen to get a barbecue ready for tomorrow night. Esther wasn't pleased with the idea of a party, but then Esther is hardly ever pleased about anything," she added with a grimace. "God only knows I'd be jumping up and down with joy if Nicolette or Mercedes came home and told me they were engaged." She looked at Neil, her expression full of warm approval. "They're my two daughters," she explained to Neil. "And I don't want either of them living the rest of their lives alone and miserable. Women were put on this earth to be loved and cherished, not to go around pretending they're as tough as men."

"But you've always been tough, Geraldine," Raine pointed out. "If you hadn't been, this ranch wouldn't be here now."

She waved a bony hand at the two of them. "That's a different sort of tough. And that's a whole other story. I want to hear about you two. Have you set a date for your wedding yet? I tried to get information from Esther, but she clammed up. I think she's ticked off because you kept her in the dark, Raine."

Raine shot a regretful glance at Neil before she turned her gaze back on Geraldine. "I'm sure Mother is upset with me. She always gets that way if I do something without telling her first or seeking her approval beforehand."

Nodding with understanding, the older woman said in an encouraging voice. "Well, don't worry about it, my dear, she'll come around by the time you have the wedding. And you are going to have the ceremony here on the ranch, aren't you? I won't allow you to sneak off to some out-of-the-way place where I can't see you in white and cry into my handkerchief."

Neil should have been squirming in his seat. After all, the last thing he'd ever expected to hear was his own wedding being planned. But since last night when Raine had implied to her mother that the two of them were more or less engaged, he'd grown to the idea of matrimony. There wasn't anything scary about planning to marry a woman when he knew the whole thing was just an illusion. He could play along and enjoy having a reason to touch and hold his fiancée.

Beside him, Raine stuttered, "I—I don't know, Aunt Geraldine. We—uh—Neil and I haven't gotten that far with things yet."

The other woman smiled gently as her gaze encompassed the couple sitting closely together on the couch. "I hope you'll accept my offer, Neil. Even though I am prejudiced, the ranch is a pretty place and we serve some of the best food around. I promise I'll see to it personally that your wedding is one to remember."

"Thank you, Mrs. Saddler. You're very generous," Neil told her.

She looked at him with keen interest. "Lex tells me you're a financial advisor. Have you been doing that type of job long?"

At least the advisor part was true enough, Neil thought. "About thirteen years."

The older woman nodded her head in an approving way. "Then you're firmly established. That's good. It makes me happy to know that Raine won't have to struggle for things she needs. Back when Paul and I first married, the ranch was prosperous, but we went through some very rough patches over the years. Especially back in the seventies when the bottom fell out of the cattle market. We had to claw our way out of debt. But then—you deal in keeping finances straight—I don't need to tell you anything about providing security for your wife."

With a fond smile, he reached over and patted the top of Raine's hand. "I'll see that Raine gets whatever she wants. Within reason."

As soon as Neil spoke the words, it struck him that he was actually telling Geraldine Saddler the truth. He wanted to give Raine what she wanted the very most—her father's identity. He realized he'd made this whole trip and agreed to go along with her charade because he didn't want to disappoint her. Simply put, he wanted to make the beautiful woman sitting next to him, happy. So what did that make him, a shadow of his father? he asked himself. No. He wasn't about to fall into the hopeless existence his father, James, had fallen into. He wasn't going to love a woman so incessantly that he would sacrifice everything to make her smile.

"Geraldine, my needs are small," Raine said. "You don't have to worry about Neil providing for me."

Raine's voice tugged his thoughts back to the moment and he glanced over to see pink color on her cheeks, but whether it was from annoyance or embarrassment, he didn't know. He was beginning to see, however, that she wasn't a spoiled young woman who'd been coddled as an only child. She wasn't out to have her way at other's expense, especially where her mother was concerned. In his opinion, she'd taken drastic lengths not to upset the woman. And that selflessness he saw in her only made him want to help her more.

"I'm not in the least bit worried," Geraldine said with a smile. "The only thing that does concern me is eventually losing you as our bookkeeper. The families have always trusted you implicitly and that's something that will be very hard to replace."

Raine awkwardly cleared her throat and Neil could feel her body tense next to his.

"I—wouldn't be worried about that, Geraldine. It will be a while before Neil and I actually get married. And even then—well, I might be able to persuade him to live here on the ranch." She looked at Neil and smiled with sweet suggestion. "Mightn't I, darling?"

Something about the plaintive shadows in her green eyes kicked him smack in the middle of his chest and before he could even think of a reasonable response, he leaned his head down to hers and kissed her softly on the lips. "Anywhere that will make you happy, sweetheart."

## Chapter Nine

Surprise flickered across Raine's face, but Neil suspected she wasn't feeling nearly as amazed by his reaction as he was. Not two minutes ago he'd been promising himself he wasn't going to get carried away with this need he felt to help Raine. Now he was vowing, in front of this Sandbur matriarch, to bend over backward to make Raine a happy woman. Dear Lord, this role he was playing definitely had enough drama to warrant an Oscar. Either that, or he needed to head to a psychiatrist's couch.

He was still gazing into Raine's wondrous expression when a movement through the doorway caught his attention and he looked up to see Esther entering the room carrying a tray of refreshments. After one dour glance at her daughter, the woman placed the tray on a low coffee table in front of the couch.

"Here're the things you asked for, Geraldine. I waited until

Cook took the brownies out of the oven. They're still hot so you might want to eat them now," Esther suggested.

"I'm so glad you brought the refreshments instead of Alida," Geraldine said to Raine's mother. "You can sit down and join us for a few minutes."

Straightening to her full height, Esther ignored Raine and Neil and headed toward the doorway with plans to exit the parlor. "I don't have time for that. Since you're planning a barbecue for tomorrow night, I need to round up Joaquin and put him to work firing up the cooker. All the mesquite wood has been used so he'll probably have to go out and cut more. And—"

"Esther! Forget about all that," Geraldine interrupted sharply. "For Pete's sake, this is your daughter. This is a momentous time in her life. You should be smiling and rejoicing with her. I was only telling Neil a few minutes ago, how happy I'd be if Nicolette or Mercedes were to come home and tell me they'd gotten engaged. Talk about parties, I'd raise the roof myself. Now come sit," she ordered.

Neil had already seen firsthand that Esther was stubborn, but apparently when it came to Mrs. Saddler, she understood she had to bend or suffer the consequences.

Her face stoic, she walked over to the armchair next to Geraldine's and sat stiffly on the edge. "Geraldine, your daughters are different from my Raine. They've been out and seen the world. Raine has been sheltered and—"

"Whose fault was that?" Geraldine interrupted, then before Esther could answer, she rose from her chair and helped herself to a brownie and a cup of coffee.

Her mouth a thin line, Esther said, "I only worry that she's doing the right thing. And how could I know the answer to that when I don't know Neil any more than I know the man who delivers groceries to the ranch."

Returning to her seat, the other woman delicately used her thumb and forefinger to lift a morsel of brownie to her lips. "You *always* worry, Esther. My God, if worry were a commodity, you'd be damned rich by now. And as for Neil, he's sitting right across from you. It's your own fault if you don't get to know him."

Hurrah for Geraldine Saddler, Neil thought. At least this woman was on Raine's side. But what would she think, Neil wondered, if she learned that Neil was really here to snoop into Esther's background. Would she be empathetic to Raine's cause? Would anyone else here on the ranch understand the desperation Raine felt to find her father?

For the next few minutes, they ate the brownies and chatted about general things pertaining to the ranch and the weather and Neil's work. With Raine's mother present, the conversation grew stilted in spite of Neil's efforts to keep things light on his end. It was a relief when the woman finally left the room and Raine announced to Geraldine that she was taking Neil to view her office.

"Whew!" Raine said under her breath as they left the parlor. "I was afraid they were going to ask you about certain places in San Antonio and you'd be staring at them dumbfounded."

Neil chuckled. "I was probably looking dumbfounded anyway. By the way, do I have black marks all over me?"

She cast him a puzzled glance. "No. Why?"

He slipped his arm around the back of her waist as they moved along a wide hallway. "Because I feel as though I've just been grilled to medium-rare."

She giggled and Neil realized he loved the sound. It wasn't one of those silly, shallow sounds, but a sound of pure

amusement and he liked that. He wanted to hear her laugh
and see her spirits lift.

"No. You still look pretty raw to me, Mr. Rankin."

Neil wondered what she meant by "raw" but he didn't
question her as the two of them traveled the hallway for a few
more feet, then took another corridor for several more before
Raine opened a door on the right and motioned for him to
follow her inside.

The room was small but very nicely equipped with leather
furniture, a wide oak desk and leather office chair, and plenty
of plants to soften the atmosphere. The blinds at the windows
were pulled open to expose a portion of the lawn at the back
of the house that was shaded by a huge live oak. Beneath the
sagging branches, a bird feeder sat on a tall marble pedestal.
At the moment, however, two squirrels had taken over the
small platform and were sitting on their haunches munching
pieces of grain while several mockingbirds were content to
sit on the ground beneath and catch the droppings.

"This is nice. Very nice," Neil said. "I could get used to an
office like this."

Leaving her side, he walked over to a built-in stereo system
and began to thumb through a stack of CDs located on a
nearby shelf. "If these belong to you, it looks like you enjoy
all sorts of music. I even see some jazz and standards here."

She laughed softly at the surprise she heard in his voice.
"People in Texas do listen to more than country music. If you
visit Austin at night, you can hear all sorts of bands playing
in the different clubs around the city. While I was living there,
attending university, I acquired a taste for all kinds of music.
That was one of the nicest things about the city. Otherwise,
well…it was an experience."

Her voiced trailed away to a mumble and he squinted a puzzled look at her. "An experience? You sound as though you didn't like it."

Wishing she hadn't mentioned that time in her life, Raine walked over to the windows and pretended an interest in the squirrels. "It was okay. I'm just not a city girl."

He studied her, his gaze curious. "Maybe not. But surely it was nice to get out from under your mother's thumb and spread your wings. That's the way most young college students feel. That they're finally free from their parents strings."

Only some of them spread their wings too far, she thought dismally. And she'd been one of them. Closing her eyes against the discomforting memory, she said, "Oh, yes, at first, I was so glad to be away from the Sandbur and Mother that I was euphoric. I'd never been away from her, even for one night and I suddenly felt like I'd been let out of prison. I couldn't see everything, do everything fast enough to suit me."

He walked up behind her. "Hmm. Sounds like fun to me."

She sighed. "It was. Until I made mistakes."

Neil reached up and brushed his fingers down the back of her hair. He'd never felt such, soft silky hair before. He'd thought all women put those gooey products in their hair to make it bigger or straighter or to stay in place. Apparently Raine's was left to its natural state and he liked it that way. The honey-brown color glistened in the sunlight filtering through the windows and sparkled with streaks of gold. He snared a lock and lazily coiled it round and round his forefinger.

"All young people make mistakes," he said gently. "It's part of growing up, learning to be adults. I'm sure yours were very minor. What happened? You got thrown in jail for upholding the habitat of the spotted lizard?"

Laughing softly, she turned to face him. "Spotted lizard? I doubt there's such a creature. And no, I didn't get thrown in jail. What kind of woman do you think I am, anyway?"

Lovely, sensitive and caring, he thought. The sort of woman he always wanted to be around. Even in those golden years she'd talked about. The realization of his thoughts stunned him a little and it was a moment before he could reply.

"Perfect. Just perfect."

Her laugh was faint and full of disbelief and then for a split second, before she looked away from him, he saw her eyes fill with dark shadows.

"What a charmer you are, Neil Rankin. You shouldn't be allowed around women. You're lethal."

Chuckling, he brought his arms around her waist. "I've been told that before. But I don't know of any woman dying from being close to me. Wanta let me prove it?"

Her eyes lifted back to his handsome face and the sexy little grin curving his lips. Yes! Oh, yes, her mind shouted the answer. The thought of being in his arms, making love to him was beginning to completely take her over. And though she'd been trying to fight the desire he stirred in her, she was slowly beginning to ask herself why resisting was so important. True, nothing could ever come of a physical relationship with him. But she wasn't looking for anything permanent anyway. Presently she was looking for her father. She needed to find the man, get to know him and the roots of her past before she could truly settle down with a husband. So what would it hurt to enjoy this time with Neil?

"Maybe. Just for a moment," she murmured, then leaned forward and laid her cheek against his chest.

Her action prompted him to draw her close and circle his

arms around her back. Raine closed her eyes and breathed in the lingering scent of his expensive cologne, the faint odor of dried sweat upon his shirt and the elusive but evocative smell of his skin.

"See. I'm not a bit fatal."

Only to her heart, Raine thought, as she snuggled her cheek a bit closer to his warm, muscled chest.

"Now tell me about it," he urged.

Tilting her head back, she glanced up at him. Did he really expect her to remember what they'd been talking about when just the touch of his hand upon her back was scattering her senses?

"About what?"

"The mistakes you made in college that still have you feeling so regretful."

She lowered her face to where all she could see was the blue plaid of his shirt. "Oh that. It was…not that important."

"I think you're fibbing to me now. I could see remorse on your face."

Daring a glance at him, she asked, "What are you, a face reader?"

The smile that crept across his face was both impish and provocative. Raine could feel her heart thumping with antici-pation.

"Of course. Do you think I'd be any good at my profes-sion if I couldn't read people's expressions? Especially beau-tiful women with sad faces?"

Leaning her head away from his chest, she looked up at him. "I'm not sad, Neil. Ashamed is more like it."

He gently shook his head. "I can't imagine you doing anything to be ashamed of."

She heaved out a heavy breath. "I was young and naive then, Neil. And like Mother told Geraldine, I was sheltered. So much so that I knew very little about being out in the real world. Especially when it came to men. But I was—let's just say I was eager to spread my wings, do all the things my mother had preached for me not to do."

"Well, honey, that's typical. Nothing to be ashamed of there."

Raine's head swung slowly back and forth. "Maybe not. But I was so stupid—so foolish. I met a guy, Scott. He was my age and a college student, too. I liked him the moment I met him and we hit it off really well. Eventually we got close—too close. But I thought he cared for me—" She made a sound of disgust in her throat. "It didn't take me long to learn that he cared about one thing and I don't have to tell you what it was."

His hand began to slip up and down her back in long, soothing strokes. "Surely you don't think you're the first young girl who's been fooled by a randy college boy. You need to forget it. Erase it from your mind."

"I can't."

His thumb and forefinger lifted her chin and forced her eyes to meet his. "Why? Because you loved him? Still love him?"

"Dear heaven, no! I'm not even sure I loved him at the time our affair happened. It's just that before I left for Austin, mother preached to me, warned me about being taken advantage of by a man and I believed she was going overboard as usual. I had always had this idea that she simply gave me these warnings because she didn't want me to enjoy myself—that she wanted to keep me caged away from life. But after the disaster with Scott I had to admit to myself that Mother had been right all along and

I'd been stupid for not listening to her advice. In fact, I think I jumped into Scott's bed because I—maybe I wanted to defy her."

Moisture clouded her eyes and Neil felt his heart squeeze with pain. He never wanted to see a tear on Raine's face. He never wanted to see her troubled or unhappy. Not if he could do anything about it.

"That's understandable, Raine. But you shouldn't be beating yourself up over what happened. You learned from the experience. And that's all any of us can do when we make mistakes. They're learning tools—not sins."

Groaning, Raine pulled away from him and walked across the small room. With her back to him, she said in a pained voice, "You don't understand, Neil. *She* was right. My mother was right about Scott, right about me getting hurt and being foolish and what if—" Her expression filled with apprehension, she whirled around to face him. "Maybe Mother is right now, Neil! I mean, about me searching for my father. Maybe I will just stir up trouble. It could even cause someone from her past to reappear and threaten her!"

"Raine, Raine," he scolded softly as he moved across the room to her. "You're getting all bent out of shape over nothing. No one knows about this search except us."

She caught her lip between her teeth. "And your client," she reminded him.

He put his hands on her shoulders and drew her body up against his. She went willingly into his arms and he smiled to himself as her hands slipped up his chest, then linked at the back of his neck.

"Believe me, he won't stir up anything. In fact, he doesn't know the details of where I am or who I'm with. He only knows that I'm somewhere in Texas looking for someone who might be Darla Carlton." His hand came up to caress her cheek. "But right at this moment I'm looking at my beautiful fiancée."

She grimaced. "Your fake fiancée, remember."

"Funny, you don't feel a bit fake to me," he murmured with pleasure.

Raine sensed the kiss was coming even before she saw his head bending down to her and this time she didn't bother asking herself whether it was right or wrong. Neil made her feel things, think things that were good. Too good to turn away from.

"You're bad, Neil Rankin. Bad for a girl like me," she whispered.

His only reply was a soft chuckle and then his lips were on hers searching every curve and coaxing them apart with a skill that left Raine only too glad to open her mouth. As she accepted the warm invasion of his tongue, she felt his hands drawing her closer until her breasts were flattened against him and the juncture of her thighs was touching the bulge inside his jeans.

A groan sounded from deep inside him and the sensual sound shot searing heat through her body like a glowing arrow leaving flames in its wake. Everything inside her began to melt, especially her common sense. And she moaned helplessly and gripped the back of his neck as her knees turned to useless mush.

"Oh, Raine, this shouldn't feel so good, so sweet," he murmured the words upon her lips. "But it does. And I don't want to stop. I want to lay you down on that couch over there and make love to you. You know that, don't you?"

Her heart was beating so rapidly in her throat that she could barely whisper her answer. "Yes."

"Your lips tell me that you want the same thing."

The fact that he'd so easily read the desire she was feeling for him was enough to shake her, yet she couldn't deny it. Not when it was so obvious to both of them.

"Yes."

The one word came out on a sigh and as it drifted away, he cupped her face with his hands and placed another long, deep kiss upon her lips that left her gulping for air and her hands clenching his shoulders.

"I've wanted to make love to you since we first met at the river. And I think you felt the same way, too."

His erotic words were painting a picture that made her heart pound and aching heat pool between her thighs. She tried to swallow, to think, to do anything but simply fall into his arms and let him have his way.

"You're crazy, Neil," she whispered fervently. "That kind of attraction takes longer than—"

"Than what?" he interrupted. "Minutes? Hours? Days? I don't need that much time to tell me that I want you."

"I'm not one of your playgirls," she managed to utter as his lips began to nibble hungrily at her ear. "I—"

"And I'm not some college boy like the one who destroyed your golden idea about love. And you're not that same gullible teenager. You're all grown up and ready to have a real relationship."

*Real.* Funny he should use that word, Raine thought, when *everything* about their relationship was pretend. Except for the way she was beginning to want him with every fiber of her being.

While she'd been trying to gather her senses, his lips had drifted downward from her ear and were now making a slow steady trail along the front V of her shirt. She was shaking inside and she expected he could hear the loud, rapid thud of her heart as he pressed his lips upon her hot skin.

"What are you calling real?" she murmured between quick sips of air.

"Go lock the door and I'll show you."

The blunt suggestion was like a hard shake to her shoulders and she reared her upper body away from his and stared at him. "Neil! We're in my office! You may use yours for sex, but mine is meant for working!"

He chuckled like a wolf on the verge of eating a tasty rabbit. "We're working. At least it's got your heart rate up."

With one hard jerk, Raine was out of his arms and heading toward the door. "Go ahead and make jokes," she flung over her shoulder. "But I'm not staying around to hear them."

Before she could open the door and scoot out of the little office, Neil caught up to her and snatched a hold on her arm. Her lips were clamped tightly together as she turned around to face him.

"Whoa, girl. What's the matter?" he softly questioned. "Don't tell me you didn't want to be in my arms. I know when a woman wants me."

No doubt, Raine thought. He'd had plenty of practice.

"I'm sure," she said shakily. "But *wanting* is as far as it's going with this woman."

Neil rolled his eyes helplessly toward the ceiling. "I don't understand you, Raine. Just a minute ago you were all warm and giving. Now you're acting like an outraged virgin. Tell me what's wrong."

She oughtn't to have to tell him, Raine thought dismally. He should already understand that if she had sex with him, she would want it to mean something. At least something more than a laugh and a few pleasurable minutes. Maybe that meant she was still naive. Or perhaps she was just hopelessly old-fashioned. Either way, she couldn't explain it. Not without making herself look and sound like an idiot.

Her shoulders sagged; her expression fell flat. "Nothing, Neil. It's just me. I made a fool of myself with one guy. I'm just not ready to…get involved again. I'm not sure that I'll ever be." She turned back to the door before he had the opportunity to make any sort of reply. "I'm going back to the house. Do you want to come along? Or would you rather look around the ranch a bit more on your own?"

He sighed. "I think I'll hang around here for a while. I might inadvertently stumble onto some interesting information."

Raine's lips were still tingling from his kisses and as she glanced over her shoulder at him, she realized with shocking disgust that she would like nothing better than to lock the door and step right back into his arms.

"All right. I'll—see you later on, then."

Nodding, he let loose of her arm and reached up to graze her cheek with the tips of his fingers. "Forgive me?"

Dear God, why did everything he did and say make her heart melt like sweet chocolate in her mouth?

Through a wobbly smile, she murmured, "Of course."

### *Chapter Ten*

In all of his dealings with women, Neil couldn't remember a time he'd let one shake or disturb him. He either wanted them or he didn't; he won or he lost. It was all just a physical game to him. But whichever way the wind blew, he could easily walk away.

So why was he still pacing around Raine's office, wondering where he'd gone wrong and wondering, too, when his hands were going to stop shaking?

Damn it, this wasn't the way things were supposed to be going, he thought. He'd come down here to Texas on a whim really. Because a young woman's sweet voice had gotten to him. And when he'd met her in person. Well, right now he didn't want to think of how bowled over he'd been the moment he'd looked into her pretty green eyes. It made him feel like a damn adolescent. And now. Hell, he should never have expected her to be just any woman. He should have known she was one of the marrying types. Not that she'd said such, but it was obvious she didn't want sex without commitment. And he couldn't give her the latter, so that meant one thing. He had to keep his hands to himself.

Yeah, right. And how was he supposed to do that, he asked himself, when all he could think about was making love to the woman. Not just once, but over and over until he got this obsessive need out of his system.

With Quito's warning about falling for a pair of pretty eyes dashing through his head, Neil left the office and looked for the nearest exit. He found it a few feet down the hallway where a door opened onto the area of the lawn that could be viewed from Raine's office windows.

There was no one about this side of the house and Neil decided the cool shade of the live oaks would be as good a place as any to place a call to his secretary.

He'd promised to call the woman yesterday when he first arrived in San Antonio, but he'd not taken the time and he figured right about now she was probably chomping at the bit to hear from him.

Thankfully his cell phone reached Connie's desk loud and clear and he smiled as her voice practically shouted in his ear.

"Neil! Why the heck didn't you call me yesterday? Are you okay? What's happened?"

Sinking onto an iron bench, he leaned back and focused on the pair of red squirrels who continued to do away with the birdseed. "Slow down, Connie. I'm okay. I just got busy yesterday after my plane landed. I meant to call, but you know how things go."

"Yeah. Things like short skirts and long eyelashes," she said dryly.

Normally Neil would have laughed at Connie's comment, but today he didn't find it funny. He was tired of being labeled as a playboy, even if it was the truth.

"There are other things that take up my time, Connie," he said more sharply than he meant to. "Now tell me what's been going on up there. Have any clients been in today?"

There was a long pause and then she said, "Since when have you ever worried about that?"

For a moment Neil wanted to throw the phone over to the squirrels and let them chomp the piece of plastic to bits. "Damn it, Connie, I'm not worried. Who said I was? I'm just curious. I shouldn't have to point out that I'm not there and I'm not psychic."

"Well, all right, Mr. Grouchy," she said in a halfway offended voice. "There've been three people in to see you already today. Mrs. Johnson was here to talk to you about her late father's estate. The other two wanted you to read abstracts. Nothing exciting, like searching for a missing woman."

"Sounds like the place is burning up with business," he quipped.

"That's the way it is. You leave the office and three-fourths of your customers show up wanting you to actually work."

He smiled in spite of his mood. "You've been my secretary too long, Connie. Your mouth is getting downright awful."

"That's what my husband says, too. But he's used to it," she said with a laugh, then added, "Oh, by the way, I paid Luther ten dollars out of the miscellaneous fund to shovel the sidewalk clear."

Luther worked as a handyman for the hardware business next door to Neil's office. "Are you talking about snow?" he asked.

"What else? You took all the bull manure with you."

Ignoring her sarcasm, Neil said, "Well, it's hard to think about snow when you're sitting here sweating, Connie."

"Hot down there, huh?"

In more ways than one, Neil thought. He was still steaming from those kisses he'd shared with Raine.

"Believe me, Connie, you'd melt."

She laughed. "Tell me what else is going on down there. Have you met this woman without a past?"

If he looked straight on, beyond the drooping arms of the oaks, he could see a portion of the horse lot. At the present, a couple of cowhands had roped a yearling and the little palomino was resisting the noose by rearing up on his hind legs and pawing the air. Neil understood just how the young horse was feeling. He didn't want to be roped in by a woman or the feelings she invoked in him. He might be letting her lead him around with this fake fiancé thing, he told himself, but when this was all over, she could put her noose around some other man's neck. He was heading back to New Mexico and peace of mind.

"I have."

"And? Do I have to drag it out of you?"

"And nothing. I'd say she has a faint resemblance to Darla, but if it is her, she's changed drastically."

"That's possible. I certainly don't look like I did nearly twenty-five years ago. If I did, you'd be chasing me around the desk and I'd probably be letting you catch me," she added with a chuckle.

"Connie! You naughty girl."

She sighed wistfully. "I used to be. And speaking of used

to be, if I remember correctly, Darla Ketchum was a beautiful, sexy woman. I can recall seeing her around Aztec on occasion and everywhere she went, she turned heads."

*Mother always lectured me to not draw attention to myself.* For some reason, Raine's words about her childhood slipped into his thoughts and it dawned on him that Esther Crockett appeared to be the complete opposite of Linc's mother. Darla Ketchum would have wanted her child to be the front and center of attention. She would have gloried in showing Raine off at social events, whereas Esther had done everything to keep attention away from Raine. Could the woman have done that on purpose? he wondered. Could she really be Darla and trying to hide herself and her daughter? Even after all these years?

"Neil! Are you there? I asked about Raine, the young woman searching for her father. How are things going with her?"

Neil swallowed as lingering desire stirred in the pit of his stomach. "She's a lovely young woman, Connie. In spite of her mother, I might add. This Esther is strange and from what I can gather she raised Raine in a very restricted way. I'm surprised the young woman is as normal as she is. If I'd been in her shoes, I'd probably already be an alcoholic by now."

"That bad, huh? I'm so sorry to hear that. But wouldn't it be nice if you could actually find her father," Connie suggested. "It might bring some real joy to her life and it sounds like the young woman deserves it."

Raine did deserve some joy, Neil thought. She was too soft, too sweet to be hurt by the likes of him. But God, how he wanted her. And would it really hurt her if they did make love?

"She does deserve to be happy. That's why I'm staying here on the ranch. With her mother, actually."

There was such a long pause on the other end of the line that Neil was beginning to wonder if his secretary had fainted. "Connie? Did you hear me?"

"Yes, I heard. But I don't believe. I thought this whole investigation was going to have to be done in clandestine fashion so that Esther wouldn't catch on to what you were doing? Now you're telling me you're staying in the woman's house! What am I going to hear next?"

A catlike smile crossed his face. "That I'm engaged."

"What!"

"Engaged. Everyone here believes that Raine and I are getting married…to each other. In fact, they're giving us a party here on the ranch tomorrow night."

"Holy cow! And you're going along with this…charade?"

"I had to. Otherwise my being here on the ranch couldn't be explained."

"Mmm. Mmm. Mmm. For you to even agree to a fake engagement is enough to make your own dear father turn over in his grave. I'm not believing what I'm hearing. This Raine Crockett must be a mighty persuasive young woman. Uh, by the way, what does she look like?"

The little palomino had decided to give up the fight and follow one of the cowboys around the dusty lot. The young horse looked almost happy to have someone leading him and stroking him gently on the head. Neil wondered if he'd ultimately be that happy if he ever gave in and allowed a woman to lasso his neck. He surely doubted it.

"That's not important, Connie. And I want to make sure that you don't speak to Nevada or Linc about any of this—not yet. I haven't really had a chance to start nosing yet and right now I don't want to make any sort of assumptions that might get the hopes up of the Ketchum's and then have them fall flat. Understand?"

"Of course, Neil. My lips will be zipped. I'm just a bit disappointed that you sound so negative, though. Ever since Raine first called the office, I had a feeling that there was a real connection here to Darla Carlton. Guess my intuition was off this time."

"Don't say that yet, Connie. Just because Esther doesn't seem like the Darla we remember doesn't mean we're on the wrong track. In fact, I've been having these odd déjà vu feelings all morning. And don't start laughing, but the family members that own this ranch remind me of the Ketchums."

"You mean they physically look like the Ketchums?"

"A whole lot like them."

"How odd. What could it mean, Neil?"

Rising from the iron bench, he wiped his sweaty brow with the back of his arm and glanced toward the Saddler house. "It might not mean anything, Connie. But I'm getting a germ of an idea. I'll call you back later—when or if I find anything."

He said goodbye to his secretary then put the small cell phone back into his shirt pocket before he made his way over to a back entrance of the house.

After a quick knock on the door, he stepped inside and found himself in a long room that appeared to be the kitchen.

A tall, thin woman with iron-gray hair coiled into a bun atop her head was sitting at a large wooden table snapping fresh green beans into an aluminum bowl cradled in her lap.

As Neil entered the room, she looked up in question. "Hello, young man, what can I do for you?"

Her eyes were so brown they were nearly black and her long fingernails were painted a bright red. Judging from the deep wrinkles on her face, she'd been on this earth many years, yet she appeared to be as spry as someone twenty years her junior.

"I'm Neil Rankin," he introduced himself. "I'm Raine's fiancé. I was just looking around the ranch and thought I might come in and beg a drink of ice water from you."

Actually he'd not known he was stepping into the kitchen, but the ice water had been on his mind.

"Nice to meet you Neil Rankin. Everybody calls me Cook. My real name is Hattie, but I've been the cook for so long that that's what I answer to." She motioned toward the refrigerator several feet away. "Help yourself to the water. There's glasses in the cabinet to the right of the refrigerator."

Neil fetched the drink and after swigging half of it down, he refilled the glass, then carried it over to the table where the old woman continued snapping beans.

"Mind if I join you, Cook?"

The old woman gestured to a chair across from her. "Glad for the company." She rested her hands on the edge of the bowl and surveyed him with her dark eyes. "Esther told me about you this mornin', but she didn't tell me you were so good lookin'. 'Course, Esther likes to pretend she doesn't notice such things anymore, but I know better." She winked and grinned. "No wonder Raine finally let loose and latched on to a man."

Down through the years Neil had heard all kinds of lines from all sorts of women, but he'd never had a woman exactly like Cook to come on to him.

"Raine actually loves me for my brain," Neil said with a grin.

The old woman cackled loudly. "Yeah. I'd bet on that."

Neil drank a bit more of the water, then glanced around the long, rectangular room. The kitchen had an old feel about it and looking at the huge gas range located in a center island of the room, he expected the appliance had been put there before he'd even been born. Yet he figured that Cook was perfectly comfortable with the condition of her workplace and preferred it this way.

"Have you worked here on the Sandbur for a long time, Cook?"

"Thirty years." She picked up another handful of beans and began to snap.

"So you were here when Esther and Raine first came," he deduced.

Cook nodded. "Yep. Raine was just a baby then. Not even walking yet. And Esther was—" She paused and scowled thoughtfully. "What is that term you young people use nowadays? Stressed. Yes, Esther was stressed out. I'd just call it plain old frazzled." She leveled a look on Neil. "Guess Raine's told you about Esther not being able to remember?"

Neil nodded while thinking he might have walked into a gold mine of information without even trying.

"Yes. That's a matter that has troubled Raine for a long time. She really wants to know where her father might be, or if she has other family elsewhere. But Esther isn't too keen on Raine making a search for her past."

Cook snorted in unladylike fashion. "That's 'cause she's always tried to act holier-than-thou and she don't want her daughter findin' out she hadn't always been perfect."

"Hmm. So you know that Esther had a wilder side?"

Chuckling, the old woman tossed down the pieces of beans and looked at him. "Not proven facts, but it was pretty obvious to me when she came here that she wasn't as innocent as a newborn lamb. Why else would someone have beaten her near to death? No, she was up to no good before she came here to the Sandbur. That's why she wants everyone to forget those days. Especially her daughter."

Neil casually drummed his fingers against the tabletop even though his mind was spinning with unasked questions. "How did you know about the circumstances of her accident? Did Esther tell you about it?"

"Lord no! Miss Geraldine and Miss Elizabeth, before she died, God Bless her soul, looked into the police reports and tried to launch an investigation of their own into the matter. But they never got anywhere with it. Esther was against it all, you see. Still is, just like you said." Shrugging her shoulder, the old woman smiled with approval.

"But now Raine has you and all that stuff don't matter. You two can make a family of your own and Esther will just have to deal with her own demons."

*Deal with her own demons.* Neil wished he knew what those demons actually were. If he did, he might just get to the bottom of Esther Crockett's past. But he couldn't question the woman herself. She was like a clam at the bottom of the sea.

"Raine loves her mother very much," Neil commented carefully.

"Raine couldn't do anything else but love her mother. That's the kind of young woman she is. Loves everybody. She'd shoo a rattlesnake from the yard rather than chop its head off with a hoe. She's been a bright spot here on the ranch for all of us. I hate to think of you takin' her away, but I want her to be happy. And from the looks of you, I don't doubt you can make her that way."

Could he? Neil wondered. If he did actually become Raine's husband, could he give her all the things she would need to make her happy? If giving a woman pleasure was meant to be a man's sole purpose in life, then God only knew how his father, James, had bent over backward trying to fulfill that goal. But he'd not managed to keep Claudia pacified, much less satisfied. Neil would be crazy to think he could do any better at being a husband than his father had been.

"Tell me, Cook, do you like Esther?"

Neil could tell from the puzzled frown on Cook's wrinkled face that she found his question strange. He supposed it was in a way, but so far he'd not met anyone who'd had anything good to say about the woman.

"Well, I guess I never thought about it really. The woman is a hard worker. She's always here early in the morning to help me in the kitchen, then she goes on to her other chores around the place. We've always got along, but Esther isn't a body you can cozy up to, you know. She keeps her feelin's to herself. I suppose I like her well enough." She grinned at Neil as she reached for another handful of beans. "Guess you're worried about what sort of mother-in-law you're goin' to be gettin', but I wouldn't fret about that, Mr. Rankin. Raine will be worth it."

Cook's words had Neil's thoughts returning to Raine's office and how passionately she'd kissed him and clung to him. The red-hot memory was almost enough to believe she would be worth loving for a lifetime.

Later that afternoon, across the ranch in Esther's house, Raine was sitting in the living room, pretending to watch a news channel on television when her mother walked in.

The moment Esther spotted Raine without Neil by her side, the woman's brows arched with surprise.

"What are you doing here?" she asked bluntly. "Where's Neil? Or has he already decided to leave?"

Even though Raine realized Neil would actually be leaving in a few days, the idea that her mother believed she couldn't hold on to a man, even for a couple of days, was degrading and hurtful.

"No. Neil is still here. All men don't run out on their wives or fiancées, Mother. He's looking around the ranch, visiting with some of the hands." She supposed, Raine thought glumly. After she'd left him in her office, she didn't know what he'd done. Other than gone off somewhere and had a good laugh about her good-girl attitude.

The other woman tossed a key ring onto a small table by the door, then crossed the room to take a seat on the opposite end of the couch from her daughter.

"Well, I'm actually glad that Neil isn't here right now. Since we haven't had a chance to talk about any of this yet and—"

Raine quickly held up her hand. "There's nothing to be said that hasn't already been said, Mother. I don't want any lectures right now. I don't *need* any lectures, either."

A pained expression crossed Esther's face and Raine couldn't help but feel guilty. She hated being deceitful with her mother, but the woman had pushed her to these lengths. Esther had never understood Raine's deep desire to find her father. She'd always insisted their lives were fine with just the two of them.

And maybe it was fine, Raine thought dismally. But having her father would make it so much better. And what if Esther had children before her accident? Didn't she want to know about them? They would be Raine's brothers or sisters.

No, Raine told herself, she couldn't let a pang of guilt stop her from finding the past. Because without the past, she couldn't see herself stepping into the sort of future she wanted so desperately.

Sighing, Esther wiped a hand across her forehead. "I guess all these years I've struggled to raise you means nothing to you. You're in love and you've forgotten all about your mother."

Raine rolled her eyes. "Really, Mother, you might as well play some violin music in the background."

Esther sat like a rigid pole on the edge of the cushion. "See! It's not like you to talk to me this way. Is that what this man— this Neil has done to you?"

Yes, Raine wanted to say. He'd given her a backbone and the strength to finally reach for the things she wanted instead of just living her life to appease her mother's whims.

"Please, Mother, let's not argue. Why can't you just be happy for me? You heard Geraldine. If it were Nicolette or Mercedes getting married, she'd be thrilled. Why can't you be thrilled, or at the very least, be pleasant about the whole thing?"

Her lips compressed to a thin line, Esther looked away from her daughter. "Because it worries me. I don't want you to be hurt."

"Like you were?"

Esther's head whipped back around and she stared at Raine with narrowed eyes. "What kind of question is that? Why would you ask me such a thing?" she demanded.

Raine didn't know where she'd found the burst of courage to ask her mother such a question, but now that she had, she was glad. For years now she'd wanted her mother to be open with her, not domineering. Maybe with a little push she could make Esther understand this.

"Because you've always discouraged me to date or get

involved with men. You obviously have something against the opposite sex. And since you won't talk about it, I can only assume that a man hurt you at some point in your life."

Esther sucked in a harsh breath. "Well, if that were the case, and I'm not saying it was mind you, a man would have had to hurt me after my—my accident. Otherwise, I wouldn't have remembered it."

Raine gave her mother a subtle nod. "I understand that."

Esther sniffed and looked away again. "I—you're all wrong, Raine. I haven't had any sort of relationship with a man. Not since you were born."

"And you don't remember anything about my father? Not even the tiniest glimmer of what your life with him was like?"

Still staring at the opposite wall, Esther said in a brittle voice, "No. And it's best that way. Twenty-four years is a long time. Things happen to people. He—your father is— probably dead."

Esther's words felt like brutal punches to Raine's stomach and she literally wrapped her arms around her waist to ward off the pain.

"Why—why would you say such a horrible thing to me? You don't know that my father is dead!"

Raine didn't wait around to hear her mother's reply. She'd already heard more than enough. Dashing back tears from her eyes, she ran to her bedroom and shut the door.

## Chapter Eleven

An hour later, after Raine's confrontation with her mother, Neil returned to the Crockett house carrying a bouquet of purple hyacinth and white daisies wrapped in green cellophane paper. Before he'd left the kitchen at the Saddler house, a florist truck from Goliad had arrived with the delivery of flowers that Geraldine ordered weekly. While the truck was there, Neil had taken advantage and purchased Raine a huge bouquet. To make up for his loutish behavior, he'd told himself. Now he could only hope the flowers would take the edge off her anger at him.

When he didn't find Raine in the living room or the kitchen, he took a chance and knocked on the closed door of her bedroom.

"Come in," she called in a muffled voice.

Neil stepped inside the small room and shut the door behind him. Raine was sitting on the bed and as he approached her, he carefully held the fragrant flowers behind his back.

"Why are you hiding in here?" he asked. "Have you been taking a nap?"

She shook her head and he noticed her demeanor seemed anything but happy. Her pretty, plush lips were compressed to a thin line and the puffiness around her eyes made him suspect she'd been crying. The idea that he'd caused her so much distress was enough to tie his stomach into a hard knot.

Frowning, he stated the obvious. "Something is wrong."

She shook her head again. "Don't worry about it."

Neil moved to the bed and gently sat down beside her on the edge of the mattress. "I knew you were angry with me, but I didn't realize you were *this* angry."

Her face turned to look at him and Neil's heart winced at the sad shadows he spotted in her green eyes.

Not waiting for her to say anything, he handed her the fragrant bouquet. "Here. Maybe these will help you to forgive me," he said softly.

Still not speaking, she took the flowers and lowered her head to sniff at the pungent hyacinth. After several long moments passed, she looked at him again and this time there was a hint of bewilderment on her face.

"You must have met the flower man," she said. "He comes every week."

"I got lucky and he drove up while I was still at the Saddler house. Cook told me that Geraldine makes a point of keeping fresh flowers in most of the rooms. Guess she's not hurting for cash," he added on a teasing note.

"No. Not hardly. But you didn't have to do this." She inclined her head toward the flowers. "I really wasn't mad at you. I was more angry with myself."

Neil hadn't realized how nervous he was until a small breath of relief rushed past his lips. "Why?"

She sighed as her elegant forefinger etched a petal on one of the daisies. "For a lot of reasons." Glancing over at him, she gave him a wistful little smile. "But mainly because I...I don't have the courage to reach out and grab what I want—like you."

As soon as her words were out, Neil wanted to take hold of her and drag her into his arms. But he restrained the urge and told himself it was best not to push his luck.

Instead he reached over and stroked his fingertips down her upper arm. "So you did want me? I wasn't just imagining the way you kissed me?"

Closing her eyes, her head jerked from side to side. "No," she whispered. "That wasn't your imagination. But that—our time in my office—that's not why you found me in here brooding. Not that I was actually brooding, but I am upset."

Neil studied her pinched features and thought how much he'd like to take her face between his hands and kiss her cheeks, her nose and chin, her eyelids and most of all, her sweet, luscious lips. If any of that would make her smile, then he'd be one happy man.

"So something did happen. What?" he asked.

She opened her eyes and met his gaze head-on. "Mother came back to the house earlier. And we had a little conversation."

His interest was instantly piqued. "Oh. Where is she now? I didn't see her when I came in."

Raine shrugged. "I don't know. She probably went over to the Sanchez house. She usually oversees the cleaning over there in the afternoon."

Neil's fingers kneaded her shoulder. "What happened? Did she lay into you about me?"

Raine's gaze dropped back to the flowers bunched in her hand. "A little. But I cut her off. I asked her why she was so against men and then I questioned her about my father. I wanted to know if she could remember anything about the man or her life with him."

"And what did she say?" Neil asked as casually as he could manage.

Raine's shoulders sagged, her head bowed. "She said that twenty-four years was a long time and things happen. She said my father was probably...dead."

The last word came out on a tearful whisper and this time Neil couldn't stop himself from pulling her into his arms and tucking her head beneath his chin.

"Oh, my little darling, you shouldn't let that upset you," he crooned as he stroked a hand down her shoulder and back. "If she has no memory of the past, then she's just making assumptions."

Swallowing at the lump of emotion in her throat, Raine tilted her head back to look at him. "But what if she does remember, Neil? Maybe this Carlton man that was found murdered down by the Mexican border was really my father and she knows it!" Shivering from that terrible idea, Raine gripped the top of his shoulders for support. "Maybe she's just trying to give me the hint that she knows my father is dead—she just doesn't want to come out and tell me the actual truth?"

Neil tightened his arms around her. "That's possible. I just don't understand why she would have said something so hurtful to you. What reason would make her say your father is dead?"

"To put me off the trail," Raine said simply.

Frowning over her head, Neil asked, "You didn't mention anything about searching for her past, did you? Or that I might be helping you look for it?"

Raine jerked her head back far enough to allow her to stare up at him. "No! I wouldn't say anything to that effect. I won't even say anything once you're gone. All Mother will ever know is that my fiancé jilted me. And believe me, that will make her gloat with happiness. She'll take great pleasure in telling me how right she always is—especially about men."

The idea that he was eventually going to leave and Raine would be left here to tell everyone on the ranch that he'd jilted her left a pain right in the middle of his chest. He couldn't bear for anyone to think he was capable of hurting Raine. But the two of them had already painted a picture and he couldn't change the last brush strokes. Not unless he changed his whole opinion of falling in love and having a wife.

"Raine, I'm thinking—it might be better if you were the one who did the jilting. Then I wouldn't be leaving a bad impression here on the Sandbur and it would allow you to save face, too."

The corners of her lips tilted up in an impish grin. "You're worrying too much about this, Neil."

No, he was worrying too much about her, Neil thought. About the way she felt in his arms, the longing he felt to dip his head and kiss her lips and most of all the deep desire he had to give her what she wanted the most—a family.

"You're probably right," he said. Then before he could do or say something he might regret, he said, "Come on. Let's go put these flowers in water before they wilt."

He started to rise to his feet, but Raine quickly caught him by the arm and urged him back down beside her. He arched a questioning brow at her and she gave him a tentative smile.

"Neil, before we go I want to thank you," she said.

His eyes roamed over her mussed hair, puffy eyes and bare lips and he shifted uncomfortably as desire began to coil deep in his loins. He didn't know why he found her to be the sexiest woman he'd ever known. She wasn't exactly glamorous. Nor was she a blinding beauty. Yet her innocence was wrapped up in sensuality and the combination stirred him in ways he'd never felt before.

"Thank me for what?" he murmured huskily.

Her hand moved across his chest and her fingers began to play with the corner of his collar. "For the flowers. But mostly for—" As she looked up at him, a veil of thick brown lashes lowered over her eyes. "For trying to help me. You didn't have to do all this. But—" The corners of her lips curled upward. "I'm glad you did. Having you here on the ranch with me and being my fiancé, even in pretense, is…very nice. Thank you for that, Neil. Very much."

He wanted to say something back to her that would be equally kind, but he found his throat had tightened around a hot lump and he couldn't utter a word. He wanted to kiss her, to lay her back on the bed and let his body tell her how much he desired her, how much he was beginning to need her. But this was Esther's house and at any given moment she might come in and interrupt them. So he settled for lifting her hand to his lips and whispering huskily, "It's my pleasure, Raine."

The next morning at breakfast, Neil was surprised to find Esther in an amiable mood and he was glad, for Raine's sake, to see the woman hug her daughter with affection and discuss the barbecue scheduled for tonight.

He didn't know what had changed Esther's frame of

mind, but it was showing him a different, more likable side of the woman and he decided this kinder, gentler Esther must be the one that Raine loved so much that she'd gone to great lengths to shield from the real reason for his presence on the ranch.

"So what are you two going to do today?" Esther asked as the three of them sat around the breakfast table, sipping the last of their coffee.

Raine looked questioningly over to Neil and he smiled back at her in a vaguely impish way.

"We're going to drive into town and have a look around," he answered. "I've never actually been to Goliad before and Raine wants to show me her apartment."

Raine's brows arched upward as she studied his handsome face. Like yesterday, she'd been staggered all over again when he'd walked into the kitchen this morning with his clean-shaven jaws, damp hair and smiling face. Dark chinos covered his long legs and he'd topped them off with a white shirt with tiny green stripes. He was the sort of man that managed to look both masculine and suave no matter what he was wearing and Raine figured most everyone on the ranch was wondering how she'd ever managed to snag a marriage proposal from such a man.

"I do?" she asked blankly, then at the sight of Neil's frown, she hurriedly went on, "Oh—uh—yes, I do want you to see where I live. It's nothing fancy, but I like it."

"Well, I wouldn't dally around town too long, Raine," Esther inserted. "Geraldine likes to start things early. And since the party is in your honor you need to be here before it gets into full swing."

"Don't worry, Mother," Raine assured her. "We'll be back this afternoon."

A few minutes later, Raine and Neil finished their coffee and Esther surprised them both by shooing them away from the table.

"I'll tend to this mess. You two go on and enjoy yourselves," she urged.

After gathering up her purse, Raine walked over to the cabinet counter where Esther was working and kissed her mother's cheek.

"Thank you, Mother. Really."

Nodding, and with something close to a smile on her face, Esther patted her daughter's cheek. "Go on," she urged. "I've got to get over to the big house and help Cook…she's probably pulling her hair out about now."

Raine and Neil left the kitchen and walked outside to where his rental car was parked.

"Was that your mother back there or her pleasant twin?" he asked, as he opened the passenger door and helped Raine inside.

"I think it was her. But I'm not really sure," Raine replied with a chuckle. But after Neil took his seat behind the wheel and started the car, she said in a sober tone, "Neil, maybe I should explain that Mother is, for the most part, a kind, gentle woman. Yes, we've had plenty of differences and arguments, but basically she's always been a loving mother. If I painted her as a shrew before, it was only because I get so completely frustrated with her."

Neil backed the vehicle onto the gravel road and headed east in the direction that would take them off the ranch.

"Well, I don't know what caused the overnight change, but it was good to see her in a better humor," he admitted. "Maybe that little confrontation you two had last night made her think twice. She probably knows she upset you and she's trying to make up for it."

Raine nodded. "You could be right." She squared around in her seat to look at him. "We didn't get much chance to talk last night after supper. Normally Mother doesn't want to sit outside after dark because of the mosquitoes, but for some reason she followed us out there. And then when we went back inside, she was right behind us. I felt like we had a shadow. And I wanted to ask you about yesterday. Did you find out anything that might help you determine whether Mother might really be Darla?"

Neil thoughtfully shook his head. "Not really. I talked to Cook for a good while because I suspect she probably knows your mother as well or better than anyone here on the ranch. But she didn't give me anything conclusive to work with. I've been wondering if you've ever tried to trace information about Esther through her social security number? I realize you might not want to dig through her private papers, but we need somewhere to start."

Raine sighed. "I've already tried the social security number. That didn't help. Apparently she acquired the number after she was released from the hospital after her accident back in 1982. I've also searched through other papers for any kind of hint of her life before that time, but I can't find anything."

Neil considered her information. "Did the police report mention anything about what they found on your mother? Any sort of papers, jewelry, anything?"

Raine shook her head. "Not that I could find. She wasn't wearing a wedding ring. And sometimes I wonder whether she was married or having an affair when she became pregnant with me." She grimaced and shook her head again. "I know

I've thrown all sorts of scenarios at you and I guess some of them sound crazy, but when you don't know the truth it allows your imagination to run wild."

He gazed thoughtfully at the dirt road ahead of them, then finally said, "I think tomorrow I should drive up to Gillespie County and see what I can find out. There could be some of the older law officers still in that area who remember the incident."

Raine studied his chiseled profile and wondered how he had the power to make her heart lift even when things around her appeared hopeless. "I can't ask you to go to that much trouble for me, Neil. Gillespie County is north of San Antonio. It's too far."

He shot her a wry grin. "Let me be the judge of that. I just wish I could openly question people here on the ranch. Especially Geraldine. It's too bad her husband, Paul, and her sister, Elizabeth, have passed on. They might have given us some sort of clues as to your mother's early years here. What about Elizabeth's husband? You said something about him being disabled, but he can communicate, can't he?"

With a sad shake of her head, Raine said, "He resides in a nursing home in Goliad and, unfortunately, it's a struggle for him to utter a word."

Neil frowned with surprise. "Oh. Well, Matt and Cordero don't seem old enough to have such an elderly father. He must have married their mother when he was an older man," he surmised.

"Actually Mingo isn't all that old. He suffered a stroke and—" She broke off as sorrow twisted her features. "This isn't something that is discussed among the family, especially with Matt, who's very close to his father. But Mingo's stroke was a result of some sort of head injury he received in a fight with a couple of men. I'm not sure what the fight was over, but Matt says the men were out to kill Mingo and they very nearly succeeded. As a result his speech is slurred and his mobility limited."

Distracted by this new story, Neil took his eyes off the gravel road to glance at her. "That's terrible. Is there any hope that Mingo will ever recuperate?"

Raine shrugged. "The doctors aren't giving the family much hope. But who knows. Miracles do happen. And we pray for Mingo all the time."

"I hope your prayers are answered," Neil told her, then reached across the seat and clasped his hand around hers. "But let's not talk about your mother or the Saddlers or Sanchezes or anyone else on the Sandbur. We're on a little journey of our own today and I want to enjoy it." He squeezed her fingers and shot her a wicked grin. "What do you say?"

Her heart thumped with anticipation as she smiled hesitantly back at him. "Before I answer, maybe I should ask you what sort of journey you're planning."

He chuckled, then said in a far too sensual voice, "I thought we'd decide that along the way."


The drive into Goliad took them a little more than thirty minutes. Once they reached the small town, Raine didn't bother directing him anywhere. He took his time driving slowly through the streets and taking in the sights of the old Spanish missions and the sacred spot where Colonel Fannin and his men were massacred by Santa Anna's army.

He asked questions about the ancient town's battle-scarred history and thankfully Raine could answer knowledgably from all her reading on the subject. But when Neil pulled into a parking slot on one of the main business streets, it was her turn to ask questions.

"What are we doing here? I thought I was supposed to show you my apartment?"

He killed the engine. "I saw a jewelry store back down the street. Let's go see if they have any suitable rings."

Raine looked at him while her mouth fell open, then popped shut. "I thought—I'd hoped you'd forgotten all about that."

He rolled his eyes with disbelief. "Forgotten? Raine, that was the whole reason for this trip to town. Remember?"

"Well, yes. But—" But somewhere in the back of her mind she'd thought the task of going into a jewelry store and purchasing an engagement ring would never actually happen. It seemed too incredible to really happen.

"But what?"

He was leaning slightly toward her and in the small confines of the car she was close enough to see the pores and fine lines in his face, smell the subtle cologne clinging to his shirt. At the moment, several locks of dark gold hair had fallen onto his forehead to frame his deep blue eyes and as she gazed into them, she couldn't imagine any woman resisting this man. So why was she even trying? she wondered weakly.

"I was actually hoping you'd changed your mind about this." She nervously licked her lips and eased back toward the door. "But I can see now that you haven't."

"Of course I haven't. Tonight is our big night." He leaned closer and placed a soft kiss on her damp lips. "Come on. You're supposed to be enjoying this."

How could she enjoy it, she wondered miserably, when it was all make believe. But did she honestly want it to be real?

Everything inside her was screaming yes, even though a small portion of her common sense was yelling out that she was crazy.

She couldn't be Neil's *real* fiancée. He didn't want one!

But the warmth of his lips and the sexy glint in his eyes made it impossible not to play along with his plans. Even if her heart might be broken later on.

"All right," she said. "I'll do my best to smile and make everyone in the jewelry store believe I'm deliriously in love with you."

"That's my girl," he said happily and placed another kiss on her cheek.

Once inside the jewelry store, Neil didn't waste any time telling the clerk what they were looking for and before Raine could hardly catch her breath, a tray of diamond rings were displayed on the glass counter in front of them.

With his arm planted firmly around the back of her waist, Neil asked, "See anything you like, honey?"

Before she could respond, a male clerk pointed suggestively to a round diamond of modest size. "Now this is a nice solitaire on a platinum band. It's been a big seller this year. And platinum is the new thing in jewelry."

Raine was about to pick up the ring for closer examination when Neil promptly began to shake his head.

"No. Platinum is too cool," he murmured gently, "Raine is a warm woman. I think she needs something in yellow gold."

Their heads were positioned so close that when he turned slightly to look at her, his lips were nearly touching her cheek. Raine could feel heat rushing to her face, but she didn't move away. She was supposed to be in love. No, she thought, she needed to correct herself on that count. She *was* in love. Somehow these past two days she'd spent with Neil had changed her. He'd become the most important thing in her life, even more important than finding her father. When this had happened, she didn't know. The only thing she was certain of was that she couldn't tell him of her newfound feelings. He wouldn't welcome them and it would only make things terribly awkward. Probably so awkward that he would race straight to San Antonio and catch the first available plane back to New Mexico.

With a little catch in her breath, she murmured, "You pick, darling, and I'll tell you whether I like it."

His blue eyes grew soft, his lips spread into a sinful smile. "All right. Let me see if I know you as well as I think."

He slowly perused the rings in the tray and eventually plucked up a large, pear shaped diamond flanked by small emeralds.

"This one." He picked up her hand and slipped it onto her finger. "The green matches your eyes."

The clerk immediately began to loudly clear his throat and Neil looked across the counter at him.

"Is something wrong? This one hasn't already sold to someone else, has it?"

"Oh, no, sir. It's just that it's rather pricey. And to tell you the truth, the diamond I first showed you is a far more perfect stone. I have papers guaranteeing there are no flaws."

He glanced at Raine who was holding out her hand and staring at the ring in a dazed way.

To the clerk, he said, "I don't care about the cost."

"Well…you…uh…okay. That's good," the clerk stuttered with surprise.

"And I don't want a perfect stone, either," Neil went on. "People aren't perfect. Including my fiancée."

Raine jerked her gaze off the ring to stare at him.

"But," he continued with a lazy smile, "her imperfections make her beautiful and lovable."

With an engagement ring on her hand and words like that slipping past his lips, Raine had to mentally shake herself to remember this was all a playact. Even so, she couldn't stop herself from cuddling close to his side and smiling up at him.

"I do like it, darling. It's unique and very beautiful."

Behind the counter, the clerk pulled a tiny square of paper from the slot where the ring had rested and handed it to Neil.

"Apparently you know what you're doing," he said with a bit of envy.

Neil barely glanced at the price tag and was about to hand it back to the clerk when Raine plucked it from his hand. After she read the exorbitant amount that was hand written in ink, she silently passed it to the clerk, then placed a hand on Neil's arm and urged him to follow her to a spot across the room where a display of Christmas gifts were piled in an antique washtub.

"What's the matter now?" he asked in a hushed tone. "Don't you like the ring?"

She shook her head in exasperation. "Don't be crazy," she whispered back at him. "I love the ring. I've never seen or owned anything like it. But I'm not about to let you buy the thing. It's outrageous! Let's go back over there, pick out something reasonable and get out of here."

His nostrils flared as he drew in an impatient breath. "Dear Raine, I appreciate the fact that you want to be frugal for my sake, but I'm not a destitute man. I'm buying the ring. Now, come on. The clerk thinks we're having an argument."

Raine rolled her eyes. "We *are* having an argument."

"Not the first and I very much doubt the last," he whispered with an endearing smile and touched the end of her nose with his forefinger. "Just some of those imperfections I was talking about."

Raine wanted to protest further, but he snaked his arm around her waist and guided her back to the jewelry case.

"It's all settled. We'll take this one," Neil told the salesman.

Seemingly stunned that he'd made such a sale with so little fuss, the clerk said, "Good. Good. I'll go get a box and write out the receipt."

"Forget about the box," Neil called after him. "She won't be taking it off her finger."

## Chapter Twelve

**M**inutes later, after the transaction of money had been made, Raine walked out of the jewelry store with her head spinning. The heavy weight of the diamond on her finger felt strange, but that didn't begin to describe the odd mixture of euphoria and fear welling up inside her. She couldn't love Neil. It was useless. Hopeless. Her heart was on a path of destruction and she couldn't think of one way to make it detour.

"Why are you so quiet?" Neil asked as he started the car and backed onto the street. "You look like you're about to be wheeled into the operating room or something even worse. I thought most women loved to buy jewelry. At least, all the ones that I know do."

Her hands were lying in her lap and she didn't lift her head to look at him. She couldn't seem to take her eyes off the diamond and emeralds as she tried to imagine what it would feel like if the ring were a real promise of his love.

"I'm not like the other women you know."

There was a grin in his voice as he said, "How could you know that?"

Turning her head his way, she shot him a faint frown. "Because it's obvious you have—certain taste. And I'm not exactly one of them."

His brows arched with surprise, but all he said was, "Tell me how to get to your apartment."

Raine directed him through the short drive and in less than five minutes they arrived at a quiet block of red brick apartments. The front of the large two-story structure was built in plantation style. The long windows were trimmed with white wooden shutters while huge white pillars supported the roof of the ground floor and the upper balcony. In spite of it being early December, pink bougainvillea and red hibiscus were still blooming vividly on the front lawn while thick trails of honeysuckle climbed the white trellis adorning the porch. Compared to the grandeur of the Sandbur, Neil realized these were nice, but modest living quarters.

"Do you live on the ground or upper level?" Neil asked as the two of them strolled down the sidewalk toward the building.

He'd slung his arm around her shoulders and Raine was acutely aware of his hip and thigh brushing hers, the way his warm fingers were curled around her bare arm. In spite of knowing it would soon end, being with him, touching him, made her heart beat with happiness.

"I requested an upstairs apartment. I like looking down at the trees and the birds—it makes me feel sorta free." She smiled at him. "And I like that."

Yes, he understood all about wanting to be free, Neil thought. While growing up he'd wanted something, anything to come along and free him from the strained, angry atmosphere that had permeated the Rankin home. And later, after he'd watched his father die of a broken heart, he'd vowed to always be his own man. He'd made a supreme effort to make sure no one, especially a woman, cornered him.

"Free as a bird. I'm not surprised to hear you say that. Growing up with a mother like Esther would have made me run and never look back."

Raine figured he'd already done a bit of that. Particularly when it came to women, but she wasn't going to think about that now. The next few days would be the only time she got to spend with this man that she'd fallen in love with and she didn't want to waste a moment.

Her apartment was located at the very end of the building where live oak branches shaded the balcony and potted plants lined the balustrade. After she unlocked the door, she motioned for him to precede her into a small foyer decorated with a large framed mirror, a deacon's bench and more potted plants.

As he followed her through to the cozy living room, she said, "Sorry about the mess. Since I haven't been around in a few days, I haven't had a chance to straighten things."

"It looks nice to me." He looked around the room at the pieces of furniture that looked mostly antique to him. Not a rich sort of antique, but rather old things that had once graced someone else's home. There was nothing modern looking about the place. Even the telephone sitting on a dark wooden end table was a replica of a rotary phone. "Although, I have to admit I'm surprised. I didn't know you were into old things."

She smiled in a minxlike way as she tossed her handbag onto a nearby table. "I like you, don't I?"

His chuckle was faintly menacing as he followed her into a small kitchen area. "That was rough. Especially when I just put an engagement ring on your hand."

Turning toward him, she rested her back against the cabinet counter. A faint frown marred the middle of her forehead. "Neil, since you didn't seem to want to argue about it down at the jewelry store, I wasn't going to bring the subject up again. But now that you have, I want you to understand that I feel very badly."

How could she look any prettier, he wondered, with her lips painted the color of a ripe cherry, the strap of her sundress falling onto her arm, and a diamond on her finger telling the world that she belonged to him. Just the idea stirred him with a desire that stunned him and he couldn't stop himself from stepping forward and slipping his arms around her.

"There's nothing to feel badly about," he said huskily. "Unless you really don't like the ring."

She groaned. "Neil. This is not *my* ring. It's yours. And I'm just afraid when you go to sell it that you won't get nearly as much back as you wrote that check for a few minutes ago."

He clicked his tongue in a shameful fashion as his hands flattened against her back and slid slowly, ever so slowly up to her shoulders. "I have no intention of selling it. The ring is yours. Do you think I give a woman something and then ask for it back?"

Maybe his heart, she thought dismally. Maybe that was the one thing Neil Rankin wasn't generous with.

"This is a different situation," she said as arcs of heat began to flow through her body. "We're not engaged. This is just a prop to make the illusion look genuine."

His head dipped and his lips brushed her ear. "Really? Have you ever thought I might want it to be real?"

The questions were suggestive, even laced with a tinge of humor, but they were enough to cause her head to jerk backward and her gaze latch onto his.

"You're not a liar, Neil. Don't turn into one now."

He rubbed the side of his face against her silky hair and Raine couldn't stop her arms from slipping around his lean waist.

"I'm not lying. Well—not exactly," he said wryly. "Sometimes when I look at you, when I kiss you, I have this thought that I always want us to be together."

So did Raine. Only she didn't have to be looking at the man. She didn't even have to be in close proximity of him. His presence had already taken up residence in her heart and something told her it was going to be a mighty big, if impossible, task to move him out.

"And then what? Sanity hits?"

He sighed. "Oh, Raine, don't be so—"

"Honest?" she finished for him.

Lifting his head away from hers, he caught her gaze with his. The sober clarity she saw in his blue eyes jolted her. He wanted her. Maybe even more than he wanted to admit to her or himself.

"Maybe that's the word for it," he conceded. "Right now, I don't much want to think about tomorrow or forever. Tonight is our engagement party. And today—" He paused to outline her lips with his forefinger. "We're all alone for the first time since we met in San Antonio. And I like it. Don't you?"

Her heart was drumming against her ribs. Her knees were

crumbling along with her resistance. She swallowed and made an attempt to break the spell that was building between them.

"It's nice—a perfect time for a cup of coffee. Want one?"

He chuckled lowly. "I'm already warm enough."

She moistened her lips and glanced away from him. She could feel the pulse in her neck throbbing and if she hadn't already been holding on to him, her hands would be shaking.

"Maybe you should go stand over the air-conditioning vent," she suggested huskily.

His hands compelled her forward until the front of her body was pressing against his.

"That's not what I really need, Raine." One hand cupped her chin and forced her gaze back to his. As he looked into her green eyes, he murmured, "Oh, my sweet, you are the most beautiful thing I've ever seen in my life."

"You're lying again. And—"

His lips suddenly swooped down on hers, blocking out anything else she might have said. And Raine decided it didn't matter. Any sort of protest she could make now would be worse than feeble. She wanted Neil as much as he seemed to want her.

He kissed her for long moments, then lifted his lips a fraction away from hers and whispered, "You talk too much. Especially when we don't need to be talking at all."

"I'm sure you have a better way of communicating."

She could feel more than see his lips spread into a sinful smile and then he was kissing her again, only deeper this time. His hands slid from her shoulders down to the small of her back, then farther down to the curve of her hips.

Raine felt her body molding to his as though it already knew what it wanted without her brain having to give it directions.

Her arms circled his neck, then clung tightly as she invited him to move beyond the heaven he was creating with her lips.

Neil had never met a woman who could rattle his senses or tilt the ground beneath his feet. But Raine seemed to have a strange effect on him. He could feel his insides quivering and a cloud of desire was fogging every part of his brain, especially the part where common sense ruled. That section seemed to have flown out the window, like the free little bird Raine so envied.

He felt as drunk as if he'd downed a bottle of Kentucky bourbon. The pit of his stomach was on fire and his hands were clumsy as he fingered the zipper at the back of her dress.

As Neil inched it toward her waist, he leaned his head back far enough to see her face. Desire and trust radiated from her eyes and the sight sent an arrow of bittersweet pain right through his heart.

"Raine, do you really want this? Me? I don't want to—"

Rising up on her toes, she pressed her lips over the rest of his words. After she'd kissed him softly, she murmured, "Now you're the one who's doing too much talking."

A thousand questions raced through his brain as his fingers tugged the zipper open and the dress peeled away from her skin, but he kept them all to himself. After all, it didn't matter what had changed her mind from yesterday to today. From the moment he'd met her, he'd wanted this to happen. He couldn't allow what bit of conscience he had left to ruin it now.

"Maybe we'd better—get out of the kitchen," he suggested.

Her face sweetly serious, she took him by the hand and led him down a short hallway and into her bedroom.

For an apartment, the room was spacious, but other than that and the old iron bedstead covered with a yellow flowered quilt, he didn't notice anything around him. His senses were already consumed with Raine and before they could even get to the bed, he tugged her dress down over her hips and watched it pool around her ankles.

To his surprise, she wasn't wearing a bra and the sight of her pert little breasts all but took his breath away. They were round and full, the nipples like two rosebuds just waiting to bloom before his eyes.

Gently he cupped his hands around the pale orbs and then lowered his mouth to the soft spot between them. From somewhere afar, he could hear her groaning and then her fingers speared into his hair and pressed against his skull.

Slowly his mouth eased up and over the mound until it reached the tight bud in the center. When he touched his tongue there, Raine let out a helpless whimper and urged his head closer.

Hungrily he used his mouth to worship every inch of one breast before turning his attention to the opposite one and by then Raine was completely lost. Her head was reeling and her hands were clinging to his shoulders in order to keep from sinking to her knees. A hot, tight ache had built between her thighs and she thought she would scream if he continued to play with her.

"Neil—oh my—please—"

Her strangled plea lifted his head and as he looked into her eyes, he took her hand and placed it on the crotch of his trousers. Beneath the khaki fabric she could feel his swollen manhood and it shocked her to think that he could want her as much as she wanted him.

"Earlier you said that you weren't to my taste," he murmured. "You couldn't have been more wrong. I've never wanted any woman like this."

"Don't tell me such things, Neil. Just—just make love to me," she begged.

Neil kissed her, then turned away to remove his clothing. Once he stepped back and pulled her into his arms, he asked in a fevered voice, "Are you protected?"

Raine nodded awkwardly. "I—er—take the pill for—other reasons," she explained.

He looked relieved and Raine felt a rush of anticipation as he finally lifted her off the floor and gently placed her on the bed.

Blinds at the windows were twisted almost closed, making cool shadows dance around the room and over the colorful quilt. Outside, beyond the balcony, among the branches of the live oaks, two mockingbirds called to each other. Neil didn't know why the sound of the birds penetrated his thoughts. Not when his mind and every cell in his body was engorged with desire for the woman in his arms.

It wasn't until moments later, after he'd entered her warm, giving body, that Neil understood. The birds didn't want to be completely free. They wanted a mate to fly beside them.

The poignant idea was not a welcome one and he closed his eyes and pushed it away even as he felt Raine's arms wrapping lovingly around him, her legs entwining with his.

"Neil, tell me what to do," she whispered fervently. "I don't know how to please you."

He opened his eyes to find her looking up at him, her face eager, and drawn with a desire that stunned him. And in that moment he realized what a precious gift she had chosen to give him. For as long as he lived, he would never forget this December morning or the precious woman in his arms.

Lifting his hand to her brow, he pushed away the honey-brown hair and pressed a kiss to her damp skin.

"You couldn't make me more pleased than I am right now," he whispered.

Her eyes widened. "But—"

"Quit talking. Just show me what you're feeling."

His basic instruction was all she needed and Raine was amazed to feel the last of her fears and inhibitions fly away as she gave her body and her heart to him.

Like a bandit racing to beat the moon, Neil snatched as many kisses and caresses as he could and cached them all inside him before this heaven on earth ended. While beneath him, Raine was certain she was floating up to paradise.

His lips, his hands and the rhythmic thrusts of his hips were doing things to her body that sent wave after wave of burning desire from her head to her toes. And though she tried to keep up with each new sensation he was giving her, she couldn't. The pleasures were too many to grasp at once. All she could do was hang on and hope this union between them would never end.

But their frenetic passion couldn't last forever and before long Neil couldn't stop his warm seed from spilling into her or push back the all-consuming feelings that were quickly flooding his heart and his mind. From somewhere far away he could hear himself groaning like a wounded animal and threaded through that sound were Raine's soft, quick gasps. He could feel the velvet heat of her body beneath him, surrounding him, while everything else was fading into oblivion.

Like a meteor on course to collide, every muscle in Raine's body tightened in anticipation of the explosion. It came like a violent jolt and then suddenly she was sailing on peaceful silver clouds, her eyes blinded by the warm sunlight pouring through her, around her.

Neil was the first to regain his senses and he quickly rolled off to one side so as not to squash her with his weight. Then lying on his side, his head nestled next to hers, he placed his hand over the region of her heart and, like a drunken fool, marveled at the rapid thump beneath his fingers.

"Are we still in my bedroom?" she finally managed to murmur.

His smile crinkled the corners of his blue eyes and he brought his lips against her damp forehead.

"We are."

"I wasn't sure." Twisting her head toward his, she opened her eyes and found his blue eyes surveying her with a look that still smoldered. "I thought you'd taken me to heaven."

A trickle of sweat was sliding down her temple. He stopped it with his finger, then moved his lips to her cheek. "You're giving me too much credit, sweetheart. I don't have divine powers."

Maybe not, Raine thought, but he certainly had a powerful hold on her body and an even stronger grip on her heart. She'd not realized how much until this very moment.

"Oh. Well, I'm glad to find out I just made love to a human."

Made love. The two simple words bounced around in his head like a rubber ball to cause him both pleasure and unease. Before Raine, he would have used the word sex to describe what had just taken place between them. Even the women in the past would have used the less than romantic term. But obviously Raine viewed things differently and he was astounded to discover that now his own thinking about the matter was being turned upside down and shaken.

She was right, he thought incredibly. There'd been a lot more than just his body involved in their union. But he wasn't going to try to analyze his feelings right now. Precious time was ticking away. He didn't want to waste a moment with her.

With decadent pleasure, one hand slid from her breast down to the faint curve of her belly where his forefinger traced a lazy outline around her navel.

"Raine?"

"Hmm?"

"Yesterday—in your office—you ran from me. From this. What made you change your mind?"

She didn't answer and when her gaze drifted away from his, he reached down and picked up her left hand. His ring was the only thing she was wearing and he couldn't imagine anything he'd rather see on her. Except a smile.

"Was it the ring? I hope to hell you weren't thinking I expected—compensation," he said in a voice muffled by the curve of her cheek.

She didn't look at him and he could feel her body, which had been soft and compliant, stiffening with defense.

"No," she said tightly. "And even if I had, I wouldn't have paid you this way."

She sounded a little miffed and Neil had to admit he couldn't blame her. But he'd had to ask. He couldn't help the way in which his mind worked. His mother had warped his thinking and he'd given up on believing he could ever straighten it out.

"I'm sorry, Raine. Sometimes I can't help being a jerk. Forgive me?"

Sighing softly, she turned onto her side and cupped her hand around the side of his face. "Of course I forgive you. And if you really want to know why I changed my mind, it was because I—"

I love you. The words were on her tongue, kicking and screaming to be released. But she swallowed them. Even after the closeness they'd just shared, it was too soon to reveal her heart's feelings to him. As far as that went, she wasn't sure there would ever be a time Neil would want to hear those words. He'd already made it clear he wasn't a love and marriage man.

"I want you," she finally finished. "I wanted you yesterday and the day before and the day before that but—this is something I've been trying to avoid. Now I—"

His lips curved upward and just looking at them made desire curl in the pit of her stomach.

"Now what?" he urged, his voice husky as he tugged her warm body next to his.

She let out a shaky breath. "I wish I hadn't wasted so much time."

Groaning, he rolled onto his back and pulled her on top of him. Her long hair swung forward to hide her face and he reached up to gently tuck it behind her ears.

"Well, we'll make up for that," he promised with an inviting grin. "We still have a bit of morning left and we can eat later—when we get back to the Sandbur."

"Much later," she whispered as she brought her lips down to his.

## *Chapter Thirteen*

That evening, as the sun dipped below the open, rolling hills of the Sandbur, the smell of roasting meat and mesquite smoke filled the backyard of the Saddler home. Numerous tables, covered with tablecloths in the image of the Texas state flag, had been set up beneath the live oaks.

To one side, a portable, wooden dance floor had been set up and strung with colorful Christmas lights. A local, four-piece band was already entertaining the crowd with country and rhythm and blues, while servants fetched and carried food and drink to the tables and the milling guests.

As for Raine, she'd been glued to Neil's side until Nicolette had come along and pulled her to one side. Now the physician's assistant plucked up Raine's hand and stared with awe at the diamond and emerald ring.

"Good Lord! Has Mother seen this yet?" She gripped

Raine's hand and laughed with excitement. "She'll say it's just like Texas—big and beautiful!"

Most all of the family and friends who were going to attend the barbecue had already arrived. As people moved about them, Raine told herself the huge crowd actually had nothing to do with her so-called engagement. Everyone in the far-reaching corners of the county loved to party at the Sandbur for any reason and tonight was no exception. Still, it made her feel guilty to allow her very best friend to believe the ring, and the man standing a few steps away from them, actually belonged to her. Maybe this morning for those few precious hours in her apartment, he had really been her fiancé. Making love with Neil had made that dream almost real to her. Their closeness had given her a sweet glimpse as to what a life with him would be like. But later this afternoon when she'd returned to the Sandbur, reality hit her hard and now she was trying to deal with a sense of emptiness.

"Geraldine has seen the ring," Raine said, trying to push light notes of joy into her voice. "She says she's jealous. Can you imagine? Your mother has some of the biggest diamonds in the state of Texas. And she doesn't even wear them."

Both women glanced across the lawn to where Geraldine appeared to be in a quiet conversation with a well-known horse buyer in the area. For a man in his sixties, he was extremely fit and darkly handsome. Raine had heard her mention the man before and she couldn't help but wonder if there was more than talk of horses between the two. She could only hope so. God only knew the woman deserved a little happiness after all she'd been through with losing her husband in a boating accident down in the Gulf.

"Jewels and riches never were important to Mother,"

Nicolette replied. "Daddy was her real love. Now the Sandbur has to fill the hole he left."

The other woman sighed a bit wistfully, before turning a bright smile back on Raine. "I don't want to think about any of that tonight. Gosh, this is your party and it's just all so exciting. I can't believe you kept such a secret from me. Especially when I've been hounding you about dating. When on earth did you ever have time to meet him?"

Raine felt her cheeks blushing, but since the shadows were growing deeper she doubted Nicolette could distinguish the color from the blush she'd carefully applied.

"It was—rather hard. But—well—this has all happened very quickly between us. I know I've shocked everyone here on the Sandbur with this news." She laughed and hoped the sound wasn't full of the nerves that were hopping around in her stomach. She wasn't exactly sure why she was feeling so edgy tonight. It wasn't like this acting thing was anything new. From the moment she'd brought Neil to the ranch, she'd been pretending to be happy, to be in love. Now that she really was in love with him, everything should be easier. But in fact, everything was much worse. Not only did she have to feign an engagement in front of her family and friends, but now she had to try to mask her true feelings from Neil. Oh God, would it ever end? she wondered miserably. "But I—I didn't want to mention Neil until I was sure and then—well, now he's here."

Nicolette turned her gaze across the yard to where Neil was standing with her brother, Lex, and cousin, Matt. The three men were talking as if they were old friends and the sight put a smile on her face.

"He's definitely here. And look how he's already fitting in. If Lex and Matt like him, then I don't have to wonder if he's a good man." She turned her attention back to Raine and once again squeezed her hand with affection. "I'm so happy for you, Raine. This is what I've been praying for you. All of that stuff with your mother and trying to find your father—I understand it's important, but I was beginning to fear that you were letting it take over your life." Her expression sobering, she peered closer at Raine. "Uh, that paper you showed me in your office the other morning—what happened? You didn't make the call, did you?"

Raine's stomach clenched to a tight fist. "Actually, I did call. But—I don't think anything will ever come of it. I guess it was just a coincidence that the woman in the picture resembled Mother."

Nicolette smiled with relief. "Well, speaking of your mother. I can't believe how well she's taking all of this. And she's so dressed up tonight that she looks like a different woman. I hardly recognized her. Neil must have really charmed her or something."

"Yes. Neil has a way of doing that," Raine replied. "But for the most part Mother hasn't been all that keen about this engagement. Right now she seems to be putting on a good front, but I'm afraid that later, after Neil goes back to San Antonio, she's going to cause me a lot of misery about the matter. So beware, I may be crying on your shoulder."

Frowning prettily, Nicolette patted Raine's shoulder. "It's going to be hard for her to give you up to any man. And maybe it would be better if you simply left with Neil. Are you planning to get married soon?"

Raine suddenly felt dead inside. She wouldn't be leaving with Neil. She wouldn't be marrying him. She wasn't even sure if she would ever get to make love to him again. The whole idea was killing her. But there wasn't a thing she could do about it. She obviously couldn't change his philosophy about marriage. And even if she could, she wasn't sure she had the courage to marry him, or any man.

"Uh, we haven't talked about a date yet. This has all happened so quickly. And I don't want to be in any hurry," Raine told her.

"Well, from the way Neil looks at you, I doubt you'll be single for much longer. In fact, he looks like he's about to come fetch you."

Neil had been looking forward to tonight and Geraldine's impromptu party. He normally loved social gatherings. Especially ones that had good food, even better beer, great music, and interesting people as this one did. But already he was wishing the celebration was over and he could take Raine to some quiet, private place and make love to her.

Forget that. He'd already gotten himself into enough trouble, Neil thought. Even so, he couldn't take his eyes off her for more than a minute. She looked like a Hollywood starlet tonight in a little black dress with its neck draped low on her bosom and her hair twisted into a sleek French twist and fastened with rhinestones. There wasn't any question that he'd thought she was beautiful before, but after this morning she was much more than that. When he looked at her now, he saw a softness, a loveliness that had nothing to do with her physical attributes.

Having sex with her was supposed to have been a pleasant experience, a nice end to the attraction that had been building between them. But their morning together had been none of those things. He was still shaken from it and he didn't know quite what to make of the way he was feeling, thinking, wanting. What did it mean? That he was falling in love with her?

Neil refused to believe that was the reason for the strange

emotions that continued to grip him. A person didn't fall in love unless they wanted to, he argued with himself. And he didn't want to. He refused to believe he could be anything more than the man he'd been thus far. It wasn't possible to change that much. And yet, he had to admit that he wanted her like nothing he'd ever wanted in his life.

"I wonder if Mom is trying to deal Grady out of that gray mare I've been wanting? He wanted a fortune for her, but she might talk him down."

Lex's comment penetrated Neil's thoughts and he turned his gaze back on the two men and tried to catch up on their conversation.

Matteo chuckled. "She has a lot better chance of talking Grady down than you do."

Lex grimaced. "Thanks for your confidence in me, cuz. I'll remember that the next time you call me in the middle of the night and want me to help you pull a calf."

It was Matteo's turn to laugh. "Well, everyone knows that Geraldine has more Ketchum blood in her veins than McCormack. That's why she's such a horse trader. 'Course, being a woman helps. Especially in Grady's case."

While the two cousins chuckled, Neil felt as if he'd just been slapped and he struggled not to appear dazed as he stared at the men.

"What did you just say?" he asked Matteo. "Did you say Geraldine was a Ketchum? What do you mean by that?"

Both Lex and Matteo were staring back at Neil as though they considered his questions more than strange.

"Yes, Geraldine and my mother Elizabeth's, maiden names were Ketchum. Their father was Nate Ketchum. Why?" Matteo asked.

The rancher might as well have slugged Neil in the gut with his fist. The revelation nearly staggered him and he quickly took a long swig of beer in hopes it would steady him.

"Uh, I, just happened to know some people by that name. I grew up with them." He glanced at Raine and blew out a heavy breath. "Like they say, small world."

"Yeah," Lex agreed. "I flew out to Sacramento last year and ran into an old friend I'd gone to school with years ago. Just happened to run on to him in the airport terminal. Guess you never know whom you might see in faraway places."

Matteo continued to thoughtfully regard Neil. "That's something. You think these Ketchum friends of yours are related to us?"

There was no thinking about it, Neil thought. He was certain they were related. It explained everything. The odd, familiarity he'd sensed the moment he'd met these people and, even more so, the missing pieces of Esther's story. She was Darla Ketchum Carlton. That's why she'd spent the past twenty-four years on this ranch. He figured she'd gotten into some sort of trouble and she'd found refuge with her in-laws. But did they have any idea who she really was? Somehow Neil doubted it. Otherwise, the facts would have reached Raine long ago.

"Well...I...couldn't really say. I will ask them, though, the next time I see them." He looked at Raine and felt his heart crack like a piece of hard candy. "If you guys will excuse me, I think I'll go dance with my fiancée."

Raine spotted Neil coming her way and quickly excused herself from Nicolette to cross the small expanse of yard to meet him.

"What's the matter?" she asked in a low voice as she took

in the frown marring his forehead. "Is attending your own engagement party becoming too much for you?"

He quickly smiled and drew her arm beneath his. "Not at all. My stomach is gnawing, that's all. I thought we might take a whirl on the dance floor while the servants finish bringing out the food."

"You mean you actually dance?" she asked as they wove their way through guests that had gathered in small talkative groups.

"Sshh!" he scolded for her ears only. "Remember, I'm your fiancé, you're supposed to know all about me."

She laughed softly as he led her up two steps and onto the polished dance floor. "Some people are married for years and never know their spouses."

He pulled her close and linked his hand with hers. "It wouldn't be that way with us," he said as he began to move her to the slow beat of the music.

His comment surprised her and she tilted a glance up at him. "Coming from a man who only wants a woman's company in small doses, that's hard to believe."

He frowned. "You believe I'm not capable of having serious feelings, that I could never stick with one woman long enough to really appreciate her."

His body was warm and hard against her and the slow rhythm of their movements only added to the sensual thoughts going around and around in her head. Being close to him like this and remembering the delights of his lovemaking made it difficult for Raine to focus her mind on anything else.

"I didn't say that."

"But you're thinking it."

A heavy sigh passed her lips and she looked up at him with an annoyed expression. "Does it really matter, Neil?"

His hand tightened against her waist. "This morning—"

"We both understand what that was. And don't worry, I'm not going to get all soppy about it."

He continued to frown. "I wasn't worried that you would. I just—"

Neil couldn't finish. He couldn't tell her that he'd been wondering how he could ever go back to New Mexico and pretend that this time with her hadn't changed him. How could he ever look at another woman, make love to her and expect it to be as good, as right as it had been with Raine?

"Just what?" she prodded.

Neil shook his head. He couldn't talk about it now. He couldn't think about it now. He had to turn his attention to Darla Ketchum Carlton aka Esther Crockett and try to figure out what the hell he was going to do about it. Telling Raine would finally give her the truth. But at what cost? he asked himself. She'd learn that her mother was a fraud of sorts and that her father was likely dead. Although, to be fair, there was no way he could assume to know who Raine's father might really be. Randolf had been an ill man just before he died, but whether he'd been too weak to sire a child was anybody's guess. That left Jaycee Carlton. Neil had never seen or met the man, but his background was murky. He didn't want to imagine Raine's father being a murder victim. But either way she was going to be devastated to learn the man was dead and it was too late for her to know or love him.

"Nothing, honey. I guess what I'm trying to say is that I still want you like hell."

Her green eyes softened and her lips tilted to a sensuous smile. "I want you, too."

Something pierced the middle of his chest and he sucked

in a deep breath and glanced away from her. His eyes settled on a couple moving around the dance floor and he was shocked to see the woman was Raine's mother.

Nodding his head toward the couple, he said, "Raine, look. Your mother is dancing. Does she normally do this?"

Twisting her head slightly, Raine glanced over her shoulder to see her mother moving around the dance floor with a man who ran the Goliad county livestock auction barn. Since the Sandbur often did business there, he was a frequent guest of the ranch's social events. But Raine had never seen her mother dance with him or anyone else for that matter.

"Dear heaven! I'm shocked that she even knows how to dance. What has come over her?"

Neil glanced down at her, then thoughtfully back to Esther. "Well, this is her daughter's engagement party. Maybe she decided she should act happy."

Raine's eyes widened with wonder. "Maybe she *is* happy, Neil. God, wouldn't that be awful?"

"Raine!" he scolded softly. "Why are you saying that? Don't you want her blessings?"

Of course it would be wonderful to have her mother's blessings. But not over a phony engagement which was soon going to end!

"Snap out of it, Neil. I don't want her to get too happy about us. Not when we're eventually going to break up, so to speak." Shaking her head, she rolled her eyes and groaned. "Can this possibly get any worse?"

She didn't have a clue to how awful it already was, Neil thought sickly. But he couldn't tell her tonight while everyone was celebrating and having a good time. He wasn't even sure he could bring himself to tell her tomorrow. Yet somehow he had to find the courage to give her the news, even though he knew it was going to break her heart.

Wanting to keep her as close as possible, Neil kept Raine on the dance floor until Geraldine announced to the crowd that it was time to eat.

The food was served buffet style and after the two of them filled their plates, they found seats at one end of a long table. While they ate, many people stopped by to offer congratulations and view Raine's engagement ring. She accepted the well wishes gracefully and, for once, since this ordeal had started, Neil watched the exchanges with regret. And it wasn't just the deception that was bothering him. He was beginning to realize how very much Raine had come to mean to him and a part of him wished they were truly betrothed and he had the rest of his life to love her.

Raine had eaten less than half the food on her plate when she glanced over at Neil. "That's all I can eat."

Tossing a soiled napkin on top of his plate, he said, "I've had enough, too."

She shook her head. "You don't have to stop eating just because I am."

He smiled wanly. "It's not that. I guess I wasn't as hungry as I first thought."

Concerned, she leaned closer and peered at him. "Are you feeling sick? Normally you have a big appetite."

Earlier this evening, Neil had been looking forward to the delicious food Cook had spent the past two days preparing. But after a few bites, he'd lost interest in everything on his plate, including the succulent smoked brisket. All he could think was that he'd found Linc's long lost mother and soon everything was going to change in a drastic way. This engagement, be it fake or real, would have to end and so would this precious time with Raine. This whole trip was not turning out the way he'd planned, he thought miserably. He'd thought he'd be spending a few pleasant days with a beautiful woman. Never in his wildest dreams had he really expected to find Darla Carlton or to lose his heart to her daughter.

"I'm okay," he said quietly. "I think—I need a bit of quietness for a moment. Do you think anyone would miss us if we took a walk?"

Smiling suggestively, she rose to her feet and reached for his hand. "Even if they do, they'll understand."

He wrapped his hand around hers and together they strolled away from the noisy eating area.

By now, the evening shadows had turned into darkness, but there was enough residual lighting coming from the Saddler house to dimly illuminate the path leading toward the horse barn. A southerly breeze carried the scent of jasmine and across the way a mare softly nickered to her colt.

The night surrounded them and as the music and the laughter began to fade into the distance, Neil said, "The party is far more extravagant than I expected. Geraldine went all out for us."

"Yes. She's a generous, loving woman."

And Geraldine could also be Raine's aunt, Neil thought, if it turned out that Randolf was her father. Raine could possibly be a true blood relative of the Ketchums! But he didn't want to think about all of that now. Not when he was finally alone with her again and his body was aching to be next to hers.

Raine glanced up at him and smiled. "Are you enjoying the evening?"

Slipping his arm around her back, he urged her closer to his side. "I am now," he assured her. "And have I told you how absolutely beautiful you look? That dress is driving me crazy. All I want to do is take it off of you."

"Neil—"

Before she could say more, he stopped their forward movement and swooped his lips down over hers.

She groaned with pleasant surprise, then rising on her tiptoes, quickly wrapped her arms around his neck

His kiss was immediately hot and hungry, telling Raine in no uncertain terms of the depths he wanted her. She clung to him tightly as flames kindled and swept throughout her body.

"C'mon," she urged when he finally lifted his mouth from hers. "I know a place we can really be alone."

Taking his hand, she led him down the path toward the horse barn. Here, a yard light illuminated a portion of the training pen. They circled the iron railing and entered the barn through a small, back entrance.

The interior was dark and the scents of horses and alfalfa hay mingled with dust. From somewhere at the other end of the barn, he could hear the restless stirrings of stalled horses and the creak of the wind against old wood.

"Aren't there guards around here?" he asked in a hushed voice. "The horses in this one barn must be worth thousands."

"They are worth thousands," she agreed. "But except for two pairs of black-mouthed curs, the Sandbur doesn't have security guards. We trust our neighbors."

Neil's worried glance suddenly darted around their feet. "Where are the dogs?"

Raine laughed softly. "Probably up at the party gorging on brisket scraps."

Placing her hand on his arm, she urged him across the darkened building, past several horse stalls, to a wide wooden door. After pulling it open, Neil followed her inside and she quickly bolted it behind him. He'd not expected her to be this bold or blunt about making love to him and the sound was like a match scraping and fire bells clanging in his head.

"Now we are truly alone," she whispered huskily.

With his hands firmly gripping her waist, he glanced around him. "What is this room?"

"Some of the ranch's tack is stored here. So watch out that you don't run into any saddles hanging from the roof."

He followed her through a shadowy maze until they reached a small cot in one corner of the room and then she pulled him down beside her. He quickly reached to drag her into his arms.

"This is decadent behavior," he whispered against her lips. "We're supposed to be out with the guests."

"We will be—later." She clasped his face between her hands. "Neil, if you're thinking that I'm behaving like a hussy it's only because…I want you."

Groaning, he kissed her hungrily as desire began to quickly grip his mind and his body. "You don't have to explain, my darling. I want you just as much. You'll never know how much. But if we lie down on this cot, we'll ruin your dress and your hair and—"

His words broke off as she pushed his shoulders down on the narrow, make-shift bed.

"Shh, you talk entirely too much," she said, using the very same words he'd used on her this morning. "And we don't have all night."

Neil was about to tell her he wished they could have all of tonight together, plus thousands more, when she suddenly hiked her dress up on her thighs, climbed astraddle of him and robbed the air right out of his lungs.

After that, he was desperate, and the only thing that mattered was getting inside her and cooling the heated ache in his loins.

With hurried movements, he unfastened his clothing and she removed her panties. Once the hindering pieces of fabric were out of the way, their bodies quickly joined and Raine let out a moan of pleasure that curled Neil's toes inside his boots.

Like a rocket shooting toward the stars, his senses soared as Raine's sweet, sweet body moved against his, her fingers stroked his face and hair, while at the same time her lips clung to his.

Raine didn't know what had come over her or where this brazen behavior had come from. All she knew was that she wanted this man with an urgency that was literally consuming her. She had to have his arms around her, his lips on hers, his body moving inside hers. And through it all she could feel her heart swelling with a love so pure, so deep that tears stung her eyes and clogged her throat.

With each passing minute the rhythm of Neil's thrusts grew more frenzied. Raine clung to him and tried to keep pace, but her lungs were on fire and her mind was already spiraling upward toward that magical place where she could float peacefully among the stars.

When she reached that place her fingers gripped his shoulders and the soft mewing in her throat turned to a guttural groan. Beneath her, Neil could feel her body tightening around him, urging him to follow her to paradise.

The delicious sensation pushed him over the edge and with a desperate growl he thrust deep within her and clutched her upper body close to his.

Long moments ticked by. With Raine's limp body draped lovingly over his, Neil's hand slowly meandered up and down her back while he attempted to draw his scattered senses back intact.

Eventually Raine was the first to stir and she sat up on the edge of the cot and began to fasten the strands of hair that had loosened from the twist at the back of her head.

In the semidarkness Neil watched her sensual movements and wondered what was happening to him. It was impossible to think that a slip of a woman like Raine could shake the very ground beneath him. For a while she'd made him forget where they were and the long minutes ticking by. She'd transported him to some ethereal place that he'd never been or seen before and he'd never felt this vulnerable in his life.

"Are you okay?" she asked.

If he hadn't felt so scared, Neil might have laughed. After all, it was the man who usually posed such a question. Certainly he'd never been quizzed in this situation.

"Not really."

He said the words more bluntly than he'd intended to and her head jerked around toward his.

"What's wrong?" She didn't wait on his answer. Bending down, she brushed her lips along his cheek. "I didn't scratch you or anything, did I?"

Dear Lord, how could he resist her when she was so sweet, so sincere? Just having her velvety breath upon his cheek was enough to send his blood back to the boiling point.

"No. I'm fine."

She raised her head and peered at him. "That's not what you just said."

He eased her away from him and after straightening his clothing, sat up and ran a shaky hand through his tousled hair.

"Forget I said that. I'm just—" He looked at her and felt his heart crack. "We need to get back to the party."

Her fingers curled around his arm. "I thought—you wanted this to happen," she said in a bewildered voice. "Now you sound angry."

He sighed. "I'm not angry. I'm just wondering if—" He paused and pressed his cheek against hers. "I just wonder what it's going to be like for both of us when I go back to New Mexico."

She shook her head and Neil felt sick as he spotted tears glittering in her eyes.

"Let's not think about that now, Neil. This is our night to be happy."

## Chapter Fourteen

The next morning Raine felt ill as she moved around the kitchen making coffee. Her head was cracking and though she'd tried to sleep past her regular time to rise, she'd woke far before daylight.

Neil was consuming her thoughts and she wished he would wake soon and join her for breakfast. She wanted to talk to him, to see for herself that he was past the melancholy mood that had come over him last night after the two of them had made love.

Once they'd returned to the party, he'd appeared normal for the most part, but Raine could sense a deep change in his mood and she knew something was wrong. All she could think was that he regretted making their relationship physical and the idea tore her heart. Her very soul had poured out of her and into him. Hadn't he felt it? Did he not want it?

Trying not to think about those questions, she downed two aspirins and walked outside to the patio with a mug of coffee.

She was glumly watching the mockingbirds and sipping the greatly needed caffeine when she heard a footfall on the brick floor behind her.

Glancing over her shoulder, Raine was surprised at the sight of her mother. She was carrying a glass of orange juice and was already dressed as though she were on her way to work.

Esther dragged up a lawn chair and took a seat next to her daughter.

"What are you doing up so early this morning, honey? You had a late night. You should have slept in."

Raine shrugged one shoulder. "You got to bed late, too. Didn't Geraldine tell you to come in to work later this morning?"

Esther nodded. "She did. But I know Cook. She'll be over there trying to deal with stacks of dirty dishes before the rest of the house ever cracks an eye. God knows if I'm not around, the old woman won't take care of herself."

"I'm glad you're thinking of her," Raine replied, then with a heavy sigh took another sip from her mug.

Esther glanced at her. "You sound exhausted. But that's not surprising. You and Neil practically lived on the dance floor last night."

"The band was great and we were…enjoying ourselves."

"Yes, Geraldine sure knows how to throw a party. She must have spent thousands on you. I hope you appreciate the fact."

Frowning, Raine looked over at her mother. "I always appreciate everything that Geraldine does for me. As for that matter, I appreciate everyone here on the ranch. Without them I—"

When her daughter failed to go on, Esther prodded. "Without them what?"

Raine's gaze dropped to her feet. She wasn't in the mood to

get into a confrontation with her mother this morning. Neil was the only thing her churning mind wanted to deal with right now.

"I wouldn't have any family," Raine blurted before she could bite the words back.

Esther stiffened in the lawn chair. "Oh. Well, what does that make me? Just someone you call Mother?" she asked with a measure of sarcasm.

Closing her eyes, Raine pressed her fingertips against the throbbing that had erupted the moment her feet hit the floor. "I'm sorry you took that in the wrong way. I meant any family other than you, Mother."

Esther didn't respond and after long moments continued to pass in silence, Raine dropped her hands away from her face to glance across at her mother. Her expression was skeptical as she inspected Raine with renewed interest.

"Okay, what's wrong?" Esther asked. "I can tell you're fretting over something."

Was her breaking heart that obvious? Raine wondered. She tried her best to smile. "I'm not fretting. I have a headache, that's all."

Esther wasn't the least bit convinced. She waved her hand in a dismissive gesture. "That's not the sort of pain I'm seeing on your face. Something is wrong."

A heavy sigh passed Raine's lips. "Mother, please don't start."

The other woman placed her empty juice glass on a table situated between the lawn chairs.

"It's Neil, isn't it?" she asked with a certainty that only made the pain in Raine's chest thrust even deeper. "Something has happened between the two of you."

If Esther had been an understanding mother, Raine might have confided in her. It would be wonderful to lay her head on someone's shoulder and know that she would receive kind and encouraging words. But Esther wasn't often guilty of showing a gentle side to anyone. She believed in dishing out strong advice and making sure Raine kept her back straight through thick and thin.

"I didn't say that," Raine replied.

A grimace tightened the older woman's face. "You didn't have to." With a resigned shake of her head, she lifted her gaze toward the early morning sky. "I knew this was all too good to be true. Whirlwind courtships never last."

Raine felt ill and she realized her face was probably as white as the moon blossoms twining up one of the porch posts. "Our courtship wasn't a whirlwind." It was more like instant combustion, Raine thought, but she couldn't explain this to her mother. As far as that went, she couldn't explain anything. It was all a farce. And the sooner she accepted the fact, the sooner she could get over this misery clouding her heart. But how could she tell herself that the love they'd made in the tack room last night wasn't real. To her, everything about it had felt right and true.

"Maybe not. But it was secretive and that's just as bad. Something is wrong with a man when you can't bring him around to meet your family and friends."

"Neil is here, Mother," Raine pointed out with exaggerated patience. "And to hear you tell it, there's something wrong with all men."

Esther sniffed. "There's no need for you to get smart with me. That isn't going to fix anything."

Raine wanted to run off weeping. But she wasn't a child anymore. Besides that, tears wouldn't fix the fact that she'd fallen in love with a playboy.

"I'm sorry, Mother, but my relationship with Neil is my business."

Her back ramrod straight, Esther scooted to the edge of the chair. "If he's causing you misery, then it's certainly my business. And from the looks of you, that's exactly what he's doing." She quickly rose to her feet and stared down at Raine. "I think I'll go have a talk with him right now. And if I don't like what I hear I'm going to send the man packing. Putting an expensive ring on your finger doesn't make him a saint!"

It was obvious to Raine that this whole conversation had escalated to ridiculous proportions and for no reason. Still, she couldn't allow her mother to continue to treat her as a child.

Rising to her feet, Raine said tightly, "You know, you're probably right, Mother. Eventually Neil may very well leave me. But at least I'll have been happy for a while. That's much more than you can say about yourself. From the time that I was born you've buried yourself and refused to live like a normal woman. I don't intend to follow in your footsteps. No matter how much you try to make me!"

Esther sucked in a furious breath as scarlet color flooded her face. "See! The man is already causing trouble between us. And—"

"I have a name, Esther. And before you start accusing me of causing problems, you might want to get your own closet in order."

At the sound of Neil's voice Raine jerked her head around to see him standing a few steps behind them on the patio. Apparently he'd heard at least the end of the conversation between her and her mother. His expression was grim and he was staring at Esther in an odd sort of way. But it was her mother's reaction that bewildered Raine even more. She was staring at Neil like a rabbit cornered by a snapping dog.

"What is that supposed to mean?" she asked after several long seconds ticked by.

Neil stepped forward and took Raine by the arm. "Think about it, Esther." To Raine, he said soberly, "C'mon. I need to talk to you in private."

He led Raine off the patio and into the house. By the time they reached the middle of the kitchen, she had gathered her senses enough to say, "All right. We're alone. And—"

"Go put on some jeans and boots. I need to say some things to you and I don't want to do it here," he said ruefully. "There's a spot on the ranch I want us to ride to on horseback."

"But we haven't had breakfast and—"

He led her out of the kitchen. "That can wait. This is important."

She had already sensed that much and his dour manner prevented her from questioning him further. Instead she hurried to her bedroom and dressed in jeans, boots and a pink short-sleeved shirt. After tying the tails at her waist and swiping on a dab of lipstick with a shaky hand, she hurried back out to the living room to find Neil waiting there for her.

Since her mother was nowhere in sight, she figured she must still be on the patio or had already left for the Saddler house. Raine hoped it was the latter. She couldn't bear another confrontation with her mother this morning.

As Neil drove the two of them over to the horse barn, Raine said, "I didn't know you rode horses."

"I grew up around horses. My good friends own a huge ranch and as kids we rode constantly. Nowadays we ride together when we can find the time."

"Oh. I guess there's a lot I don't know about you."

She sounded a little lost and even more sad. The notion pierced his heart, yet he told himself he couldn't think about that now. If he did, he might just turn the vehicle the other way and drive the two of them straight off the ranch to a place where no one or nothing could come between them. But there wasn't such a place, he realized. After a while reality would intervene, their lives would have to go on and he would have to tell her about Esther.

Giving her the best smile he could, he said, "You're learning."

At the horse barn, two stable boys quickly saddled a couple of trusted geldings and after they'd mounted up, Neil urged Raine to join him in a northerly direction. He realized that the beaten-down track could have been covered in a vehicle, but he'd needed the fresh air and slower pace to help prepare him for the distasteful job ahead of him.

For ten minutes they rode in silence and then he saw the tree up ahead. A massive live oak with branches so old and heavy that in some places the crooked arms rested upon the ground. Lex and Matteo had told him about the tree and that it shaded the family burial grounds.

A frown marred Raine's forehead as she stood in her stirrups and peered up ahead of them. "We're headed toward the Sandbur cemetery. Is that where we're going?"

Neil nodded soberly. "There's something there I want to show you. It will help explain what I have to say."

The lines of confusion deepened on her face. "I don't understand. This is crazy, Neil. You hurried me away from the house as though there was some sort of emergency. We could have ridden out here anytime."

*Anytime.* The word implied that the two of them had the rest of their lives to spend together and a huge part of him wished it could be so. But that wary side of him, the side that had kept him safely cocooned for many long years was screaming it didn't want to hear anything about love or forever.

"I know. Just bear with me, honey."

The horses were traveling at a brisk walk and in less than five minutes they had reached a small private cemetery surrounded by a low fence made of scrolled iron.

After dismounting his own horse, Neil helped Raine to the ground. For a moment, as she stood in the loose circle of his arms, Neil wanted to forgo his mission and simply lower his head and kiss her. But he realized one kiss would never be enough and the two of them would wind up making love again. And once that happened he'd never be able to tell her that she was really an heiress and that her mother had more than likely been deceiving her for years.

"How did you know how to find this place?" Raine asked as he guided her over to the fence.

The tree provided such a dense shade that the air was much cooler beneath it. Raine slipped the hat from her head and ran a hand through her mussed hair.

"Lex and Matteo told me. Last night, before the dancing started, we were talking about our fathers and one thing led to another." He looked down at her. "Do you come here often?"

Raine shook her head. "No. It makes me too sad. I loved Paul and Elizabeth. I don't like to be reminded that they're gone. As for the others that went years before, I'm too young to have known them."

The name Ketchum was carved into each headstone and Neil pointed to the one resting over Nate's grave before turning his gaze back on her. "Raine, last night I discovered something that—it's incredible really. And I suppose I should have told you last night. But there was our party and I wanted you to enjoy it. And frankly, I needed some time to absorb the truth myself. I'm still not sure I've taken it all in yet."

Her features wrinkled with confusion as her head slowly turned from one side to the other. "I'm not understanding anything you're saying, Neil. Is this something about us? About us—being together?"

He realized she meant the two of them making love and he could only groan in response and draw her into his arms.

"Oh, no, honey. That was—wonderful. Too wonderful." He smoothed his hand over the top of her hair, then bent his head and kissed the shiny crown. "This is about your mother."

Instantly her head tilted back so that she could look at him. "Neil, I'm so sorry. I don't know what you heard her saying about you, but—"

"No, Raine. It's not about this morning. That's not important. What I'm trying to tell you is that I—I've discovered something about your mother's past."

Her eyes rounded with shock. "How? What?"

With his hand on her shoulder, he turned her slightly so that she was facing the cemetery. "See the family name. Ketchum. That's really Esther's name, too. Not Crockett."

She stared up at him in stunned silence until she was eventually able to stutter. "Wh-aat?"

Nodding soberly, he said, "Look, Raine, up until now I haven't told you who my client was back in New Mexico. There was no need and I respect his privacy. But now everything has changed. I have to tell you who my client is so that this will somehow all make sense." His hand slid to her upper arm and he guided her toward one of the park benches positioned a short distance away from the graveyard. "Let's sit down while I try to explain."

Once the two of them were sitting side by side, Raine reached for his hand and clutched it tightly. "Neil, this is— there's no way. My mother can't be a Ketchum. Everyone here would have known it."

Neil shook his head. "Not necessarily. You see, they apparently don't know about the New Mexico Ketchums. One of whom is Linc Ketchum, my client and dear friend. His mother was married to Randolf Ketchum. Shortly after he died she married Jaycee Carlton. They left the area and Linc only heard from her once or twice before the contact ended entirely."

Her expression took on a look of wonder. "But couldn't the name be just a coincidence? Who's to say these Ketchums are even related to your friends?"

He drew in a bracing breath. "Because I happen to know that Randolf and his brother Tucker had family somewhere here in Texas in the San Antonio area, but many years ago there was a rift that spilt them apart. I don't know all the details, but it's obvious to me that Geraldine and her late sister, Elizabeth, are the two men's sisters."

Raine literally began to shake as though a northerner had just blown across the ranch and was chilling her straight to the bone. "How—how can we know for sure, Neil? I'm not sure how Geraldine and the rest of the family will take all this!"

He cupped his hand gently against the side of her face and Raine wanted to simply fall against his chest and huddle to the warmth of his body.

"We're not going to approach Geraldine about this yet. We're going straight to your mother."

Raine's green eyes swept over and over his face as she tried to digest the meaning of his words. "How could she know? She had amnesia and—"

Groaning softly, he stroked his fingers along her cheek. "Raine, my little darling, think. It's too much of a coincidence. She came here knowing these people were her in-laws."

The implication that her mother had been lying all these years hit her like a fist and she slapped a hand against her stomach as pain radiated through her. "But why? And why would she pretend? Why would she let me think that she didn't know who my father was? Why would she try to stop me from finding him? Why—"

The questions stopped as hot tears began to spill from her eyes and Neil quickly folded her into his arms.

"Don't cry, Raine. We have to go back now. And I want you to be strong when we face your mother. Can you do that?"

Slowly Raine eased away from him and looked grimly toward the tombstones. Was that her family lying there, she wondered? She had to know the truth once and for all.

Back at the ranch, they discovered Esther at the Saddler house. She was still helping Cook contend with the leftover party mess. When the woman first spotted Raine and Neil entering the kitchen she appeared surprised, but then she quickly assumed the two of them had come over to the big house in search of a meal.

"You two decided you didn't want to make your own breakfast this morning?" Esther asked.

Cook, who was washing dishes at the deep double sink, said to Esther, "I'll cook them some hotcakes. You take over here."

"Don't bother, Cook. We're here to see Mother." Raine stepped toward Esther and marveled at the fact that she could stand, much less speak. Her whole body was trembling and she kept wondering if she was actually in some sort of nightmare from which she couldn't wake. "Uh, could you come outside with us, Mother?"

Esther glanced from her daughter's strained face to Neil's grim expression. "I'm busy here. Why don't you come back in about an hour or so," she suggested.

*I want you to be strong when you face your mother.* Neil's words were the only thing keeping Raine going at the moment. She repeated them over and over as she straightened her shoulders and drew in a bracing breath.

"Because I don't have an hour," Raine said firmly. "We need to talk now."

Esther's brows lifted in surprise, then she shot an accusing glance at Neil before she finally made a move toward the door. "All right," she said, then glancing over her shoulder at Cook, she added, "I'll be back in a few minutes."

"Never no mind this mess," the old woman assured her. "We got all day."

The three of them trooped outside and stood just beyond the view of the kitchen windows. In the distance Raine could see Lex and Cordero crossing the ranch yard together. The two men were both dressed in chaps and long sleeved shirts which could only mean they would be rounding up cattle today. The sight of them suddenly made her heart ache with bittersweet wonder. Were they really her cousins?

"All right," Esther said, breaking the tense silence. "What's this all about? Are you two ending your engagement or something?"

Raine couldn't look at Neil for his response. It was far too painful.

"We're here for the something else," Neil spoke up, then placing his hand against Raine's back he said in a gentle voice, "Go on, Raine. Ask her all the things you want to know."

Sensing something out of the ordinary was going on, Esther opened her mouth to speak, but before she could Raine said stiffly, "I've found out who you really are, Mother. Do you want to hear? Or would you rather tell me yourself?"

Esther's hand flew to her throat and her mouth fell open. "Wh-at—what are you talking about? I'm Esther Crockett, everyone knows that."

Raine swallowed as emotion threatened to overtake her. From the moment she was old enough to remember this was the woman she'd loved and trusted. To think all those years had been riddled with lies was cutting straight to Raine's heart.

"Really? I always thought Esther Crockett was a made-up name. When you were found on the highway you didn't have any identification. And since you had amnesia you had to come up with some sort of name to use. At least that's what you've always told everyone."

Esther suddenly took on an offended look. "Are you, my own daughter, trying to say I'm a liar?" She shot a daggered glower at Neil. "You've put this into her head, haven't you?"

"Don't try to spin this off on him, Mother. This is about you and me and the lies you've been living. Your name is really Darla, isn't it? Darla Ketchum Carlton."

Even though her face had gone deathly white, Esther tried to laugh. "You must be joking. I've never heard of the woman. This ranch is owned by the Ketchum family. Don't you think they'd know if I were related?"

"Not if you came from New Mexico—from the T Bar K ranch," Neil interjected. "I suppose you've never heard of Linc Ketchum, either. Or the late Randolf."

The moment Linc's name came out, Esther's face began to crumple and suddenly she was crying. Something Raine had never witnessed before.

"Oh God. My little boy. My son," she whispered hoarsely. "Is he—" The accusation on her face had evaporated and now she looked pleadingly at Neil. "Tell me that he's okay."

"He is. No thanks to you. He's still on the T Bar K and recently married."

The woman looked visibly relieved. "Thank God."

As Raine stood next to Neil, she realized she was seeing an entirely different person than the one she'd known as her mother and she didn't know whether to be frightened or happy or angry. As it was, all three emotions were raging a war inside her and she felt so weak from the turmoil she had to lean against Neil to stay upright.

"Then you are Darla," Raine stated dazedly. "You've been lying to me for all of my life!"

Esther quickly stepped forward and started to reach for Raine, but she avoided her mother's touch by clinging even closer to Neil.

"You don't understand, Raine. I had my reasons. Maybe I was wrong—I mean, yes, I was wrong. But at the time I thought I was doing the right thing. Then later—it was too late to change and I was too afraid to try."

Raine felt so stunned she couldn't say anything. Finally Neil suggested they walk over to a group of lawn chairs shaded by a cluster of crepe myrtle trees.

"Why don't you start from the beginning, Darla-Esther or

whatever you want to be called," Neil said to her after the three of them were seated.

Raine watched her mother mull that thought over and realized with stunned fascination that she'd gone all these years with a false name and a life left behind.

"Maybe—maybe you'd better call me Darla. I think it's time I quit hiding."

Feeling a spurt of strength returning, Raine scooted to the edge of her chair so that she was facing her mother head-on. "Hiding? Is that what you've been doing all these years?"

Darla nodded, then glanced knowingly at Neil. "You're not really from San Antonio are you?"

Neil shook his head. "You probably don't remember me, I only met you in passing once. But I was Linc's buddy when we were growing up as kids. I was on the ranch that day you left with Jaycee Carlton. Linc and I watched from horseback as you drove away. He never saw you again. He figured you were dead. Or—that you didn't care."

Esther pushed a shaky hand through her graying hair. "Oh, I cared all right. But Linc was like his father—he loved the T Bar K more than he did me."

Amazed at what he was hearing, Neil stared at her. "You shouldn't have put him in a position of choosing between you and his home. Especially when you were going off with a man he didn't even know!"

More tears oozed from Darla's eyes as though all the heartache she'd been feeling the past twenty-four years was trying to escape all at once.

"You're right. I was not a good mother back then. Oh, I tried to be, but I was getting so much grief from Randolf that I'm afraid I neglected Linc. I'm sure he'll never forgive me for that or—anything else," she said, her voice trailing away to a whisper.

"Tell me, Mother, is this Linc my brother? Just who is my father?" Raine demanded.

Darla dabbed at her eyes and tried to collect herself. "Linc is your brother, honey. Your father was Randolf Ketchum. Your grandparents were Nate and Sara."

## Chapter Fifteen

Raine gasped and jerked her head around to stare at Neil. He looked equally stunned. The two of them had been standing over Nate's and Sara's graves less than an hour ago. At the time, neither of them had been certain of the connection, but now the truth was finally out. He reached for her hand and squeezed it tightly.

"Then—then my father is dead," Raine whispered painfully. "All of this—only to find that's he gone. I'll never have the chance to know him!" Her head snapped around and she stared at her mother with accusation. "Why didn't you tell me all this before? How could you let me wish and hope and wonder? How could you be that—that cruel to me?"

Darla shook her head with remorse. "I wasn't trying to be cruel, Raine. I didn't know what else to do. You see, when I was discovered nearly dead on the side of the highway, I hadn't been in a car accident as you'd assumed, I'd been beaten by two men. I'm sure their intentions were to kill me and no doubt when they left me there, they figured I was dead."

"Wait a minute," Neil spoke up. "Just back up and explain from the beginning. How did these men get to you and what was the connection? Where was Jaycee in all of this?"

Groaning, Darla said, "I'd better start even before Jaycee, because my problems started long before he came into my life. As you know, I was married to Randolf for years and I loved the man with all my heart. But unknown to a lot of people he was just like his brother, Tucker. He loved women and didn't think twice about playing around, the only difference Randolf had with his brother was that he kept his adulterous behavior hidden. As the years wore on, I begged him to leave the ranch and go elsewhere. I thought, foolishly I suppose, that if he was away from his brother's bad influence, he might change his ways. But Randolf refused and I didn't want to leave him because I loved him. He was the father of my son and Linc adored him. I didn't want to tear up the family.

"Then Randolf developed a heart condition. It seemed to be worsening and I begged him to leave the ranch to see a specialist. He promised that he would and also promised to change his ways. He said that he'd always loved me and that the other women had never meant anything to him. We made love in spite of his ill health, and for the first time in years I felt there was hope for our marriage. But that newfound happiness only lasted a few short weeks before he died of a heart attack."

Raine released a painful sob and Neil slipped a comforting arm around her shoulders.

Darla wiped at her tears and continued. "Randolf's death left such a hole in me that I latched on to the first man who came across my path. Unfortunately it was Jaycee Carlton. He'd been passing through Aztec on his way to Colorado. He owned a construction company in San Antonio and had plenty of money, so he said. He promptly promised me the moon and I fell hook, line and sinker for everything he said. Little did I know that he'd been robbing his own company and was also involved with a Mexican mafia. He owed them money. And lots of it."

Neil looked at her as he tried to keep the story straight in his mind. "So is that who finally caught up to you?"

Darla nodded grimly. "I think so. They ran us down on the highway, jerked me out of the car and started using their fists. Before I lost consciousness I saw them drive away with Jaycee and later I heard they'd found him dead down by the border."

Neil nodded. "That's right. I was able to gather that much information. But no one knew what had happened to Darla."

Heaving out a heavy sigh, she turned her attention to Raine and her eyes were full of sorrow. "When I first woke up in the hospital in Fredericksburg, I truly did have amnesia. I didn't know my name or anything that had happened. But after a few days when everything began to heal, my memory returned and I was terrified. The doctor told me I was pregnant and I knew for certain that Randolf was the father. I didn't want anyone to search me out and harm my unborn child. Nor did I want them to trace me back to Linc or the T Bar K. I was afraid they would either harm him or try to extort money. That's why I made up the name Esther Crockett."

Raine numbly shook her head. "You say you know for certain that Randolf was my father. How? If you were married to this Jaycee person—"

"But I wasn't," Darla quickly interrupted. "Everyone back

in New Mexico thought we'd gotten married. But actually the ceremony hadn't happened yet. We were going to travel to Las Vegas and have a quick wedding there. The two of us never actually—we never had a physical relationship. I was holding out until the ceremony and later, after I realized I'd been duped—well, I was glad I'd been old-fashioned."

Raine couldn't say anything to that. Not when she'd made the mistake of giving herself to Neil without any hope of marriage. Oh God, why had she been so foolish? He was only passing through, too. She'd known that, yet she'd not been able to stop her heart from tumbling straight into his hands.

Doing her best to shake her thoughts away from her situation with Neil, Raine asked her mother, "What about Geraldine and the other Ketchums here on the Sandbur? Do they know who you really are?"

Darla shook her head. "No. It was just by chance that I wound up working in a bank that they used in San Antonio. It didn't take me long to figure out they were Randolf's sisters, so when they offered me a job here I jumped at the chance. It made me feel safer to know I was among family and I have always hoped that the people who killed Jaycee would never track me to this ranch."

"So no one else here on the ranch, including Geraldine, knows about the Ketchums in New Mexico?" Neil asked with a bewildered frown. "How can that be?"

By now Darla had collected herself somewhat. Even though her face was pasty-white, her tears were dried. "It's a long story and I don't know everything that happened, but it had something to do with Nate's death. It caused the family to split and the two Ketchum sons left out on their own. From what I've been able to glean from Geraldine, and Elizabeth before she died, they were told their brothers died in some sort of plane accident down in Mexico."

"How very strange," Raine murmured.

Neil glanced at her and smiled. "Honey, it sounds like that's a whole other mystery. But at least we have yours solved."

Her head dipped as she swallowed a lump of hot tears. "Yes. My father is dead. But thankfully I now know who he is."

He squeezed her shoulder. "You're missing the good part, Raine. You have a brother. A wonderful brother, I might add. He's going to be so happy to find out about you."

She lifted her head and looked at him through a glaze of tears. "You really think so?"

"No doubt."

Across from them, Darla cleared her throat. "Well, I'm sure Linc will never want to see me. I can't—blame him for that. But at least I can keep up with his life through Raine now. That's more than I had before."

Neil looked at the woman and was surprised to feel a pang of sympathy for her. By all rights, he should hate her for what she'd done to his best friend, and to Raine. Desertion and deception were hardly noble traits, especially when it came to dealing with one's own children. But he could see that Darla had paid dearly for her mistakes. Maybe now that the truth was out, their lives could move forward. That was all he'd ever wanted for Raine, to give her a measure of happiness.

"I wouldn't be so swift to assume the worse, Darla," Neil told her. "Linc asked me to search for you. And now that I've found you, I'm sure he'll want to see you. Hopefully you two can start over. That is, if you really want to."

Darla's expression grew tender as she glanced from Neil to Raine. "I've wanted to start over for twenty-four years, but I never had the courage to try. I think you two have just given it to me."

Rising from her seat, Raine went over to her mother and put her arms around her. "It's time we all started over, Mother."

The rest of the day passed in a chaotic blur. After a lengthy discussion between Raine and her mother, the two decided the only choice they had was to tell Geraldine and the rest of the family of what Neil had uncovered. The revelation had reverberated around the ranch like a shock wave after an earthquake. Everyone was stunned to hear Darla's secrets, but in the end they were happy to discover that Raine was their cousin and that there were more family members in New Mexico.

During all the mayhem, Neil had called Linc at the T Bar K and given him the news. Raine had spoken to her new brother over the telephone and the exchange had been so emotional that Neil had been forced to swallow several lumps in his throat. But now the lumps were back and no amount of swallowing would make them go away.

For the past hour he'd been pacing around his bedroom, trying to relax, and most of all trying to reassure himself that everything was going to be fine. He could go back to Aztec knowing he'd accomplished his job.

Job, hell. None of this had been a job, he realized. He'd followed Raine here to the Sandbur like a cat stalking a mouse. And when the time was right, he pounced. He'd caught the prize and now he had to face the fact that he didn't want to give her up.

But he had to, he argued to himself. His home was far away, and he was too set in his bachelor ways to change now. And Raine deserved more, much more than a loner like him.

Minutes later, Raine was in her bedroom, lying across the bed, gazing wistfully at the diamond and emerald ring on her finger, when a knock sounded on the door.

She quickly rose to a sitting position and called, "Come in."

As Neil strode into her room, the sight of him instantly filled her heart with love and pain. He'd changed her life in ways that could never be measured and now she had to think about letting him go. The whole idea was weighing on her like a dark, heavy rain could.

"I was hoping you weren't in bed yet. Am I intruding?"

Shaking her head, she patted a spot on the side of the mattress. "I know it's late, but I'm still too wired up from all the excitement to sleep. Come sit."

He eased down beside her and let out a long sigh. "What a day."

"That's an understatement," she said.

"Are you doing okay?" he asked gently.

She nodded and Neil watched her gaze drop to the ring he'd placed on her hand. That moment in the jewelry store, and later at her apartment, seemed like it had happened eons ago. Still, it was caught in his memory forever and he knew that even when he went back to New Mexico, he would remember and ache.

"I'm all right," she answered. "Actually I'm glad you came to my room. I was thinking—it's time I give this back to you."

She started to remove the ring from her finger, but Neil quickly caught her hand before she could slip it off completely.

"No!" he said flatly. "I told you that the ring was yours to keep. Nothing about that has changed."

With a heavy sigh, she tilted her face toward the ceiling. "Everyone knows we're not really engaged now. There's no need for me to keep it."

"Other than the fact that I want you to."

His words brought her face back around to his and she searched his face for long moments. The soft, gentle light he saw in her green eyes made his breathing so slow his lungs began to burn with pain.

"All right," she murmured. "If that's what you want, I'll keep it."

He pushed the ring back in place and folded his hand around hers. "Raine, I'm very glad that I was able to give you the truth about your father and the rest of your family. I hope you're glad about it, too."

A wobbly smile quivered her lips and all Neil wanted to do was cover them with his own mouth and kiss her until nothing else mattered.

"Of course, I'm glad. I just need time to absorb it all." Her free hand lifted to his face and she traced a gentle pattern upon his cheek. "Thank you, Neil. You've changed my life. You realize that, don't you?"

Not nearly as much as she'd changed his, Neil thought. Before he'd met Raine, he'd never believed he had the ability to care about a woman this much, to care about anyone this much. He'd allowed the wounds of his childhood to heal into a callous scar, one that had hardened as the years went by, until he'd found himself just experiencing things on the surface. But she'd opened that scar and now he was feeling far more than he'd ever wanted to feel.

"Well, I only wish I could have given you a live father, one that you could get to know and love. But at least you have family to tell you all about him."

She bit down on her bottom lip and glanced away from him. "Mother said he was an adulterer. Is that really true?"

The idea that her father was less than all she'd imagined was obviously tearing at her. Neil tried to answer as kindly and truthfully as he could.

"Back then Linc and I were just young kids, Raine. I didn't know anything about his parents' personal life. I never heard Linc speak of his father's transgressions, but then he might not have known about them."

Nodding sadly, she glanced at him. "I guess I shouldn't dwell on that, should I?"

Smiling wanly, he slid a hand over her silky hair. "No. Just concentrate on the good."

Her gaze dropped to her lap. "So what now?"

He wanted to close his eyes and shut out the beautiful sight of her. He wanted to close down his mind and forget the passionate way they'd made love, but he could do neither.

"Uh, that's why I came to your room. I wanted to tell you, away from your mother, that I'll be leaving in the morning. It's time I got back to New Mexico and see if I have a practice left."

Pain struck Raine deep and she couldn't bring herself to look at him. "I understand. You never planned to hang around here for very long. And now everything is...over."

Suddenly his fingers were beneath her chin, forcing her to lift her face. She blinked her eyes and thanked God that they were dry. At least she could hold on to a bit of her pride.

"For what it's worth, Raine, I'm not really happy about it. I've come to care about you and I'm going to miss you."

Care, but not love, Raine thought dully. "I'm going to miss you, too. But it's better this way." She tried to smile, but the muscles in her face refused to work. "You don't want a wife or a family. And now, after everything I've learned, I'm not sure I want to have a relationship with any man."

He frowned. "Don't turn into someone like me, Raine. You have too much to give to a husband and children."

Not without you, she wanted to cry. "Maybe we can write to each other and—still be friends."

Friends? How could they ever be friends, he wondered wildly, when all he wanted was to throw her across the bed and make love to her. Apparently this whole thing between them had been one-sided and he'd been on the losing side.

"Yeah. Friends. That's for the best."

She nodded and Neil forced himself to ease off the bed and walk out of the room.

Two weeks later, Raine was sitting in her office in the Saddler house, gazing sadly out the window as she recalled the morning Neil had driven away from the Sandbur. The skies had been clear and beautiful that morning, but she'd hardly seen them through her tears.

For the first time in her life that morning, she'd thought of pretending to sleep through the jingle of her alarm clock in hopes that he would go without saying goodbye. But Raine had never been a coward and she'd realized that if she ever had any hopes of going on with her life, she had to face the fact that Neil was walking away from her. So she'd shared a small breakfast with him, then strolled to his car and allowed him to kiss her one last time.

Throughout the past days Raine had hardly been able to think of anything but Neil. Even the wondrous fact that she now belonged to a large family was not enough to outshine the despair she felt over losing the only man she could ever love.

*Love.* The word made her ponder and a deep frown furrowed her forehead. She'd been terribly afraid to say the word to Neil. She'd sensed that he had not wanted to hear anything that equaled ties or commitments. Yet these past days she continued to wonder if it would have made a difference if she'd revealed her feelings to him.

The word love was something that had hardly been spoken to her throughout the years. Darla had never been a sugary person and Raine had come to accept that her mother's actions spoke her feelings. She supposed she'd been hoping that Neil would consider the time she'd spent in his arms as a conveyance of her love. But if he had, it had made little difference in the end.

The door of the office suddenly swung open and Darla walked in carrying a small tray loaded with snacks, an urn of coffee and two cups. Since the secret of her past life had been revealed, Raine could safely say her mother was quickly emerging into a different woman than the one she'd known all these years. She was more relaxed and smiles came easier to her. She'd been making an effort to spend more time with Raine in hopes they could mend all their differences. Lunch together had become a habit for them.

"Ready for a little grub?" Darla asked as she placed the tray on the corner of Raine's desk.

Quickly dashing at the tears on her cheeks, Raine jumped up and hurried over to turn down the stereo. "Grub?" she repeated with a forced smile. "I never heard you call it that before."

Darla laughed. "That's ranch lingo for food," she teased. "That's what your father used to call it. He'd say, 'Give me some grub in my saddlebags and a horse under my seat and I'm a happy man.'" Her smile rapidly faded into wistful acceptance. "Strange, how much I still miss him."

Even though the tears on Raine's face were gone, her heart was still crying. She hoped her mother couldn't see.

"If you love someone and they go away, you never stop missing them," Raine said.

Darla sighed as she picked up the urn and filled two mugs. "You're right, honey. And I guess for all these years I tried to pretend that I was someone else. I told myself that I'd always hated Randolf and our home on the T Bar K so that I wouldn't hurt. But all the pretense couldn't take away the truth."

She passed Raine one of the mugs and offered her a paper plate. With a shake of her head, Raine said, "I'm not hungry. You go ahead. I'll just have the coffee."

With thoughtful concern, Darla watched her daughter sink onto the leather couch and cross her legs.

"You're getting too thin, Raine. You need to eat."

"I can't. It lodges somewhere between my throat and my stomach."

"Maybe you should let Nicolette take a look at you. She can prescribe something for you to take."

Raine stared out the window and watched the squirrels play. The same way they were playing when Neil had suggested she lock the door and make love to him. Oh God help her, she prayed.

"Medicine won't help. I've already tried."

Darla began to place several finger sandwiches onto a plate. "And why do you think that is?" she asked gently.

When Raine didn't answer, she looked around to see her daughter's head was bent, her shoulders shaking.

"Oh, Raine. Raine."

Her mother's arms came around her and Raine let her head fall against her shoulder.

"Don't mind me, Mother. I'm just being—a little emotional."

Darla gently patted her back. "It's been obvious to me and

everyone else on the ranch that you've been brooding about something. We've all been very worried about you, honey. Is it me? Has this whole issue of being a Ketchum gotten you down?"

Raine lifted her head and looked at her mother with surprise. "Oh, no! I couldn't be happier that you're being open with me and that I have a family now."

"You certainly don't look happy." She worriedly studied Raine's tearful face. "It's Neil, isn't it? You miss him."

There was such a lump of hot pain in Raine's throat all she managed was a woeful nod. "Terribly."

Once she'd gotten the husky word out, Darla asked, "Have you heard from him?"

"No. I haven't tried to contact him, either. I decided it wouldn't help matters. All I can do now is try to forget him."

"Why?"

The simple question caused Raine to wail with frustration and jump from the couch. "Mother, you were right all along."

"Which time?"

The fact that her mother could make a joke now, or anytime, amazed Raine. She tried her best to smile.

"All the times you warned me about men. I should have listened."

"And why do you say that?" Darla asked.

Raine shrugged, then turned and walked over to the window. As she stared unseeingly at the blooming roses, she said, "You have to ask? My father was an adulterer and the man who would have become my stepfather was so unscrupulous he nearly got you killed. If that doesn't make them bastards, then I don't know what does!"

"Raine! Please don't talk that way. Don't even think it!" Darla left the couch and hurried over to her daughter. "Honey,

I understand where your bitterness is coming from. But it's wrong. I was wrong! I chose the wrong men in my life and I made bad choices trying to fix my mistakes. While I was raising you, I let all of that color my judgment. And that's the worst mistake I could have made. All men aren't bastards. Neil is a good man. Even I could see that. And if you love him, as I think you love him, then you need to let him know you don't intend to give him up."

Raine looked at her in wonder. "Do you really mean that, Mother?"

Smiling, she cradled Raine's face in her hands. "I want you to be happy, Raine. I don't want you to lose years of your life being bitter and calloused. Now get on the phone and call the airport. I'll drive you up to catch the plane."

"But you never leave the ranch!"

Darla shook her head with more regret. "I was always afraid to. Afraid those henchmen might somehow spot me. God, all that fear I had was so wasteful. No one from the past would recognize me now. I've turned into an old, ugly woman."

Raine shook her head, then leaned forward and pressed her cheek against her mother's. "No," she whispered through her tears. "You'll never be that to me."

## Chapter Sixteen

One. Two. Three. The darts swooshed through the air and stabbed the heart of the target hanging on a wall in Neil's office.

Throwing darts was something he'd done since his early childhood. The first set Neil had ever owned had been given to him by his father, a gift he'd had to keep hidden from his mother, who considered it far too dangerous for an eleven-year-old boy. Down through the years, he'd mastered the sport and only a few months ago had won a dart tournament at Indian Wells, a favorite tavern on the outskirts of Aztec. He'd taken on slews of competitors and slaughtered them all with ease.

Yeah, he was good at darts and he was a decent lawyer, but he was a failure with women, particularly one woman with honey-brown hair and Ketchum green eyes. Walking away from her had been more painful than anything he'd ever had to do and now after two weeks and two days, Neil was still wondering when the numbness was going to go away. Was he ever going to be the man he used to be?

He was pulling the darts from the board and mulling over the hopeless question when the door between his office and Connie's opened. Glancing over his shoulder, he saw his secretary stepping into the room. A coat was slung over one arm and her handbag hung from one shoulder. She was obviously leaving for the day and he hadn't even realized it was time for the office to close.

"What are you doing? Practicing up for another tournament?" she asked, eyeing the darts in his hand. "I thought you'd be ready to lock up. It's nearly six. Haven't you noticed it dark outside?"

Two wide windows dressed the back wall of his office, but he'd not bothered to open the drapes covering the expanse of glass. It didn't matter if the sun was shining or not. He always felt in the dark.

"Sorry, Connie. The time got by me. Just give me a minute to pack up a few briefs and I'll follow you out."

He walked over to his desk and began to stuff several legal papers into an accordion folder. Connie moved deeper into the room and watched him with a thoughtful eye.

"We were very busy today," she said. "In fact, ever since you came back from Texas, we've been overrun with business. Guess that's making you happy."

"Yeah. I like keeping busy."

"The title company called this afternoon about the Coley abstract. They want to close on it soon. When do you think you'll have it read?"

"Tomorrow or the next day. I don't know what in hell they're pushing me for when we all know they're the ones dragging their feet, waiting until the last minute to contact me. If they mess with me, I'll throw the thing in their lap and let them find another lawyer."

Connie didn't make any sort of reply to that and her silence was so unusual, he paused in his task to look up at her.

"What's the matter? Why are you looking at me like I've turned into the devil incarnate? You know I'm right on this one. The title company wants me to hurry and make up for their lost time."

"Of course you're right, Neil. But it never used to make you angry. Come to think of it, I can't recall much of anything that made you angry. Now your blood stays at the boiling point."

Neil dropped the heavy folder back on his desk and stared impatiently at his secretary. "Do you have to start in on me tonight?"

She let out a laugh of disbelief. "Oh, so now you realize it's nighttime and I've already worked an hour overtime for you." Stepping forward, she looked at him with open disappointment. "I'm sorry, Neil, but I'm beginning to think I'd better start looking for another job. You're not the same and, frankly, I don't like this new Neil Rankin. He's an unfeeling bastard."

Neil opened his mouth to shout at her, but the realization that she was right struck him before he could make a bigger fool of himself and he shook his head with remorse.

"I'm sorry, Connie. I really am. Forgive me."

The older woman walked over to him and laid a hand upon his arm. "I don't know what happened with you and Linc's sister down in Texas, but it's ruining you."

His face went void as he reached down and tied the folder shut. "I don't want to talk about it, Connie."

"Why not?"

"Because talking won't help."

"Maybe you need to do more than talk. Maybe you need to head back to Texas and see what you can do to make things right with her."

Disbelief swept over his face. "Make things right? Nothing is wrong, Connie. I want my freedom and so does she. We went our separate ways, just the way we wanted."

"I've never heard such a stack of manure in my life. You're miserable."

He was miserable all right, Neil thought. Every waking moment he was thinking about Raine. His sleep was filled with tormenting dreams of her. "I'll get over it, Connie. You know me, I've gotten attached to women in the past. This time it's just taking a little longer to get over the affliction."

Connie rolled her eyes. "Keep talking and we'll be up to our eyeballs in manure. And don't tell me this was just an attachment. You obviously love the woman. If you didn't, you'd already be back to your sunny self."

Stepping around her, he snatched up his darts and began to sling them viciously at the board on the wall. "Since when did you become an expert?"

She jammed her hands on her hips. "I've been married for thirty years. I ought to know a little about the subject."

*Thirty years.* Even that wouldn't be enough time to spend with Raine, he thought. The silent admission caused his shoulders to slump and he turned a miserable look on his secretary.

"I've never wanted to love anybody, Connie. I never thought I'd ever want a woman for more than a weekend or two." He speared a weary hand through his hair, making the gold-brown locks stand on end. "Marriage isn't for me. It makes people act crazy."

"And you're not acting crazy now?" With an understanding

smile, she patted his arm. "Go home and pack your bags, Neil. I have plenty of excuses to give to the title company, mainly that you've gone to spend Christmas with your family."

Connie didn't wait to hear his response. She waved goodbye and quickly left the office, leaving Neil behind to stew on her advice.

Connie was right, he thought. He wanted to spend this Christmas with Raine and every Christmas to come with her and the family they hopefully might have. Raine had said she didn't want a relationship with any man. But he wasn't just any man. He was the man who loved her.

Neil's home was north of town, nestled in high desert hills covered with juniper and pinon pine. Normally the drive took about twenty minutes, but tonight his truck needed gas and he stopped at the last station on his way to fill up the tank.

Since this morning, the weather had taken a nosedive and the whipping north wind held bits of sleet and snow. As he hunched between his truck and the gas pump, his thoughts turned to south Texas and the Sandbur. Winter flowers would still be blooming there; the nights mild. He supposed that if he'd stayed a few more days he would have become acclimatized to the warmth and a few other things, like loving a woman and planning a lifetime with her. Instead he'd run like a scared cat from the swat of a broom. It had been easier than staying and trying to tell her that he loved her.

He was five minutes away from home when he spotted the headlights behind him. Since he lived on a private dirt road with no neighbors, the vehicle was obviously coming to his place. He could only hope it wasn't someone who needed legal advice tonight. Now that he'd decided to fly to San

Antonio, he didn't have time for work. He had to pack and plan and figure out how to persuade Raine to marry him.

Once Neil was out of the truck, he dashed to the porch and stood waiting for the car to stop and the driver to emerge. A nearby yard light illuminated the path to the house, but the foul weather made it difficult to distinguish the figure approaching. Until that person reached the steps and then he was so shocked he dropped his briefcase.

"Raine! Is that you?"

She was bundled in a dark coat and a matching fur-edged cap. She was hugging a shiny Christmas package and her teeth were chattering.

"Yes. It's me."

Hurrying toward her, he grabbed her by the arm. "Watch the steps. There's sleet."

"I know," she exclaimed. "It's freezing! I was afraid the roads were going to become slick."

Once Neil had her standing safely on the porch he gathered up his briefcase and quickly unlocked the door.

"Sorry," he said, "I just now got home from work. But the house is warm." He shoved the door open and ushered her in. "How did you know where to find me?"

"Linc gave me the directions to get here," she replied.

A dim night-light illuminated a small living room with wooden floors, braided rugs, leather furniture and a fireplace at one end. Near the windows she could see a blue spruce decorated with silver tinsel and hanging ornaments. There were no gifts underneath the tree, but she quickly changed that by walking over and placing her package under the drooping boughs.

After he'd switched on a couple of lamps, he shucked his

jacket and tossed it on the end of the couch. Across the room, kindling and firewood were already stacked in the fireplace. Squatting on the hearth, he struck a long match and stuck it to the under pieces of kindling. The pine quickly ignited and once he saw the flames licking up the logs, he straightened to his full height and turned to face her.

Still shivering, she took a few halting steps toward him and blurted, "I'm—sure I've surprised you. I should have warned you I was coming."

Neil's heart was pounding, his throat tight as he walked over to where she stood. She looked incredibly beautiful with black fur framing her tanned face and her brown hair glistening with bits of ice. All he wanted was to close the few inches between them and gather her into his arms. But first he had to know if she'd come to New Mexico to see him or her brother.

"This is—more than a surprise," he admitted. "I was expecting to see one of my clients with an emergency."

Her gaze clung to his as she reached to unbutton her coat. "This is an emergency. I—"

"Just tell me one thing, Raine. Are you here in Aztec because of me? Or your brother?"

The wary shadows in her eyes turned soft with yearning. "For you," she whispered.

Hope, relief and hungry need rushed through him like a hurricane and he groaned as he reached for her. "Raine. Oh, Raine."

She stumbled eagerly into his arms and their lips came together in a desperate reunion that had her clinging and arching her body fervently into his. The physical contact shoved away all the questions rolling around in Neil's head. For now it was enough that she was here in his arms.

Unable to temper his craving, his mouth ravaged hers until

her lips were swollen and he was gasping for air. As he regained his breath, he quickly went to work removing her coat. After tossing it toward the couch, he led her over to the fire, which was now snapping with orange flames.

"Are you still cold?" he asked.

"No. But Neil—"

"Later," he mouthed against her lips. "Tell me later. Right now—just love me. Love me."

His urgent pleas were like golden sunshine raining down on Raine. She opened her lips and melted against him. "That's all I want."

Reaching up, he removed her hat, then slid his fingers into her glossy hair. She clasped his face with her hands and kissed him with a hunger that took his breath away. Raw need wrapped around him and he tried to touch her everywhere, kiss her lips, her face and hands.

The zipper in her dress was in the back. In a matter of seconds Neil had the clasp tugged to her hips and the dress off her shoulders. By the time he lay her down on the braided rug, she was completely naked and as he stood to remove his own clothing, his eyes drank in the sight of the glowing flames sparking amber lights in her hair and stroking golden fingers across her belly and breasts.

And moments later, as he knelt over her and entered her warm body, Neil suddenly understood the true meaning of coming home. In Raine's arms, he felt whole and full. The ache in his heart was gone. Joy buzzed along his veins and sang in his ears like a Texas mockingbird.

"I love you, Raine. Now and for all time," he whispered against her cheek.

His declaration stung her eyes with emotional tears and as

they slid down her temples and into her hair, she vowed in a husky voice, "And I love you, Neil. I had to tell you. I had to feel you like this—again."

If he'd had any lingering doubts in his head about her intentions, they were all washed away with her words and for the next several minutes, he thought of nothing but the hot, delicious thrust of her hips, the sweet, honeyed taste of her lips and her hands moving up and down and over his heated skin.

Quickly, effortlessly, she took him to an incredible place that no woman had ever taken him before and as he floated and floated among the sparkling clouds he thought his heart would burst. He could hear himself crying her name like a mantra until it became impossible to speak and he fell against her in weak, sated exhaustion.

Later, after their ragged breathing smoothed back to a normal pace, Neil rolled to his side and pillowed her head on his arm.

"I thought you said you didn't want a man in your life," he said with wry humor. "Guess this means you've changed your mind."

Languidly Raine reached up and traced her fingertips along his cheekbone. "Forgive me for that, Neil. I was so upset. I'd just learned my father was an adulterer. And that the second man my mother intended to marry was worse than devious. He was a crook and probably several other things to go along with that."

"And you thought I could be like them?" he asked in disbelief.

"No. Of course not. But you'd told me you were leaving. And you'd insisted you didn't want to have a wife or family. I felt like everything I'd ever hoped or imagined about men was suddenly crushed."

Neil looked at her with regret. "Raine, I'm so very sorry that the truth wasn't all you'd hoped it would be—that I wasn't what you'd hoped for, either."

She rested her palm against the side of his face. "Don't be sorry. Mother made me see that her troubled life with my father and Jaycee were mistakes that she had made. And now that I've had time to think clearly, I know that you could never be like the men who hurt my mother."

Surprise lifted his brows. "Your mother talked to you about this?"

Raine smiled drowsily. "She actually encouraged me to come here to see you. She thought I ought to tell you that I love you. And thankfully, this time, I took her advice."

Clearly amazed, Neil said, "I can't believe it."

"She's changed, Neil. Thanks to you. And so have I."

His hand slid possessively from her shoulder to her hip and back again. "In what way?"

She rolled forward so that the front of her body was nestled against his. Her fingers played with the hair on his chest. "I've spent all my adult life dwelling on the past. I'd always believed that if I could only find my father, then all my doubts and insecurities would disappear. I used to picture him returning to my mother and together they would both teach me how to become a woman, a wife and mother. But now I understand that's something I have to learn on my own. And I'm not afraid of the future now, Neil."

Bending his head, he rubbed his cheek against the top of her hair. "Raine, that day I left you on the Sandbur, I believed I could come back home and my life would return to how it was before we met. It hasn't worked that way. I've been in such a wretched mess that my secretary threatened to quit tonight. I've turned into such a bastard that she can't stand me and I honestly can't stand myself—without you."

Tilting her head, she pressed a kiss on his chin. "All day, on the way up here, I wondered and tried to imagine what I would do if you didn't want to see me. But I had to take a chance, Neil. I've been terribly miserable without you."

Rubbing his cheek against hers, he admitted, "Tonight, Raine, before I left the office, I'd already decided I was going to fly down to San Antonio in the morning and try to set things right between us. When Connie pointed out that I was acting crazy, I realized she was right."

"Hmm," she purred with happy contentment. "You're secretary threatened to quit and Nicci was threatening to pour castor oil down me."

He laughed and shuddered. "I hope she doesn't try that on her real patients."

She chuckled with him, then eased her head back far enough to gaze into his blue eyes. "Oh, Neil, I loved you long before you left the ranch. But I was too afraid to tell you. I figured you wouldn't want to hear it. You'd told me several times that you weren't a family man and I—well, after the impulsive affair I had in college, I was afraid to love, afraid I'd be hurt. But I fell in love with you anyway and I didn't know what to do. I've behaved like a ninny."

His fingers stroked down her hair and onto the soft skin of her back. "I've been pretty stupid myself, Raine. For years now I wouldn't let myself forget my parents' unhappy marriage. I hated my mother for it and blamed her for my father's death. It was easy to blame all my insecurities on her. Especially when my best friend had terrible issues with his own mother. Linc and I were comrades in misery—wronged by our mothers, and determined to never make the mistakes our father's had. But then Linc met Nevada and he changed."

"He married her," Raine replied. "And from what he tells me, he's very happy."

Both his hands were on her shoulders now, holding her close to his heart. "I talked to him yesterday and he said he's planning to fly down to Texas over the holidays and meet his mother. I think basically he's already forgiven her and he's happy to have her back in his life. That hit me hard, Raine. It made me think. If he has the courage to forgive Darla then surely I could find the courage to ask you to marry me." He eased her back on the braided rug and then stroking the tumbled hair off her face, he asked, "Will you marry me, Raine?"

He was saying the words she never thought she would ever hear and they rang in her heart like church bells on a clear Sunday morning.

"I'm still wearing your ring, Neil," she murmured softly. "I wanted it to be real then and now it will be."

A smile crooked his lips as he lifted her hand to see his diamond glittering on her finger. "What about the Sandbur?" he asked. "You have lots of relatives there. You might not want to make your home up here with me."

"I have lots of relatives up here, too," she reminded him. "Especially a brother that I'm eager to get acquainted with." Catching hold of his shoulders, she tugged him closer and whispered, "But you're the only reason I need to move to New Mexico. You and the children I hope we have soon."

Love was in his eyes as he brought his lips down to hers. "Welcome home, darling. And Merry Christmas."

She smiled against his kiss. "Oh, yes, my love, this Christmas is going to be the merriest of all."

* * * * *

# Special
## *moments*

We hope that the Special Edition novel you have just
finished has given you plenty of romantic
reading pleasure.

We are thrilled to have put together a section of
special free bonus features, which we hope will add to
the entertainment in each Special Edition novel from
now on.

There will be puzzles for you to do, exciting
horoscopes glimpsing what's in your future, author
information and sneak previews of books in
the pipeline!

Do let us know what you think of these
special extras by emailing
specialmoments@hmb.co.uk

For you, from us…
Relax and enjoy…

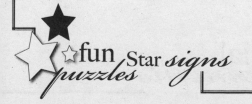

**fun** Star *signs*
*puzzles*

Dear Reader,

Several books ago, when I first began spinning tales about the Ketchum family, I was particularly drawn to their lifelong friend and lawyer Neil Rankin. Through thick and thin, he's the kind of guy who remains steadfast and devoted to his friends, and the sort that will tell them the truth of the matter, even when it hurts. His lonely heart cried out for that special woman, and while he travels all the way to a south Texas ranch to find her, he also uncovers a startling secret about the Ketchums that will change his life – and theirs – forever.

Christmas is a gift for love and hope, and Neil is lucky enough to experience both while he's in south Texas. As for me, my family and I are blessed to enjoy the yuletide season here on the coast with balmy weather, homemade tamales, parades of shrimp boats decked with lights and Santa on a riding lawn mower!

God bless and Merry Christmas, y'all!

*Stella*

# Author *Biography*

## STELLA BAGWELL

Stella began her writing career almost by accident. Although she always loved reading romances, she never thought to write one herself. She was a hairdresser but, ironically, Stella developed a severe allergy to hairspray and was forced to resign.

With time on her hands, she remembered a school English teacher telling her she could be a writer if she wanted. Armed with that notion and an old manual typewriter, she went to work. The result – her first book. After that, Stella became a full-time writer and today has more than sixty published novels.

At seventeen, Stella married her school sweetheart: Harrell. They have celebrated their twenty-ninth wedding anniversary. One of her greatest joys was to see Jason, her only son, graduate from college with two degrees.

Recently, she and her husband moved from the hills of Oklahoma to Seadrift, Texas, a sleepy little fishing town located on the coastal bend. Stella says the water, the tropical climate and the seabirds make it a lovely place to let her imagination soar and to put the stories in her head down on paper.

Next to writing, travelling is one of her most favourite activities. Yet, because the southwest is dear to her heart, she sets most of her books there in rough, rugged ranch country. She feels it's essential to know a place before writing about it; that philosophy gives her more reason to plan trips!

Stella's plan for the future is to continue writing romance novels as long as there's an audience to enjoy her work.

## Killer B's
Copyright ©2007 PuzzleJunction.com

| **4 letter words** | Bible | **7 letter words** |
|---|---|---|
| Baby | Brass | Babylon |
| Bats | Bribe | Bellini |
| Beam | Burma | Bifocal |
| Blob | **6 letter words** | Bristol |
| Boer | Baboon | Brittle |
| Born | Bamboo | **8 letter words** |
| Bran | Baobab | Baronage |
| Bulb | Bedaub | Beefiest |
| **5 letter words** | Bewail | |
| Babel | Blends | |
| | Buoyed | |

# Sudoku

To solve the Sudoku puzzle, each row, column and box must contain the numbers 1 to 9.

| 7 | 8 |   |   |   |   |   |   |   |
|---|---|---|---|---|---|---|---|---|
|   |   | 9 |   |   | 5 |   |   |   |
|   | 1 |   |   |   | 9 | 7 |   | 4 |
| 4 |   | 7 | 2 |   |   |   |   |   |
|   |   |   |   |   |   | 5 |   |   |
|   |   | 8 | 9 |   |   | 3 |   |   |
|   |   | 2 |   |   | 3 |   |   | 6 |
| 8 |   |   |   | 6 |   | 4 |   | 9 |
|   |   |   |   | 7 |   | 8 | 3 |   |

Dadhichi is a renowned astrologer and is frequently seen on TV and in the media. He has the unique ability to draw from complex astrological theory to provide clear, easily understandable advice and insights for people who want to know what their future may hold.

In the twenty-five years that Dadhichi has been practising astrology, face reading and other esoteric studies, he has conducted over 8,500 consultations. His clients include celebrities, political and diplomatic figures and media and corporate identities from all over the world.

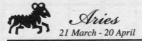

### *Aries*
21 March - 20 April

You're deeply interested in investigating the possibilities for your life during November. Your mind is focused, deliberate and less prone to superficial involvements. On the 13th, 18th and the 24th and 25th you could uncover some valuable information which will help you achieve some new success in the coming months.

### *Taurus*
21 April - 21 May

The Sun and Mars will de-stabilise your relationships this month so it's important to be less reactive. By the 11th, you'll observe extreme mood changes in your spouse and this requires more understanding. Relationships with children on the 21st are touchy so your test this month is to remain peaceful and non-reactive.

# Special *moments*

## Gemini
*22 May - 22 June*

This is a romantic month but don't be compulsive. On the 14th be less possessive if someone wants more independence. The 14th to the 22nd is an excellent time to pursue a new hobby and discover the hidden talents you've overlooked. The health of a relative on the 25th may concern you but should clear up quickly.

## Cancer
*23 June - 23 July*

Outdoor activities and physical exertion are necessary to relieve you of stress this month. On the 20th, make a greater effort to do your exercise or yoga class. You'll feel so much better for it. Balance your physical and emotional appetites on the 25th so that you have enough energy for social interaction and a fun night out on the 29th.

## Leo
*24 July - 23 August*

Don't let the past haunt you. Let go of unsavoury experiences that you have no control over. Your mind will be dwelling on someone or some situation. Make that phone call, speak your mind and then put the matter to bed. The 10th, 16th and 25th would be ideal days to do that.

## Virgo
*24 August - 22 September*

This month shows just how capable you are of achieving so much with so little. Industriousness and resourcefulness will be evident on the 12th, but you mustn't push others to their limits. On the 13th and 14th changes in your professional environment will be welcomed and offer you centre stage.

## Libra
### 23 September - 23 October

Arguments over money must be avoided this month. You are in a spending mood and this is probably because it's nearing Christmas. On the 12th, study your credit card statements and don't live beyond your means. A profitable period is forecast from the 18th but on the 20th turn down that attractive bargain when shopping.

## Scorpio
### 24 October - 22 November

Your words of kindness and compassion will have the desired effect on the 8th when sparks of romance will fly. An unexpected meeting with a stranger or someone you're introduced to could pave the way for a new love affair. The 11th and the 21st should be put aside to deepen your affection for them.

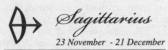

## Sagittarius
### 23 November - 21 December

Your monetary concerns should be all but cleared up now. Additional income, unearned commissions and interest from savings should be better than expected. An oversight on the 14th might create a glitch in your bank balance, but don't let this deter you from moving forward to bigger and better things.

# Special moments

# Capricorn
*22 December - 20 January*

A long-lost lover may return or you will be reminiscing about someone you haven't seen in a while. On the 8th, re-connect with those people who just happen to be popping up in your mind. Extending your knowledge of electronic devices and communication is likely after the 8th. Romance flourishes between the 15th and the 24th.

# Aquarius
*21 January - 18 February*

A new social group is what you need. Connecting with a bunch of fresh new faces will lift your spirits and broaden your view of the world. Watch your health on the 6th when your lower energy levels will be telling you something. You will feel refreshed by the 14th and can expect a stroke of good luck around the 23rd.

# Pisces
*19 February - 20 March*

You're restless in love but should count your blessings and be grateful for what you have. You could experience some stresses around the 19th and 20th but if you look at the upside, you will start to feel much better by the 23rd. The attitude of gratitude seems to be the moral of the Piscean story in November.

# Word Search

```
D X H Y D R A P O E J V S
T R T D L W V C H E C K R
E T A D E N V I S I O N O
F R J J Y G K F M M F X O
P N D T G N D W K R C M D
B K U N I T D E A L E R W
K D A T E B Z F G N C N S
C T Z I I T X T E H G E R
B R R B N M N T N W K E Y
T F O O Z O E E T A K V R
E W V S U R M M T C F T V
R G E T S B E U E G K R K
U T R T K A L D E C A F M
T A Q R N C M E K N Z D V
A L G I R L A M G X P E R
E K N W K R T B B V H B G
F G R T K T D V N K Q G L
```

©2007 PuzzleJunction.com

| | | |
|---|---|---|
| AGENT | DOORS | MEANING |
| BACK | DUTY | OVER |
| BED | EDGED | PNEUMONIA |
| CHECK | ENTENDRE | TAKES |
| CROSS | FACED | TALK |
| DATE | FEATURE | TIME |
| DEALER | JEOPARDY | TROUBLE |
| DECKER | KNIT | VISION |

Special
moments

# Connect-it

## It's Greek to Me

*Copyright ©2007 PuzzleJunction.com*

Each line in the puzzle below has three clues and three answers. The last letter in the first answer on each line is the first letter of the second answer, and so on. The connecting letter is outlined, giving you the correct number of letters for each answer (the answers in line 1 are 4, 6 and 6 letters). The clues are numbered 1 to 8, with each number containing 3 clues for the 3 answers on the line. But here's the catch! The clues are not in order - so the first clue in the line is not necessarily for the first answer. Good luck!

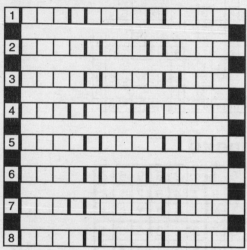

Clues:

1. Mate.  Bass horn.  Greek capital.
2. Greek fabulist.  Hear.  Danger.
3. Ascend.  Chess piece.  Greek philosopher.
4. Greek epic poem.  Musician.  Green fruit.
5. Direction.  Greek marketplace.  Long river.
6. Greek island.  Mistake.  Hogs.
7. Field or water game.  Greek mountain.  Push.
8. Dock.  Greek theatre.  Debacle.

## KRISSKROSS

```
B A O B A B   B U L B     B
A     A   O   E     A     R
B E A M   E   D     R     A
Y     B U R M A   B O R N
          O   A   O
B A B O O N   B E W A I L
R   I         G
R   F   B   B A B E L
B U O Y E D     A
E   C   E       T       B
    A   F   B R I S T O L
B E L L I N I           E
L       E   B A B Y L O N
O       S   L           D
B R I T T L E   B R A S S
```

## SUDOKU

| 7 | 8 | 4 | 1 | 2 | 6 | 9 | 5 | 3 |
|---|---|---|---|---|---|---|---|---|
| 3 | 6 | 9 | 7 | 4 | 5 | 2 | 1 | 8 |
| 2 | 1 | 5 | 3 | 8 | 9 | 7 | 6 | 4 |
| 4 | 3 | 7 | 2 | 5 | 8 | 6 | 9 | 1 |
| 9 | 2 | 1 | 6 | 3 | 4 | 5 | 8 | 7 |
| 6 | 5 | 8 | 9 | 1 | 7 | 3 | 4 | 2 |
| 5 | 4 | 2 | 8 | 9 | 3 | 1 | 7 | 6 |
| 8 | 7 | 3 | 5 | 6 | 1 | 4 | 2 | 9 |
| 1 | 9 | 6 | 4 | 7 | 2 | 8 | 3 | 5 |

387

# WORDSEARCH

```
D X H Y D R A P O E J V S
T R T D L W V C H E C K R
E T A D E N V I S I O N O
F R J J Y G K F M M F X O
P N D T G N D W K R C M D
B K U N I T D E A L E R W
K D A T E B Z F G N C N S
C T Z I I T X T E H G E R
B R R B N M N T N W K E Y
T F O O Z O E E T A K V R
E W V S U R M M T C F T V
R G E T S B E U E G K R K
U T R T K A L D E C A F M
T A Q R N C M E K N Z D V
A L G I R L A M G X P E R
E K N W K R T B B V H B G
F G R T K T D V N K Q G L
```

# CONNECT-IT

| 1 | T | U | B | A | T | H | E | N | S | P | O | U | S | E |
|---|---|---|---|---|---|---|---|---|---|---|---|---|---|---|
| 2 | A | E | S | O | P | E | R | I | L | I | S | T | E | N |
| 3 | C | L | I | M | B | I | S | H | O | P | L | A | T | O |
| 4 | K | I | W | I | L | I | A | D | R | U | M | M | E | R |
| 5 | A | G | O | R | A | M | A | Z | O | N | O | R | T | H |
| 6 | S | W | I | N | E | R | R | O | R | H | O | D | E | S |
| 7 | P | O | L | O | L | Y | M | P | U | S | H | O | V | E |
| 8 | W | H | A | R | F | I | A | S | C | O | D | E | O | N |

*Enjoy this sneak preview of*

**Sierra's Homecoming**
*by New York Times bestselling author*
*Linda Lael Miller*

*Available in December 2007*

# *Sierra's Homecoming*

### *by*

### *Linda Lael Miller*

Soft, smoky music poured into the room.

The next thing she knew, Sierra was in Travis's arms, close against that chest she'd admired earlier, and they were slow dancing.

Why didn't she pull away?

"Relax," he said. His breath was warm in her hair.

She giggled, more nervous than amused. What was the matter with her? She was attracted to Travis, had been from the first, and he was clearly attracted to her. They were both adults. Why not enjoy a little slow dancing in a ranch-house kitchen?

Because slow dancing led to other things. She took a step back and felt the counter flush against her lower back. Travis naturally came with her, since they were holding hands and he had one arm around her waist.

Simple physics.

Then he kissed her.

Physics again—this time, not so simple.

"Yikes," she said, when their mouths parted.

He grinned. "Nobody's ever said that after I kissed them."

She felt the heat and substance of his body pressed against hers. "It's going to happen, isn't it?" she heard herself whisper.

"Yep," Travis answered.

"But not tonight," Sierra said on a sigh.

"Probably not," Travis agreed.

"When, then?"

He chuckled, gave her a slow, nibbling kiss. "Tomorrow morning," he said. "After you drop Liam off at school."

"Isn't that…a little…soon?"

"Not soon enough," Travis answered, his voice husky. "Not nearly soon enough."

\* \* \*

*Don't forget*
Sierra's Homecoming
*is available next month!*

## BRIDES OF PENHALLY BAY

Medical™ is proud to welcome you to Penhally
Bay Surgery where you can meet the team led by
caring and commanding Dr Nick Tremayne.
For the next twelve months we will bring
you an emotional, tempting romance – devoted
doctors, single fathers, a sheikh surgeon,
royalty, blushing brides and miracle babies
will warm your heart…

*Let us whisk you away to this Cornish coastal
town – to a place where hearts are made whole.*

Turn the page for a sneak preview from
*Christmas Eve Baby*
by Caroline Anderson
– the first book in the
BRIDES OF PENHALLY BAY series.

## CHRSTMAS EVE BABY
### by
### Caroline Anderson

Ben crossed the room, standing by the window, looking out. It was a pleasant room, and from the window he could see across the boatyard to the lifeboat station and beyond it the sea.

He didn't notice, though, not really. Didn't take it in, couldn't have described the colour of the walls or the furniture, because there was only one thing he'd really seen, only one thing he'd been aware of since Lucy had got out of her car.

Lucy met his eyes, but only with a huge effort, and he could see the emotions racing through their wary, soft brown depths. God only knows what his own expression was, but he held her gaze for a long moment before she coloured and looked away.

'Um – can I make you some tea?' she offered, and he gave a short, disbelieving cough of laughter.

'Don't you think there's something we should talk about first?' he suggested, and she hesitated, her hand on the kettle, catching her lip between those neat, even teeth and nibbling it unconsciously.

'I intend to,' she began, and he laughed and propped his hips on the edge of the desk, his hands each side gripping the thick, solid wood as if his life depended on it.

'When, exactly? Assuming, as I am, perhaps a little rashly, that unless that's a beachball you've got up your jumper it has something to do with me?'

She put the kettle down with a little thump and turned towards him, her eyes flashing fire. 'Rashly? *Rashly?* Is that what you think of me? That I'd sleep with you and then go and fall into bed with another man?'

He shrugged, ignoring the crazy, irrational flicker of hope that it was, indeed, his child. 'I don't know. I would hope not, but I don't know anything about your private life. Not any more,' he added with a tinge of regret.

'Well, you should know enough about me to know that isn't the way I do things.'

'So how do you do things, Lucy?' he asked, trying to stop the anger from creeping into his voice. 'Like your father? You don't like it, so you just pretend it hasn't happened?'

'And what was I supposed to do?' she asked, her eyes flashing sparks again. 'We weren't seeing each other. We'd agreed.'

'But this, surely, changes things? Or should have. Unless you just weren't going to tell me? It must have made it simpler for you.'

She turned away again, but not before he saw her eyes fill, and guilt gnawed at him. 'Simpler?'

she said. 'That's not how I'd describe it.'

'So why not tell me, then?' he said, his voice softening. 'Why, in all these months, didn't you tell me that I'm going to be a father?'

'I was going to,' she said, her voice little more than a whisper. 'But after everything – I didn't know how to. It's just all so difficult –'

'But it *is* mine.'

She nodded, her hair falling over her face and obscuring it from him. 'Yes. Yes, it's yours.'

His heart soared, and for a ridiculous moment he felt like punching the air, but then he pulled himself together. Plenty of time for that later, once he'd got all the facts. Down to the nitty-gritty, he thought, and asked the question that came to the top of the heap.

'Does your father know it's mine…?'

She shook her head, and he winced.

'Have you had lunch?' she said suddenly.

'*Lunch?*' he said, his tone disbelieving. 'No. I got held up in Resus. There wasn't time.'

'Fancy coming back to my house and having something to eat? Only I'm starving, and I'm trying to eat properly, and biscuits and cakes and rubbish like that just won't cut the mustard.'

'Sounds good,' he said, not in the least bit hungry but desperate to be away from there and somewhere private while he assimilated this stunning bit of news.

She opened the door, grabbed her coat out of the staff room as they passed it and led him down the stairs.

They walked to her flat, along Harbour Road and up Bridge Street, the road that ran alongside the river and up out of the old town towards St Piran, the road he'd come in on. It was over a gift shop, in a steep little terrace typical of Cornish coastal towns and villages, and he wondered how she'd manage when she'd had the baby.

Not here, was the answer, especially when she led him through a door into a narrow little hallway and up the precipitous stairs to her flat. 'Make yourself at home, I'll find some food,' she said, a little breathless after her climb, and left him in the small living room. If he got close to the window he could see the sea, but apart from that it had no real charm. It was homely, though, and comfortable, and he wandered round it, picking up things and putting them down, measuring her life.

A book on pregnancy, a mother-and-baby magazine, a book of names, lying in a neat pile on the end of an old leather trunk in front of the sofa. More books in a bookcase, a cosy fleece blanket draped over the arm of the sofa, some flowers in a vase lending a little cheer.

He could see her through the kitchen door, pottering about and making sandwiches, and he went and propped himself in the doorway and watched her.

'I'd offer to help, but the room's too small for three of us,' he murmured, and she gave him a slightly nervous smile.

Why nervous? he wondered, and then realised that of course she was nervous. She had no idea what his attitude would be, whether he'd be pleased or angry, if he'd want to be involved in his child's life – any of it.

When he'd worked it out himself, he'd tell her. The only thing he did know, absolutely with total certainty, was that if, as she had said, this baby was his, he was going to be a part of its life for ever.

And that was non-negotiable.

\* \* \* \*

**Brides of Penhally Bay**
*Bachelor doctors become husbands and fathers –
in a place where hearts are made whole.*

*Snuggle up this festive season with*
Christmas Eve Baby
*by Caroline Anderson
– out in December 2007!*

MILLS & BOON

# *Special* Edition

## On sale 16th November 2007

### A TEXAS CHRISTMAS
*by Cathy Gillen Thacker*

All lawman Kevin McCabe wants for Christmas is to get closer to Noelle Kringle. But he knows she's hiding something. Noelle knows that secrets in her past mean she can never be with the sexy deputy. Then again, maybe she's underestimating the power of Christmas…

### THE SUPER MUM
*by Karen Rose Smith*

Though she was known around Danbury Way as Supermum, Angela Schumacher was at her wits' end raising three kids and working at two jobs…until her son's irresistible 'big brother', sports coach David Moore, offered his *very* personal support. But would her ex-husband's interference alter David's affections?

### SIERRA'S HOMECOMING
*by Linda Lael Miller*

After moving to the family ranch, single mother Sierra McKettrick had enough trouble fending off handsome caretaker Travis Reid, without having to worry if the house was haunted! Yet strange events led her to discover she was leading a parallel life with her ancestor, who offered Sierra a lesson in love and hope.

## MILLS & BOON
# *Special* Edition

## On sale 16th November 2007

### IT TAKES A FAMILY
*by Victoria Pade*

Penniless and raising an infant niece after her sister's death, Karis Pratt's only hope was to go to Montana, and find the baby's father, Luke Walker. Did this small-town cop hold the key to renewed family ties and a bright new future for Karis?

### CALL ME COWBOY
*by Judy Duarte*

When children's book editor Priscilla Richards uncovered evidence that her father had long ago changed her name, she hired sexy PI 'Cowboy' Whittaker to find out why. Soon they discovered that her mother was alive – and that Cowboy wanted to mend prim-and-proper Priscilla's broken heart.

### UNDER THE MISTLETOE
*by Kristin Hardy*

No-nonsense businesswoman Hadley Stone had a job to do – modernise the Hotel Mount Eisenhower. But the manager Gabe Trask stood in her way, guarding the landmark's legacy. Would the beautiful Vermont Christmas – and meetings under the mistletoe – soften these adversaries' hearts?

# FREE

## 4 BOOKS AND A SURPRISE GIFT!

We would like to take this opportunity to thank you for reading this Mills & Boon® book by offering you the chance to take FOUR more specially selected titles from the Special Edition series absolutely FREE! We're also making this offer to introduce you to the benefits of the Mills & Boon® Reader Service™—

- ★ **FREE home delivery**
- ★ **FREE gifts and competitions**
- ★ **FREE monthly Newsletter**
- ★ **Books available before they're in the shops**
- ★ **Exclusive Reader Service offers**

Accepting these FREE books and gift places you under no obligation to buy; you may cancel at any time, even after receiving your free shipment. Simply complete your details below and return the entire page to the address below. You don't even need a stamp!

**YES!** Please send me 4 free Special Edition books and a surprise gift. I understand that unless you hear from me, I will receive 6 superb new titles every month for just £3.10 each, postage and packing free. I am under no obligation to purchase any books and may cancel my subscription at any time. The free books and gift will be mine to keep in any case.

E7ZEE

Ms/Mrs/Miss/Mr......................................Initials ....................................
**BLOCK CAPITALS PLEASE**

Surname ..........................................................................................................

Address ...........................................................................................................

..........................................................................................................................

...................................................................Postcode ...............................

Send this whole page to:

The Reader Service, FREEPOST CN81, Croydon, CR9 3WZ